BRIAN LEYDEN was born in Roscommon in 1960. He won the RTE Francis McManus Short Story Award in 1988 and the *Irel* *'s Own* short story competition the following year. He a o devised and performed a one-man stage show on W. B. Y called *Experiments in Magic*. A regular contributor to ac , his RTE documentary, *No Meadows in Manhattan*, won Jacobs Award in 1991. He has been hailed as a unique new in Irish writing, especially since the publication of his story collection, *Departures*, "a book which calls out for ng". *Death and Plenty* is his first novel.

In the Valley of the Black Pig dreams gather

Death and Plenty

Brian Leyden

First published in Ireland and Great Britain in 1996
Brandon Book Publishers Ltd
Dingle, Co. Kerry, Ireland

ISBN 0 86322 218 8
British Library CIP data is available for this book.

The author very gratefully acknowledges receipt of an
Arts Council of Ireland bursary in literature, which saved his bacon
during the writing of this book.

Published with the assistance of the
Arts Council/An Chomhairle Ealaíon

"Wintry Dawn" is reproduced by kind permission of the author
and Gallery Press. From *Collected Poems* (1995) by John Montague.

Cover design by The Public Communications Centre, Dublin
Printed by Colour Books Ltd, Dublin

For their faith, inspiration and generosity this book is dedicated to Imelda Peppard and Cillian Rogers.

DEATH

THE AFFAIR BECAME a legend. Like so many things that grow more colourful over the years, its roots began in darkness, the darkness in which an audience sat ready to be entertained.

It was the last night of the show and Grace O'Connor watched from the wings with the stage-hands and crew. The auditorium was hushed, the charged atmosphere of a full house. Grace inhaled the smell: a compound of old carpet and people packed in shoulder close, dusty floorboards, make-up, painted flats and hot lights – a familiar, throat-burning, dry heat. A perfume of success. It had been a good run, a re-working of an Oscar Wilde play elevated to a gaudy and popular Broadway musical. Now, the out-of-towners were slipping out of that involved state with the performance and thinking about the safest way back to their midtown hotel rooms, booked along with the show at a discount rate. The final curtain was just minutes away. Kenneth and his stage partner Pamela were hamming it all the way to the finale in their period flounces and brocades.

"I, who had shut my eyes to life, came to the brink. And one who had separated us – "

"Darling, we were never separated."

They moved left of stage to the crimson velvet chaise-longue and locked eyes. Ploys rehearsed in detail now a matter of routine. Even the costumes Grace had designed for the show looked tired and worn out. Or perhaps she had just lost interest in her job; dressing up actors to play these games of make-believe.

"O Arthur, don't love me less, and I will trust you more. I will trust you absolutely..."

Grace watched in silence as they delivered the closing lines. Her arms were wrapped tightly around her body, but the unease she wished to contain was betrayed by the nervous tapping of her left foot. Tony, the production hair stylist, was standing beside her. When she turned to go, he nudged her in the ribs.

"You're not leaving?" he whispered.

"I have costumes to look after."

"What about the party?"

"Tell Kenneth I have a headache. I'm going back to the apartment as soon as I finish with wardrobe."

She did not stop at the dressing rooms but continued up the narrow, dimly lit corridor. The team in wardrobe could get by without her interference. She needed to walk. She needed air. She needed space to get things straight in her head. Leaving the theatre by the side door she stepped out into the bitumen city drizzle.

A gloss of rain on the night time avenue mirrored the lights of the theatre canopy and the passing cars. This electric glare swelled to daylight brightness at the intersection of 7th Avenue, Broadway and 42nd Street. Why did they name it Times Square, she had once puzzled, when it's really a triangle?

Crowds of people were leaving the movie houses and theatres. In their wake she caught the waft of eau-de-Cologne and expensive perfume, the distilled fragrance of money and position. Inside the shadowy margins of Broadway, the hair-thin divide between wealth and dereliction was never more apparent, with a concentration of money and glamour in the theatres up the street, the patrons all bunched together for safety as they fled homewards after the show. Fortunes going up and fortunes coming down, they all met at this sleazy and dangerous intersection.

Grace entered the human traffic with no clear direction in mind, going with the hustle and drift. In the years she had been away, the square had changed profoundly. She was a stranger now, roving amongst the vanished haunts of her childhood. She was not that hungry kid any more, who came to grab fast food, to gawk and wonder at the spangled and dizzying spectacle of Times Square after dark. No more giggling at the Japanese tourists ducking in and out of the sex shops and the live action shows. No more swapping street banter with the dark men over their ponderous games of chess, arranged on top of busted orange crates.

Like so many citizens of this town she had always been repelled and yet drawn to the sad and the brash excesses of the square: the lurid shop-fronts, the giant billboards, the demented movie theatre hoardings and dazzling corporate logos; and below them, the army recruitment post, the bag-ladies out on the street, the hookers, the pan-handlers and the teenage runaways. This old playground for the children of the ghettos was cleaning up its act, but it was hard to say if the cold and impersonal towers going up all around were any improvement on its once reeking atmosphere of fast-food, its edge of violence and sex for sale.

She dropped a buck to a vagrant squatting on the side-walk with a hand-printed cardboard sign around his neck saying: "Spare a Dollar for Psychedelic Research".

Up the street she stopped for a cappuccino in an old roost, then took a window seat in the dairy cafeteria to watch the passing crowd. Catching that fresh coffee and cinnamon aroma, she reflected that this neighbourhood wasn't all sad memories. As a kid her mother had brought her to the square to witness the New Year's Eve parties, and then on to Bethesda fountain to view the fireworks and the line of evening-dressed joggers crossing Central Park at midnight. The fantails of exploding light, the warmth of the crowd, the rain of coloured paper and the scent of gun-powder, park greenery and her mom's face-powder furnished one of the happiest memories of her childhood, and gave her an abiding love of noisy carnivals and costumed parades.

Her mother's acting career had brought them back to the theatre district so often it became an ever more familiar and unmagical part of their lives. Sharing rooms in low rent boarding houses Grace had her first brush with the pain of failure and the hunger for attention that came with this territory. She had sat up countless nights sharing the broken ambitions and passing success of others, finding excuses along with them for the poverty and the mental strain they endured.

Her mother had been one of the lucky few. Her career took off, Hollywood called, she took the chance, made it work, and carried Grace along in the slipstream of her success. It had been a timely escape. The last years in New York had seen the poison of hard drugs pollute the old sub-culture of the square. The underworld of hookers, hustlers, hobos and peep-shows had been invaded by a pestilent breath of addiction, murder and a killer virus. City Hall had set about demolishing the plague houses without ever tackling the source of the plague, and the square began to resemble an old hooker who had lost all her charm.

What had this place been all along but a safety valve for the violent life force that drives a big city? New York, the big blur. This demented experiment in crowding human beings and their complications in impossible numbers.

"Honey, if you can't cut it, it's time you got out of town. Another show-biz burnout," Grace said, and caught herself talking out loud like one of those bag-ladies lost in Central Park.

She had delayed long enough, and worked herself into a suitably black and unforgiving mood to face the final night party. She dropped her change on the table-top and crossed the street to hail a cab. The taxi-cabs had all melted away in the rain, but the boisterous street gangs still jostled on the corners and in the doorways, preening and putting on loud-mouth displays of young male defiance. In the years Grace had been away, this naked aggression had become more un-stable, the kids more wild-eyed and unpredictable. Or was it just a sign that she was growing older and more fearful?

At last a broken-down yellow cab swung into the kerb. The driver was a confused and unintelligible soul not long arrived from some famine district on the other side of the globe. Eventually they negotiated an address on the upper West Side.

She entered the marble and glass insulated calm of the lobby, where her face was known to the doorman, and took an elevator to the twelfth floor. From the elevator she stepped into a studio apartment that was all discreet lighting and loud voices. She had come to a decision out on the street and set a course of action in her head. Now her whole body tensed before what was to come.

The atmosphere was a mixture of happiness at the success of the show, and the hollow sensation that there would be no call to work tomorrow for many of those at the party. There was a black-tie contingent, but no worried backers grimly holding on to their cocktails. The run was over, the money banked. People could let their hair down with no agonising duty to appear relaxed or confident while the early make or break reviews went to print. This was a self-congratulatory affair, and Grace was probably the most up-tight person in the room.

Tony was standing near the door, a thin, fastidious figure in black. He signalled hello and seemed genuinely surprised to see her.

"Hi there," he greeted and rushed to bring her a drink. His eyes made a darting search of the room while he fussed around Grace, holding out a chilled cocktail glass and a tray of hors d'oeuvres.

"What happened to your headache?" he asked.

"Isn't he here yet?"

A square-featured, elderly man with grey, oily hair and shiny spectacles approached. A pocket-sized George C. Scott. He took her hand and shook it. "I loved your designs for the show. Great. A terrific production. Wonderful."

"Thank you," she said.

"I'm sorry I couldn't make it to your mother's funeral service. Obligations. You know how it is!"

She shrugged off the apology, but her eyes were hard. The loss was a painful open wound and she didn't want to be reminded. The man sensed he had put a foot wrong. He placed his free hand over the back of Grace's hand, squeezed for sincerity, nodded and moved off.

"He's a nice man," Tony cautioned.

"It's been two months. What did he want me to do? Break down?"

"Why not? I love a good cry."

"I'm not the type."

She had been studying each face in the room. Now she turned directly to Tony.

"Where is he?"

Tony looked at the floor.

"Where, Tony?"

He would not answer and she did not press him. She left him holding her empty glass and pushed through the crowd, avoiding eye contact. It was the producer's apartment and she knew the layout from previous visits. The bathroom was at the end of the hall. Three closed doors in between.

She tried the first door. The room was dark, but the light coming in over her shoulder revealed the heap of coats on the bed. The next door was locked. She crossed to the other side of the corridor, stood to take a deep breath, then tested the handle. She slipped in without a sound.

Pamela had her back turned to the door. Her legs straddled her partner on the bed. Kenneth's trousers were down around his ankles, one hand inside the open front of Pamela's dress, the other out of sight. Drinks had been finished and the empty glasses knocked over. The dresser top was scattered with the messy afters of a coke binge. Pamela was utterly lost to her surroundings, her head thrown back, her blonde hair in disarray. Kenneth's eyes were screwed tightly shut, his face creased in a worried frown. A bubble of saliva foamed at the corner of his mouth while he huffed and panted to keep pace with the convulsive demands of his partner.

They were not aware of Grace standing in the doorway, and she had seen enough. She slammed the door hard to shut out the sight. The muscles of her throat locked in a painful spasm. Her eyes burned but remained wilfully dry. It was rage, not self-pity, that drove her up the corridor and away from the party. Before the elevator she stopped and called back to the figure in black, loud enough for everyone in the room to hear.

"It's what I expected. Another second-rate performance from Kenneth."

GRACE SAT OUT on the porch of her mother's beach house on Long Island, a place in the Hamptons, bought years before as a hideaway and a springboard to their old stomping grounds in the city. Her eyes were closed and her feet were curled up in a padded cane chair. The sea had always been a source of renewal, yet its vastness filled her with an aching want. It was not a feeling she could put into words. All she had were these tantalising impressions of a coastline she knew in her soul, but had never visited. A place lodged in the deeper memory: remembered for the perfect clarity of the sea-light, the intense salt tang in the air, the seductive whisper of sand-grains under her bare feet, in what must have been another and a better life. A paradise beside which this present retreat was a pale imitation.

She sat there soaking up impressions as the sounds of the neighbourhood drifted up to the house. Youths playing soft-ball. The encroaching tinkle of ice-cream vendors. Raised voices around hot-dog and orange-juice stands, and the endless march of feet reverberating along the board-walk. The whole area was going steadily down-market, but the mellow warmth, the oyster-coloured sky, and the shimmer of sequined light far out on the water only increased her longing for that quiet and tranquil shore of her dreams.

She rose and went inside. The sea-breeze and the scavenger gull cries of the children followed her through the screen door.

She had found a buyer for the house and they had closed the deal. Her leave-taking was down to last personal things, things she found it hard to face, like this chore of packing away small, emotionally loaded objects and keepsakes. Her mother's personal effects. Simple things. Cosmetic jars, backstage trinkets. A scrap-book of folded cuttings, reviews and date-stamped photographs, following the public career of the stage and screen actor, Eleanor O'Connor.

Grace felt that all of these things, bar the scrap-book, had to be got rid of. You could not bring back the dead by holding on to the intimate things they once used. With the death of their owner, objects, too, lost their meaning. Disposing of her mother's property was the right thing to do, and still it felt wrong, even traitorous.

She had worked her way through all of her mother's belongings in the weeks following the funeral, and now she stood before the pine dresser in the bedroom. The final resting place of her mother's passport, jewellery, scented Irish lace handkerchiefs, the oldest family documents and photographs.

She spread these last effects on the dust-sheet draped over the bed. Her mother was dead and still this felt like an invasion of privacy. Since the funeral every item before her had been sifted and scrutinised for clues, and still the sensation of being an intruder remained. She was a small child again poking through her mother's things while her mother was out of the house.

Once more she selected the framed photograph of the man in the American Marine uniform. She had studied this face in secret many times when she was growing up. If she shared any likeness to this stranger, it wasn't noticeable then or now. Enough. She turned the print over in her hand. Her mother had never married. Grace did not even bear this man's second name. "He was a good man, and a lot of fun." That was all her mother ever had to say about the stranger in the photograph, along with the admission that he was Grace's natural father.

The notion that her father had been a "good man" and a soldier plucked too soon from life was so theatrical it was barely credible. Often Grace was tempted to believe the whole story was a fantasy concocted by her mother on her way to the theatre as she passed the army recruitment post at the centre of Times Square. This man might just as easily be a matinee actor, the uniform a theatrical costume. Whoever he was, he had played no part in her life. And following the death of this soldier-lover all her mother's affairs had been short-lived, one-sided and high on drama. A pattern repeated in Grace's own emotional tangles.

She unrolled her mother's birth certificate and scanned the details. Father also unknown. The last official document was her grandmother Sarah O'Connor's death certificate. As Grace was smoothing the paper under her hand, images of the sea invaded her imagination. A ship-board smell filled her senses, and she experienced a terrible sense of loss. It was a sudden, intense and mystifying sensation, and not the first time this odd sense of communion with another life had occurred. These visions of ocean passage had started about the same time Grace had set about unravelling her mother's family beginnings. She put this waking dream effect down to her recent bereavement, followed by the ferry crossing to Ellis Island: the place where the search into her family roots had become such a compulsion.

"Hi there? Anyone home?" a familiar voice called from the front porch to break the eerie spell of another, older world present in the room with her.

"In here, Tony."

With the instincts of a faithful hound Tony had tracked her down. He was even dressed for the territory in brand new espadrilles, peaked cap and dark glasses dangling from a cord around his neck.

"Have you heard the news?" he gushed. "A new production. Another Irish play."

"Yes."

"And?"

"I'm hired. If I take the job."

He moved to hug her. They had worked for several years as a team back stage. Outside work Grace practised Tai Chi while Tony perfected the art of backstabbing gossip in the locker room. He was a considerate but featherweight presence in her world.

"I'm going back there," Grace said with her head rested on his shoulder. Tony took a step away from her.

"Back to Kenneth?" he said surprised.

"No, to Ireland."

"What!"

"I'm going to Ireland."

"Are you feeling okay?" he said biting at the nail of his first finger and studying her closely.

Grace fanned out the items on the bed. "I've been doing some detective work out on Ellis Island."

"The Immigration Museum?"

"After a visit there I decided to look up the records. Immigration records. With people's names and the places they sailed from."

"You want to find your ancestors?" he mocked.

"Yes, Tony. Yes I do."

His expression changed. "You're crazy. What about the new production?"

"I can't say."

"Why can't you say?"

"Mom is dead, Tony. She's gone. And this time she won't be back. Not after three months, not after six months away on tour or on location. And I don't know what to do. Do you understand? My job was to make her and any production she appeared in look good. She had voice trainers, choreographers, manicurists, wig artists, turban women, make-up artists and dressers. I was her costume designer. Her chaperone. Her personal servant. That was my role."

"Why are you saying this? You've got a talent. You've got a career – "

"All I ever had to do was make her look good."

"That's not true, and you know it."

"Remember the night of the party to close our first big show without her. I went for a walk about the old theatre district. Broadway. Times Square. And I found I wasn't needed. I didn't belong there any more. I didn't belong anywhere. I was just another sad drifter."

"I'll bring you a cold beer," Tony offered. He went out to search the ice-box.

Grace looked at the personal trinkets scattered on the bed. From the pile she selected a fine gold chain with a lucky charm fixed on the end. A tiny gold pig. A crazy sort of relic, or heirloom, but it had been passed on from her grandmother to her mother, and now it had come down to her. The first and last names in the government records and documents formed no more than broken links with the past, but this was something she could grasp in her hand. A physical connection with her family past. A past she was determined to unravel and know.

Tony came back from the kitchen with two chilled beers. He handed one across. "Tell me this isn't about Kenneth?" he asked.

She shook her head. "I'll let you in on a secret. Kenneth always had a name for what he had between his legs. Willy, Dick. John. You know why? Because he didn't want a total stranger doing all his thinking. We're through. Finished. I never want to see him again."

"If it's not Kenneth, what is it?" Tony pleaded.

"I love you guys and the shows we've done together, but I'm getting out. I'm lonely. Lonely as Christ. And staying here, doing what I've always done, is only making it worse.

I've got to do something. Find a space."

"It's too soon after your mother's funeral. You're still upset. You need to talk to someone."

"Maybe it's just a break I need," she mellowed. "I haven't told anyone about this yet, but I've traced my mother's family back to Ireland. I know where my grandmother was born."

"How?"

"I had a notice printed in the Irish newspapers: an appeal for information about the O'Connor family. These guys got in touch with me. They knew the house where my grandmother was born. They were really kind: sent photographs in the mail, papers, maps. They even took care of the legal side."

"The legal side?" Tony said nervously.

"Yeah, they fixed it so I could buy back the property."

Tony looked at her aghast.

Grace looked back at him from the edge of the bed and met his eyes directly, grateful for his concern, but her mind made up. "You don't have to worry about me," she said. "It's going to be a surprise visit, and I'm bringing my lucky charm. See..." she dangled the tiny gold pig on the end of the chain. "I want you to have the apartment while I'm gone. All you've got to do is clear up the mess."

"What mess?"

"I made a bonfire out of Kenneth's CD collection of Broadway musicals. You'll find them with the rest of his things in the trash can."

"Oh, Grace," Tony said and rushed to hug her again. Tears rolled down his cheeks. "I'm sorry," he sniffed, "but I love a good cry."

TWO

THE DARK AND undulating coastline was pin-holed with lights. The street lights, kitchen and front room windows of Belmullet, Kilalla, and Ennismuck. Ireland's first recorded inhabitants were a shore dwelling people who had populated these Atlantic headlands. Their descendants had later shaped this landscape to mirror their religion, with ambitious earthworks, monuments and standing stones. Over the passing centuries new invaders built tower houses and stone castles and left other fortifications scattered about the district.

Unlike its neighbours, the early Irish estuary settlement of Ennismuck had been largely overlooked by these regular invasions, land wars and uprisings. Only in the last century had it evolved a minor reputation as a family holiday resort, its one notable innovation being a seaweed bath-house built along Edwardian lines and opened the year the Titanic sank.

The pristine beach was its most outstanding feature: a perfect sweep of empty coastline, golden sand and glimmering sand dunes, the grandest of these known locally as the Valley of Diamonds. Opal-capped sapphire breakers lapped this precious shore, and the only man-made feature was a blunt concrete pier paved with flagstones, built at the town end by the local authorities to make a harbour for the lobster, shrimp and salmon fishing boats. The harbour road finished at a cobbled slipway, and a series of linked pedestrian paths snaked down a steep, grassy embankment to meet the promenade, with its terraced cement steps leading into the water. There was a caravan park amongst the dunes: a line of low-roofed mobile homes with bay windows facing the sea, two tennis-courts and a little, fenced-off playground for children, modestly equipped with slides and swings. The resort provided no electronic amusements or game machine arcades; just a scatter of tiny, brightly coloured seasonal souvenir and sweet shops, which sold ice-cream and plastic buckets and spades during the summer months, and put up their shutters for the winter.

After the terraced guest houses that offered bed and breakfast accommodation overlooking the beach, the town proper stood with its back turned to the sea. An enclave of narrow dwelling houses and small shop fronts, a bar and a general providers, all faced around a square with an empty plinth in the middle to mark the town centre. The plinth was empty because a bomb had been planted under the original occupant. In a gesture of solidarity with a beleaguered neighbour, a local landlord in the last century had imposed on the town a statue of Captain Boycott. The response was a midnight demolition job: the only known guerilla incident in the history of Ennismuck. Afterwards, it was decided the plinth should remain empty in a town where a public monument could arouse such explosive feelings.

Despite the glorious strand, and a harbour opening to the resources of the sea, Ennismuck was not a thriving place. There was a palpable sense of unease amongst the population. A feeling that wrong decisions had been made and wrong turns taken.

This general sense of disquiet was heightened by the grinding mechanical noise that throbbed from an unseen source high above the town. In the table of mountains, a volcanic ridge known as the Caledonian folding, which ran all the way from Norway to the County of Mayo, a four hundred million-year-old eruption, was said to have left mineral wealth in the district. Now fresh rumbling had started. An industrial noise that carried with it a fearful undercurrent. A sinister, persistent energy, mechanical but alive, like a great animal burrowing into the side of the mountain, feared all the more for being out of sight.

Every night the sky above the town was searched by probing fingers of light from the gold mine company yards. A constant movement of large trucks, humped and warted with earth, moved through the hours of light and darkness in silhouette along the rim of the hills. A wide incision opened in the mountain, but no local had been given a part in the operation, though several hundred well-paid jobs had been promised.

All that came from the mountain was water. Torrents of white water, grinding age-old boulders down to pebbles and gold-flecked sand, where the head-waters joined to make a broad river that met the tidal estuary.

The pounding water from the mountains and the smooth sea-swell came together that night under a crescent moon. The slow suck of swirling water at high tide, and the occasional call of the wild birds along the water margin, were reserved at such a late hour for the sensitive ears of night prowlers and hunters.

Into the timeless rhythm of this river world came a sudden splash and the flash of scales in the moonlight. Another splash. Then several. The salmon were returning. They sported before the rapids, playful and still vigorous, though they had shoaled the wide Atlantic and singled out the mouth of this one estuary from a thousand miles of jagged coastline. From the ice-water bays of Canada and the Davis Straits, they came each year to this empty country, back to age-old spawning beds and first origins, blindly compelled by their ancestry.

The man with the gleaming-black beard, big bones and ox-broad shoulders was stationed and ready. He had been watching for days for this salmon run. The half-bottle of *poitín* beat hot in his blood, a liquid armour against the icy water that soaked his work-shirt and trousers. It gave him the necessary will to push against the numbing strength of the current in which he stood up to his thighs. He moved with steady purpose, wading up the middle of the river, his quick eyes searching the black pools and eddies. In his right hand he held a crude, forged-iron harpoon with a blunt snout, its twin prongs flashing in a fiery light.

A second man, a tall and shambling figure with wild silver-black hair in natural dreadlock curls, wearing a waxed-cotton jacket, wool cap and unlikely bright red boots walked the river-bank. He followed his friend's progress up the churning river. In one hand he carried a large Hessian sack. In the other hand he held aloft a torch made from a straight blackthorn branch with a sod of blazing turf soaked in diesel fuel oil tied on the end with electric fence wire.

The harpoon struck and the prongs went deep into the water. Still holding the shaft, the big man wading the river plunged below the surface of the water. When the man on the river-bank saw his friend go under he planted the shaft of the torch in the soft ground and opened the top of the sack.

For what seemed like a full minute the big man remained submerged. Finally he broke surface, his fingers wedged in the gills of a fine salmon. He tossed the salmon heavenwards to be netted like a basketball in the waiting sack.

"Nice one, Oliver," his friend called, inspecting the fish.

"Keep your voice down, Mulcahy. How many is that?"

"Twelve. I think we could call it a night."

"One more, before the heat of the *poitín* wears off."

"Don't push your luck," Mulcahy warned and he searched the darkness in both directions. Several minutes had passed since he had last checked for signs of danger. From the darkness any threat might spring, but the real mark of trouble was a flashlight beam exploding out of the night into your stunned face and the bailiff shouting: "Got you!"

Oliver pushed on, wading the river. Mulcahy picked up the torch and the sack and moved with him. Again the harpoon hit the water and Oliver's hand followed the shaft below the surface, feeling towards the restraining prongs, and the muscular struggle of the salmon trapped there. As he bent into the current, he went lower in the water. The river reached his chest and then up to his shoulders until, once more, he was out of sight.

Mulcahy had the sack open when he heard a new sound over the steady rhythm of tumbling water, and the distant rumble from the company mines. Up river he caught the glint of flashlights moving at a run towards the blazing torch.

He searched the river, but there was no trace of Oliver.

He waited and watched for a break in the surface of the water. A salmon leaped further up by the waterfall. The lights on the other side of the river were closing fast. He could hear the yelps of the dogs clearly now and the determined call of their handlers.

A streaming head broke surface and Oliver stood up, blowing like a walrus.

"Oliver!"

"What's up?"

"Bailiffs!"

"Where?"

"On the far bank and closing."

Mulcahy took the sack to the river's edge, but Oliver tucked the fish under his arm and started for the embankment. In an effort to wade straight across to where Mulcahy waited, the big man stumbled into a deep place and lost his footing. The salmon began to struggle in his arms and threatened to knock him completely off balance. He tightened his hold on the floundering fish in one arm, and used the harpoon in his other hand for support. There was a fringe of foam-spattered sedge along the bank. Oliver tossed up the fish, followed by the harpoon, and scrambled for a hold. The oozing stems slipped between his fingers and he found that the clay had been undermined by winter flooding. A weak section of the bank crumbled under his weight. He went tumbling back into the river.

A firm hand grabbed him by the scruff of the neck and hauled him safely on to dry land. "Stop acting the maggot and come on," Mulcahy urged.

Oliver collected the fish and swung the sack over his

shoulder while Mulcahy rescued the harpoon. The bailiffs on the far bank had fanned out to search for a safe crossing place. Mulcahy gave them a last glance, plucked the shaft of the burning torch from the ground and tossed it far out over the river. As it hit the water Oliver and Mulcahy turned for the empty bog land and its covering darkness.

THE BLIND SNAPPED open and the strong morning light entered through the moulded plastic window. Grace O'Connor yawned and looked out. She saw land below through the drifting wisps of cloud. Ochre and khaki coloured mountains were dimpled with small sky-reflecting lakes. In the valleys the green pasture land was divided into tiny fields. White bungalows stood apart. The sun flashed on the glasswork of the early morning traffic.

Past experience of airline mix-ups had taught her to bring everything she considered vital in her hand-luggage. Nervously, she glanced to her left. There was no cause for alarm. The tan, travel-worn valise was there with all her documents, the equipment essential to continue her work while she was out of the country, her toothbrush, cosmetics and a change of underwear. The flight was on time. The journey was going according to plan.

The flight attendant appeared in the aisle to clear away the coffee cups and to take back the little bag of salted peanuts. His hair-cut was a mistake and Grace was not impressed by the designer uniform, styled like the gift wrapping on a Christmas hamper.

"Good morning," he said. His smile was fixed and grating. "We will be landing shortly at Knock airport. If you would like to clear your personal belongings from the table and put your seat in the upright position."

"Sure," she said.

She gathered the pile of papers from the table; a combination of new fashion and show-business journals, legal documents of conveyance and other official paperwork. A photograph of an Irish country cottage. A road map. And a list of handwritten directions taken over a transatlantic telephone connection.

"Your first visit to the West of Ireland?" the attendant enquired.

"Yes," she said sorting and returning the documents to her bag.

"A working holiday?" he asked hovering.

Grace snapped the lock tight.

"Family business," she said.

She considered what she'd said to the flight attendant. "Family business." But what business was that? This trip across the Atlantic had been guided purely by an instinct to understand the sway and influence of her family past, and to exorcise a ghost that had entered her life after a visit to the immigrant processing station on Ellis Island.

She had a small town called Ennismuck circled on the map, a property secured by law through the documents stashed in her hand-luggage. She had no idea what to expect when she got there.

OLIVER KNOCKED BACK another hefty swig of *poitín* from a clear glass lemonade bottle, snorted as the spirit went down, and then shivered off the memory of their escape from the bailiffs. A rough jog up to their knees in soggy ground, interrupted by heather stems as tough as trip-wires, and the crack of shin bones against buried rocks, brought them to the bog road and the safety of his pickup truck, which was already faced for home. He had waited until they got back to the cottage to throw off his wet clothes and change into a pair of oil-stained dungarees. Now, after each scalding swallow he set the bottle of *poitín* aside and shook a yellow metal cylinder, stirring up the sediments of rust at the bottom, along with the last dregs of liquid cooking gas.

Mulcahy had three freshly carved salmon steaks simmering on a black iron frying pan. He stood by the gas cooker in the cosy and, until their arrival, neatly arranged cottage kitchen. The flames under the pan rose and fell while Oliver wrestled with the cylinder.

"There's a heel left in this bottle," he offered.

"Finish it," Mulcahy said. "I have too much to do today. I need a clear head."

Outside the air was brightening, the filaments of grey fog clearing to blue. Oliver polished off the bottle. The door to the top bedroom opened.

An old man stooped to come through the low doorway and then straightened to look around his kitchen. He had a natural gaunt elegance and his fine white hair hung behind his shoulders in a pony tail, but his skin had the pale, brittle pallor of the very ill. He surveyed the two men with discerning grey eyes and saw the Hessian sack, the home-made harpoon and the ring of water circling the discarded clothes on the floor.

"Gentlemen," he said.

"Breakfast is ready, and your name is in the pot, Theo," said the woolly-haired man standing by the cooker.

"Poaching again, Mulcahy?"

"It's been a lean month."

Oliver gave the gas cylinder another shake. Theo went around the table and gathered up the sandpaper, the rasp and the pocket-knife used for hand-carving that lay amongst a bed of clean timber shavings and sawdust from the night before.

"One of these days – " he warned Mulcahy as he moved around the poaching equipment to put away the tools.

"My ass will be grass, with those bailiffs for a lawn-mower," Mulcahy finished for him.

"I've heard the dogs. It isn't a game to them."

"You taught us all the tricks, Theo. Were you ever caught?"

"I knew when to quit."

Mulcahy juggled the pan to catch the dying flames.

"What the hell! In another couple of months none of this will matter," he said.

"He's right," Oliver agreed. "When that mining outfit on the mountain have finished, there won't be a fish left in the river. We might as well take what we can get now."

"There are all kinds of laws to protect our rivers from pollution," Theo reminded them.

Mulcahy turned the salmon steaks over to cook the second side. "There are laws against poaching, too," he said.

Silenced by the remark Theo went to the dresser. He opened the cutlery drawer and the door to the bottom compartment and began to set the table for breakfast. With old world exactness he left out a much used, though once fine and hallmarked silver setting, along with matching bone china tea-cups, saucers and breakfast plates.

"Why do the mine owners hire thugs for bailiffs if they have no regard for the river?" Theo asked when the settings were correct. "It doesn't make any sense."

"Some people consider it a great honour to join the company fishing parties," Mulcahy said. "After a good supper and several brandies, the deals are made."

"Even though they know the company doesn't care what happens to the river?"

"In a nutshell, it all comes down to jobs," Oliver said. "People have been promised well-paid jobs."

"And if it's a choice between poverty or poison," Mulcahy said, "they'll swallow the poison."

"You daren't open your mouth about what's going on," Oliver nodded.

Theo waved a bread-knife in the air, clearly vexed. "When did a regular job ever matter to you, Mulcahy?" he asked. "You were the one who said any fool can work for a living. Why have you not protested?"

"Save your breath to cool your porridge," Mulcahy replied. "Everyone knows backhanders were paid to get around the regulations."

"What about political pressure?"

"Not as long as John Charles Leddy our local TD is in power. Leddy and his cronies have been buying up land around the mine where access roads will have to be built. As for Tom Giblin's so-called campaign against the mine: all he does is shout from the floor at every public meeting. The others are only in it for the *craic*, an excuse to get out of the house on the long nights, and down a few pints and start an argument."

"They need guidance."

"Theo, the outcome is already decided. Mark my words, the mine owners will be here until the last ounce of gold has been ripped out of that mountain."

"He has them well read," Oliver agreed sadly.

"You can't change human nature," Mulcahy went on. "I know. I've signed more petitions, been to more meetings. Not just this time, but the last time, and the time before that. All my life I've fought the good cause and I've changed nothing. Gold is still more precious than honest-to-God drinking water."

Theo cast a look of appeal to Oliver, but the big man shook his head.

"Ordinary five-eights have no say in these things. We're not important."

"You have the power to change things if you really want to," Theo insisted.

"Power! I'll tell you about power," Mulcahy said. "At the height of his campaign, Daniel O'Connell was stopped on the side of the road by an old fellow breaking a pile of stones. 'How is the campaign going?' the old timer asked the Great Liberator. And O'Connell said, 'It doesn't matter to you who gets elected, you'll still be here breaking stones.'"

"Jasus, Mulcahy! You're a bitter article," Oliver remarked.

"But polluting the Moyle, one of the finest salmon rivers in Ireland, is an outrage," Theo said fiercely. "Something must be done."

Mulcahy turned back to the gas cooker to hide the sympathy he felt for the old man.

"Theo," he said, "when I think of those magnificent creatures navigating the Atlantic on the journey home to the head-waters where they were spawned, it seems like a crime against nature to cut that journey short. Then I re-member what the poet Kahlil Gibran said: 'By the force that consumes you, I too shall be consumed.' So I go out and I poach."

"But you have a sense of honour. You do it the hard way. You test your skill with an old harpoon and not the hooligan's nylon net."

"It's still poaching," Mulcahy pointed out.

"You take only what you need." Theo would not give in.

"And the company and their kind take what they need," Mulcahy said. He lifted the salmon steaks with his fingers and brought three separate plates to the table. "Now eat."

IT WAS A four-way junction, but the only signpost was a brown and white notice that pointed across the fields to a "Giant's Grave." There were no signposts offering anything as real as a direction or a route number. The name of the nearest town or village remained a closely guarded secret.

Grace pulled the car over to the side of the road. Knock Airport, tiny, informal and high up on a mountain top, had looked like a first cousin of the make-shift airports of South America; but the exit from the plane had been speedy, and the rental car she had ordered through the travel agent had been waiting for her in the lot. Driving on the left-hand side of the road was a nuisance, but after a few goofs she adjusted to the change. The begrudging number of sign-posts had proved a real brain teaser, and her journeys had seemed to expand and contract at will, until she realised that distances were sometimes given in miles, and at other times in kilometres.

She opened the bag resting on the passenger seat and

pulled out the road map and the set of hand-writtendirec-
tions. She had never before seen such a spider-web of tiny
roads, and the directions she had been given, that had once
seemed so reassuring and detailed, were useless in practise.

"Help me here," she said to herself.

When she looked up she was startled to find an odd-
looking individual standing beside her car. He was leaning
against a rickety old bicycle, with a rain-coat and a rolled up
newspaper tied in a bundle on the back. He wore a battered
hat over an ancient pin-striped suit. His boots were muddy
and the cuffs of his trousers were rolled into his socks.

Grace lowered the window on the driver's side. "Hello
there," she called.

He wheeled closer and leaned towards the open window.
His eyes were the same light blue as the sky, but rimmed
with red, his chin stubbly with a three-day beard, the pores
of his skin sallow with ingrained dirt.

"Hi there," she tested nervously. "Can you tell me the way
to Ennismuck?"

He studied her a full minute.

"Ennismuck?" she repeated.

He massaged the colourless growth of beard under dirty
fingernails.

"Ennismuck," she tried once more.

"You'll not get to Ennismuck from here," the old timer
volunteered at last. "Go on another couple of miles."

"Pardon?"

"The nearhand way is over the mountain," he pointed.
"Up left and turn on your way down."

"Sorry?"

"There's a heap of stones on the side of the road – you
leave them there," he winked. "Then left again at the cross
and you're home and dry."

"Thank you so much," Grace said. She skidded away,
leaving the old man standing in the middle of the road. He
had been sincere she imagined, and even willing to oblige,

but the language he spoke made even less sense than the average New York cab driver.

The next branch road going up into the mountains seemed the nearest thing to the directions offered. She began the climb. It was early yet, and even if she went astray there would surely be a grocery store or a gas station where she could ask for directions.

MULCAHY SLAPPED HIS hand down on the roof of Oliver's pickup truck, shouted good luck through the open window, and stood back as it pulled away. Another poaching expedition done. Thirteen fine salmon, minus the one shared with Theo, to be disposed of through the black economy and the money split two ways. It was not enough to keep the wolves from the door, but at least he wouldn't have them chasing him around the kitchen table. The day was moving on. He had delayed too long with Theo. He needed to make up time.

He collected the empty gas cylinder and loaded it into the bottle-green Wolseley. It was an old-fashioned and impractical car, but he cherished the rich leather seats, the walnut trim and the heavy chrome ornamented bodywork, at a time when every other car on the road was uniformly streamlined to resemble a soap-bubble.

"I'll bring a new cylinder when I get paid for the fish," he called to Theo.

The old man had come outside to lean on the stone wall that surrounded the pig-sty at the gable of the cottage. He was breathless after the exertion and he did not answer.

"You should go back to bed for a few hours. You need the rest," Mulcahy urged. "Did you hear me?" he shouted again as he sat into the car. Theo turned and waved him off, a gesture to indulge Mulcahy.

ALONE WITH HIS thoughts, Theo went on watching the pigs in the sty. He enjoyed their company and the way they stopped short and cocked their heads at a curious angle to weigh-up an onlooker. He approved of those fleshy ears and the comical twist of their short, curly tails. He admired the pig especially for being the most immediate, stubborn and earthy of creatures, and yet the inspiration for such a rich vein of folklore and legend. Roast pig was an age-old source of nourishment, the centre-piece of every proper banquet. But even the domestic pig was seen as a devourer of its young, and the wild boar was a bristled and ferocious messenger of death in the Celtic order of things.

These pigs were of a mixed and humble variety, but he watched in fascination as they snouted and fussed and made something precious of the clay. Soon, he, too, would be clay. He had dedicated his entire life to the study of myth and legend and to the business of self-knowledge; that opening of the soul to the mysteries of existence. So why hold on? Why this grim persistence, this urge to continue?

"But who does not fear
   the bristling boar of death
  the bustling black
    hog of his own death."

He recited the lines by his favourite poet to his attentive listeners.

In these final days he had been visited by dreams of unusual force. Dreams like vibrations, or shock waves, that started on the edge of the web of consciousness this incarnation had woven around him. He interpreted these intense emotional vibrations as a signal that the entire web was on the brink of collapse. It was easier to interpret these troubling dreams as a sign that the end was close, than to accept that they pointed to a sense of loss he was destined to take to his grave.

MULCAHY'S CAR BUMPED out the lane towards the mountain road, his mind on Theo. How much time had they left? The old man was sinking very fast. He ought to be spending more time with him. He cursed the bank loans and duties that kept him away. These last hours were so precious, and yet he was being forced to run around the country like a blue-arsed fly, just to scrape up enough money to put food on the table of a dying man.

Visibility was poor at the junction where Theo's lane met the public road, and Mulcahy was distracted. He had pulled out on to the road before he saw the truck. A huge haulage truck on its way to the gold mine with a load of steel vats and pipes. The driver had no intention of stopping. Mulcahy jerked the gearshift and the car shuddered into reverse. The big wheels of the truck came within a hair's breadth of the car. The truck rolled past. A lumbering and intrusive beast in this landscape of stunted hawthorn trees, low dry-stone walls and narrow bog roads.

"Shit!" he swore.

He would be stuck behind the heavily loaded truck until the next turn-off. Until then he would have to suffer the cloud of dust and diesel fumes and loose stones thrown up in its wake. He dropped back and waited to get out by the truck at the next passing place.

GRACE WAS TRAVELLING fast, enjoying the clear blue sky against the craggy mountains, the great sweep of open bog land, the fresh air and the high empty road. She drove with the window open, to feel the breeze, and to blow away the jet-lag, one elbow cradled in the frame. It had been a good decision to take the road less travelled, she thought happily, and reached for the volume dial on the radio. She was still fumbling with the dial when she swept around the bend and met the truck.

There was no time to stop or pull over. She swung the wheel hard. The car swerved wide and tilted violently as it mounted the ditch. The steel hubs of the truck's enormous wheels chewed along the side of the car as it squeezed through the impossibly narrow gap, and then spat the car out against the ditch.

Everything moved in slow motion. Every detail of the accident was inscribed on Grace O'Connor's brain. She heard the sound of splintering glass and the dull, emphatic thud of metal being crushed against rock. Then the car fell back with a dreadful lurch. The terrifying momentum had barely eased, but by some miracle she had got around by the truck. Her car was still bouncing out of control along the road when immediately in her path she saw the oncoming car.

MULCAHY HAD A clear view of the disintegrating car and the whey-faced driver as she jerked the wheel in horror to avoid a second head-on collision.

"Here we go!" he shouted and hit the brakes hard and braced for the impact.

When he felt the car slide he released the brake pedal and then pumped the pedal hard a second time. The tyres squealed and gripped, and the car shuddered to a halt. His head lurched towards the dashboard. The safety belt caught. A fish went flying past and smacked off the glass.

He looked up, but there was nothing in front of him. He checked the rear-view mirror in time to see the other car mount the opposite ditch and take flight over the edge of the mountain.

The salmon had tumbled free from the sack on the back seat and fallen all around him. The engine had cut out. But there was no other evidence of what had very nearly been a fatal collision. Ignoring the mayhem it had caused, the truck continued on its way, turned the corner and disappeared. Mulcahy jumped out and ran up the road to the spot where the other car had vanished.

He followed the skid-marks to the edge of the road and looked down. The car had landed on its roof in the bog. A wheel was slowly spinning. He stood frozen in his tracks, looking down at the smashed car, stunned by the speed of events. When the wheel finally stopped spinning the mountain became intensely still. Mortuary silent. He steadied himself for a terrible duty.

A tan leather bag came sailing out of the open window on the driver's side of the crashed car. A woman's arm reached out. A head crowned with dark hair appeared, and the driver crawled free from the upturned wreck. She got to her feet, dishevelled, wet and muddied, but apparently unhurt.

"Hello. Are you all right?" Mulcahy shouted from the road.

"All right?" Grace yelled. "Do I look all right? Look at my car. Look at my things..." She spun around in the soft ground in a tantrum of shock, indignation and protest.

She had no broken bones anyway, Mulcahy decided. "Take it easy. You're still in one piece," he said. He scrambled down the embankment calling to her. "You just ran out of road."

"I did not run out of road, I was run off the road," Grace raged. "I'm calling the cops."

Mulcahy was relieved to find the girl unharmed. He felt sorry for her, but he had to think of himself. He had no fishing rod, no license, no permit and no club membership. To invite a big inquisitive guard on the scene with a tape-measure and a notebook would be a recipe for disaster. Once the guard had the details of the accident, and discovered that no one had been injured, his attention would inevitably turn to the chief witness, Mulcahy.

"I never knew any situation so bad a policeman couldn't make it worse," he bluffed as he arrived beside her.

"What?"

"I said, let me take a look."

Grace could hardly keep up with her emotions. First there had been the holiday sensation of the open road, followed by the horror of the accident. Then the relief to find that she had escaped uninjured. The appearance of another slack-jawed yokel standing there watching the whole episode had brought a burning rush of temper. This fury was quickly giving way to a sense of bewilderment and disbelief.

"That truck made no attempt to avoid a collision," she insisted. She followed Mulcahy as he circled the car on a tour of the damage.

"It was up to you to pull over. The smaller vehicle is supposed to give way."

"This is my fault? Is that what you're telling me?"

Mulcahy scratched his jaw in thought, and eyed her from the other side of the upturned wreck. "You could send for the police," he said. "But you'll be stuck here for hours waiting for them to arrive, because all we have in Ennismuck is a talking door."

"What are you talking about?"

"There are no guards on duty in the town, only a green intercom on the door that connects you to a bigger station. The other station is a long way off, and they won't exactly call out the emergency response unit for a car in a bog hole. And let's suppose you do bring the guards in on this, and the case goes to law. In six months time you'll have to come back here to give evidence in the District court before a sour old District Justice. The Justice has a serious brandy hangover from the night before. The company who own the truck and, co-incidentally, the stretch of river and guest lodge where the Justice does his fishing and brandy drinking, have the truck driver swear he met a confused American woman driving on the wrong side of the road."

"I swerved to avoid a collision."

Mulcahy went back to his inspection of the car, leaving Grace to draw her own conclusions. He wouldn't swear to the truth of what he'd said, but he didn't want his name on any official report or police file. Not that he was wanted by the law, or anything: he just didn't need the hassle. Guards were like Rottweilers, great to have on your side, but they could also turn on you without warning.

Grace studied the stranger's thin build. His manner was

self-effacing yet defiant. Unruly hair. Shuffling walk. Ragged but colourful woollen sweater, woolly cap, muddied jeans and a neckerchief tied at his throat. If she had been asked to costume an arrogant, anti-social misfit she would have been pleased to arrive at a similar get-up.

She flicked a strand of damp hair from her eyes and looked at all that was left of her car. "I picked it up at the airport this morning," she said. "What are the rental people going to say? This is terrible."

"No accident in this life is ever too bad if you can walk away from it," he said.

"But what am I going to do?"

"Leave the car here and we'll go for help."

Her head was in a spin, but it dawned on Grace that she was in no position to turn away any offer of assistance – no matter what form it took. Her hands and face were smeared with dirt, her clothes were wet and torn and she was stranded on the top of a mountain. She might have to wait a long time before another person showed up. Even then would they stop to give her a ride looking the way she did?

She remembered the advice given by her Tai Chi and fitness instructor: clarify your goal and focus on your next move.

"Okay," she began a rapid pep talk to herself. "So you've written off your car. But you've escaped serious injury. You're still in one piece. There's no blood and no major injuries, and this guy has offered to give you a ride back to civilisation."

She broke off to shout to the stranger.

"You got a name?"

"Mulcahy," he said.

"All right, Mulcahy," she said. "My luggage is in the trunk."

The car had hit the ground fender first and then belly-flopped to finish top down in the soggy ground. The soft landing had spared Grace but there was a lot of damage from the earlier collision with the truck. They tried and failed to force open the damaged lock securing the trunk.

"Stuck," Mulcahy said.

Grace felt her resolve cracking. "Great. That's just wonderful," she exploded. "What next? An avalanche?"

Mulcahy rested one hand gently on her shoulder.

"Leave it," he said. "I have a friend with a garage. He'll rescue the luggage, salvage the car, and sort out everything for you with the rental people. He'll have you back on the road in no time."

Grace picked up the bag thrown from the car and allowed herself to be led away. Mulcahy took her hand and helped her up the last steep part of the embankment. When they reached the road she withdrew her hand and stopped to look back at the crashed car stranded in the wilderness of bog. What a lousy, stupid mess! It was just typical of her luck to be singled out for disaster only hours after she had arrived in the country.

THREE

ULCAHY STUDIED HIS silent passenger. He had been afraid she might have to be treated for shock, but thirty minutes or more had passed since the accident without any recognisable symptoms. He was surprised she had not called for a doctor, or told him to drive her straight to the nearest hospital, but he did not force the issue. She could make up her own mind. He said nothing, and used the lull to look her over.

He was impressed. The crash had barely knocked a feather out of her. Once she had been persuaded to leave the car behind on the mountain, she had regained her composure quickly. Now she seemed willing to follow whatever course of action he suggested to get her transport back on the road and her day up and running again. With luck, and a little bit of help from Oliver, the whole episode would waste only a couple of hours. He could have done without the complication, but it was nothing to get too wound up about.

"Are you feeling all right?" he asked to confirm his reading of the situation.

She nodded, but said nothing.

Her arms were folded around the bulging leather bag rescued from the car.

What did she have in that bag? She held on to it the way a small child might cling to a comfort blanket or a precious stuffed toy. Her hands were small, manicured and flighty, always touching her hair or tugging at her clothes. The clothes were expensive, and her jewellery so discreet it must have cost a fortune. Her make-up had been spoiled by the crash and her chestnut copper hair was in a tangle. A damp bob hung over her forehead down to her lively eyebrows. Her mouth was large and her nose slightly too big, but her cheek bones were high and her hazel eyes responsive and quick. Attractive? Yes. Beautiful? Well that was a matter of opinion. She certainly had an open, animated and appealing face – if that was any indication of her real nature. Irish American, he decided, with a dash of sailor's blood somewhere along the way.

He still hadn't asked her name, but why bother? She was a native of a more colourful climate, accidentally blown off course, and much too exotic to be doing anything more than passing through this neighbourhood. She had the appearance of someone cut out for a better life in a better place than this.

GRACE IGNORED HER new acquaintance and his attentions and maintained a quiet reserve, looking straight ahead. She felt several slow, tingling shivers crawl along the length of her spine. A throbbing ache had started in her neck and in her right shoulder, but the last place she wanted to be was a hospital. Not so soon after her mother's death. She took deep, regular breaths, holding the air in her lungs, and allowed the pain to pass. She was determined to remain in control. It was useless feeling sorry for herself. Her thoughts and emotions were like mud mixed through water; they would have to be given time to settle and clear.

The old-fashioned car crested the mountain and the road dipped towards the sea. Grace found the scenery a perfect antidote for the trauma of the accident. The sunlit heather went on for miles. In the distance the mountain ridges were splashed with magenta, cobalt and Prussian blue. Below her there appeared a thinly populated community, separated from the sea by miles of greensward and long sandy beaches. A white band of breaking waves stretched the length of the coast, while inland the tiny fields were arranged like a stamp collection, the boundary hedgerows a bright haze of May blossom. Thickets of brushwood with saffron-coloured flowers and an abundance of other lace-delicate wild flowers lined both sides of the road as they dropped towards the valley.

She was still taking in the view when the smell in the car – the smell of spirit-based glue and old upholstery, damp floor-mats and fish – reached her nostrils. Yes, definitely fish. The scent led her attention to the open sack on the back seat. Several large salmon with their mouths agape, their eyes frozen in a permanently startled expression, hung out of the top of an old gunny-sack. Another loose fish lay at her feet.

When she looked up Mulcahy was watching her. She felt she had to say something.

"Do you fish?"

"No," he said.

She imagined some errand outside the law, and it flashed through her mind that her accident on the mountain had been deliberately engineered. She had been run off the road with a purpose. Kidnapped. Of course. Why not? The luck of the O'Connors.

No. She had to control the paranoia. Ever since this man Mulcahy had arrived on the scene of the accident, his manner had been so cool and dismissive it verged on hostile. He was a reluctant Samaritan, forced by circumstance into helping her. Her accident was a nuisance. Having to look after her was a huge inconvenience, interfering with whatever low-life business had brought him her way this morning.

One look at his thin build and Bohemian appearance told her he was the type whose own needs come first. Broadway and the acting profession were crowded with his sort.

"The minute I'm out of this mess, pal, you're free to get on with your own squalid little affairs," she told herself, and the promise increased her resolve to put this entire episode behind her as soon as possible.

At the foot of the mountain they came to a four-way crossroads. There was a large mound of earth and stones in the field opposite the crossroads. Short grass grew up the sides of the mound, but the top was heaped with bare rocks.

She recognised it as a pre-Christian burial mound. Beyond the green mound a river looped and glistened. Not without a sense of irony, she spotted the black and white signpost pointing left to Ennismuck. Mulcahy turned right.

"The village is the other way," she objected.

"I have a small chore to do," he said.

Rather than alarming Grace, the detour only confirmed everything she had guessed about him: his own interests first, naturally.

After a couple of miles they left the main road and turned up a stone-paved driveway planted on either side with young trees. An old building loomed before them. From the outside it appeared to be in ruins, nothing more than a rambling, three-storey, stone shell. The outlying wings were windowless and roofless, the courtyard stood empty and there were gaps in the perimeter walls. Only the centre of the building appeared remotely inhabitable.

Mulcahy stopped inside the walled courtyard with the car facing a high wooden door. The door was freshly painted with black and secured by a heavy metal bolt.

"Where are we?" Grace demanded.

"My place," he said.

"You're kidding?"

He did not answer but twisted about to pick up the open sack from the back seat.

While Mulcahy collected the loose fish and replaced them in the sack, Grace surveyed the building. She found it impossible to place its purpose. She guessed from the stonework and the state of disrepair it was over a hundred years old, but it did not look like any castle or stately home she had ever seen. It lacked the fortifications of a barracks or a jail, and it was not typically industrial, though she felt the building had elements of all these things.

"What is this place?" she asked finally.

"It used to be a Poor Law workhouse."

"Where they took in homeless people during the potato

Famine?" she asked, annoyed that she had not been able to identify the purpose of the building sooner.

"You know about that?"

"My grandmother was Irish."

Mulcahy shot an interested glance in her direction, but then grabbed the door handle.

"This will only take a minute."

She watched him go to a small service entrance set in the larger main door. The latch key was already in the lock, and he left the door open after he went through. She allowed him a full minute and then, hesitant but intrigued, she took up her bag and got out of the car.

She stood in the doorway and listened. The inside of the building was silent. She stooped and stepped through the small door and cautiously looked about. She had entered a vast room with a high ceiling. The floor was paved with red brick, and the space appeared to be unfurnished and used only for storage. She paused for her eyes to adjust to the darkness. In the gloom, and between the shafts of natural light coming through the high narrow windows that were squared into tiny panes, she could pick out a host of giant figures. There was a horseman mounted on a stallion, which reared up in the air dwarfing her. Beside the horseman a poet sat enthroned with an open book in his lap. They were constructed on the same grand scale as the main doorway. Around them giant heads, a witch with an empty cage tied on her back, and an abundance of mythical creatures that Grace could not name, were gathered in the half-light. They stood in silent ranks, huge, colourful, bizarre, and completely at odds with this sad building's original purpose.

Her breathing quickened at the unexpectedness of the discovery, and she was led deeper into the building by the whole dreamlike spectacle.

She touched papier-mâché surfaces and textured fabrics to be sure the things before her were real. Then she looked about to get her bearings. She was in a long hall that appeared to be divided into several chambers with old, flaking remnants of paint on the walls. She continued through to the next chamber where there was more light. The ceiling was just as high, but here there were hanging strip lights and this space was clearly used as a workshop. The timber shelving along the walls was packed with wood-work and metal working tools, paint tins and brushes, bolts of fabric and parcels of bamboo canes, coils of wire and bundles of stiff marsh reeds. Here too were half-made fig-ures, painted wooden stilts and crêpe paper lanterns. It was like looking into a circus trailer, with the show packed away in moth-balls, but ready to explode on to the green again at the first opportunity.

The next compartment was walled off with a regular door standing open.

"Curiouser and curiouser," she chuckled to herself and went through.

She had entered the living area. The massive timber beams that supported the high ceiling, and the woodwork over her head, had a more finished appearance. The sheer walls were painted smooth white and hung with enormous works of art, metal sculptures and nameless farm implements. There was a huge stone fireplace with a patterned rug in front, and two old chairs on either side. A woven reed basket, the size of an average family car, was used to store the fuel. It was like stepping into the reception hall of a great castle.

Then she noticed that one entire side of this enormous room was divided into a series of living compartments. The timber units were stacked like a child's building blocks and connected by an open-plan stairway and landing. It was a house within a house.

Marvelling at the ingenuity of this conversion, and con-sumed by curiosity, she lifted the latch of the plank door and went through into the first-floor unit. She stepped into a kitchen paved with large black flagstones. The ceiling was low and the rafters hung with every kind of odd and remarkable item: lamps and jugs, bottles and hand-tools, coils of rope and brass beer taps. An impossible hoard of nameless antiques. Only the most dedicated collector could have assembled this Aladdin's cave of wonders and curiosities.

Grace was so taken with the decor she did not immediately notice Mulcahy bent over the drainer, gutting and cleaning the fish.

"I wondered where you'd got to," she blurted to cover for the intrusion.

"Sorry, this is taking longer than I thought."

She was relieved to find he did not object to her walking in on him. "Quite a place you have here," she went on quickly.

"It takes people by surprise the first time they see it," he said. He gave her a half-welcoming glance over his shoulder before turning back to the fish.

"That stuff on the way in – what's it all for?"

"Festivals, parades, floats, that kind of thing," he said.

"Is that how you make your living?"

"I wouldn't exaggerate," he said as he cleared the fish entrails away with his fingers.

"The Workhouse – it's a neat address for a starving artist."

Mulcahy did not bother to answer. She guessed he had heard the remark too many times before. "Hey, I was an art student once!" she said defensively.

"Fine art?" Mulcahy enquired. He put the last fish down flat with the others in a crate.

"Design," she said.

He dried his hands and turned to look at her, still holding the towel. "What do you do now?"

"I'm a costume and a production designer. Film and stage work mostly. Hollywood. Broadway."

"What's the name?"

"O'Connor. Grace O'Connor."

Mulcahy shrugged to let her know he hadn't heard the name before. He threw the hand towel aside. "You make a living at it?"

"I do okay."

Mulcahy considered his visitor. The workhouse had stirred her interest, but then the place had that effect on a lot of people. Some felt it was the work of a madman; others were dazzled. She was an arty type and would probably want to see more, but he found her attractive and that was a problem.

However, he could not ignore the way she had begun to shiver. Several times now he had seen her stamp her feet and rub her hands vigorously along her upper arms for heat. He reached out for a woollen sweater hung over the back of a kitchen chair. He tossed it across.

"Try one of my costumes for size," he said. "It doesn't look great, but it'll keep you warm until we collect the rest of your stuff."

Grace put down the bag and caught the flying garment. To find the sleeves she had to shake the sweater open. It was torn in several places, splattered with paint and matted with wood-shavings. It was the most shapeless and off-putting article of clothing she had held in her hands for a very long time, but she felt cold, shivery and bruised, and she would be grateful for any comfort. She raised her arms and pulled the old sweater down over her head. Her shoulder hurt, but by the time she had fixed the roll neck in place the warmth of Mulcahy's sweater surrounded her like an embrace.

"The bathroom is next door," he said, "if you want to get cleaned up."

"Thanks."

It was a man's bathroom. Not as clean as it should be. A razor in the tooth glass, the top open on the toothpaste, soap melting in the water. A dog-eared poster against animal testing of cosmetics on the back of the door. But there were traces of a woman. The half-used bath oils in fancy bottles, a discarded hairbrush, a novelty jug holding a range of cosmetic brushes, and several other little touches only a woman brings to a bathroom. It didn't look like she lived there, just stayed over sometimes, or perhaps she had lived there for a while and they had broken up.

The instinctive inspection over, Grace went to the mirror. She looked bedraggled and shaken. She washed her hands and dabbed water on her face. Later she would shower and rest. Her make-up was in her bag, but when she tried to re-apply lipstick and eyeliner her hands were shaking too much. Before leaving the bathroom she looked in the mirror again and bolstered her spirits with the thought that she didn't look too bad considering all she'd been through.

"You look terrible," Mulcahy said when she returned. "Are you sure you don't want to see a doctor?"

"I'm okay, really," she said peeved.

"If you say so."

He picked up the crate with the fish and led off. Grace followed him out of the kitchen and allowed the latch to drop back on the plank door. It was an eye-catching return journey and she stalled to see more. In the workshop she stopped beside an enormous set of antique, cast-iron weighing scales.

"It's like stepping into a Hollywood backlot," she said, fingering the heavy chains that supported the twin iron pans.

"Those scales were used to weigh in the meal to make gruel for the starving inmates here at the height of the Famine," he said.

Grace could not say if the answer was meant as a rebuke, or delivered as an historical fact.

"We're standing in what used to be the workhouse kitchen. Next door is the refectory," he continued in the same tone. "If you look over there you'll see what's left of the stoves, and the big iron pot where the gruel was cooked." As he pointed he moved steadily towards the door.

"It's incredible," she said. "There's so much history here."

"Too much old history," he said. He stood at the threshold with the smaller service door held open and waited for Grace to catch up. She stepped out around him into the morning light. He closed the door firmly, but left the key in the lock. Then he crossed the courtyard to load the crate in the back of the car.

"I have a lot to do this morning," he said to cover for the haste.

"Maybe I can have the tour another time," she prompted.

"This is where I live," he said. "It's not really open to the public."

FOUR

THEY DROVE STRAIGHT through the crossroads marked by the ancient mound and took the coast road to the village, a breathtaking stretch of dips, rises and winding bends. Grace was ready to forget the driver, and enjoy the roller-coaster ride in a vintage car with spring-flowering pasture-land on one side, and the open sea on the other, fringed by mile after mile of mountainous backdrop. A scattering of stunted thorn trees, their branches combed away from the prevailing gales, were all that stood before magnificent views of the Atlantic.

She had brushed up on her Irish history and folklore for this trip, and raided the Strand and other bookstores for coffee-table volumes showing Irish country life and customs. Having done this background reading, she considered herself up to speed on this little island, but the Ireland portrayed in the books had been deceptive.

How could she have prepared for the enormous industrial truck that almost took her life on a quaint and narrow bog road? A Famine workhouse full of giant carnival figures? Or these weird-looking roadside bungalows with their Spanish arches and Texas ranch-house attachments, built right next door to the most beautiful but neglected traditional farmhouses. One house they passed had a family large enough to fill an entire wash-line with numbered football jerseys drying in the sea breeze. She would have taken the next dwelling for an abandoned shack it appeared so sad and run-down, but through the open front door she glimpsed a table and a kitchen chair, and an old man with a face smoked a tea-leaf dark colour by the open fire.

The margins of the road were teeming with delicate and abundant wild flowers, and yet the spread of garbage and wrecked cars was reminiscent of New York's poorest ghettos. Wind carried plastic shopping bags and banners of torn black plastic hung in tatters from the trees and the barbed wire fences. Then there was an immaculate garden, a lovingly restored cottage, cropped fields and mile after mile of rugged and wonderful dry-stone walls.

Another surprise was the large number of farmhouses with FOR SALE boards posted in the front yards. She began to watch for these boards and counted five within a short distance.

"There's such a lot of property for sale," she remarked. "In America you could only dream about owning a home somewhere this beautiful. Even if you found the right place you'd have to be a lawyer to pay for it."

"Not around here, you wouldn't. This place is on its last legs," Mulcahy said bluntly.

"But it's so beautiful."

"You can't eat scenery."

Grace saw a pale modern church spire and a cluster of rooftops in the distance, but Mulcahy pulled up outside a stone cabin on the outskirts of the town.

The once white walls of the cabin were streaked with green after several rainy winters. The tin roof was painted grey, but the rust had holed right through in patches. Broken and dismantled hulks of cars were piled up all around the yard, the aftermath of time's demolition derby.

Mulcahy got out of the car and Grace followed. She noticed a stack of used horseshoes hanging on a nail over the cabin door. Several fire-blackened twists of iron rested against a water barrel beside a blacksmith's anvil. These were the only indications of trade.

"This isn't a service station," she said.

"Oliver... hello. Oliver... you about?" Mulcahy called, ignoring her. The front door was closed, but not locked, and he walked straight in, obviously on familiar terms with the owner.

The inside walls were black with soot. Taking up one entire end of the building was a cow-hide bellows that resembled a pleated and brass studded leather lung. It was connected to a forge with a scorched steel hood, a funnel-shaped chimney, and a grate full of cold cinders. On a stand beside the forge stood a second anvil embossed with bright hammer strokes. There was also a long wooden bench, pushed back against the wall, and used to display hand-made iron candlesticks and brass tripods; the sort used to burn scented oils.

These hand-crafted items stood in contrast to the cog-wheels, engine parts, electric motors and mechanical debris assembled on a wooden table in the centre of the workshop. A whole area had been given over to trial inventions, engi-neered after the free-hand blue-prints sketched on scraps of paper, beer-mats and torn ends of cardboard, and scattered around the floor. Drawings like dead flower heads shed by a frustrated imagination. The product of a teaming mind curbed by a lack of money, encouragement and common sense.

Everything about the place seemed crude, experimental and wayward. Grace began to have serious misgivings about letting whoever was in charge of this alchemist's den look after her car.

Luckily, Mulcahy was having trouble locating the owner.

"Maybe we should go to a proper repair shop," she sug-gested. "The rental people will – "

"Oliver. Where are you?" Mulcahy shouted across her, and this time Grace caught a hint of worry in his voice.

As they waited in silence for an answer, they heard a low moan. A second dull groan led Mulcahy to a canvas cover in the far corner of the forge. He pulled back the cover.

"Oliver!"

The owner of the forge stirred groggily. A tell-tale glass bottle escaped from a fold in the canvas and took off across the floor.

Oliver's eyes flickered open and he looked up.

"Sally. Is that you?" he squinted towards Grace, where she

stood in silhouette against the bright light coming through the door.

"Get up you dirty eejit. It's me, Mulcahy."

"What's up with you now?" Oliver said, twisting his head painfully to meet the voice.

"You have a customer."

Bleary-eyed and shaky, Oliver sat up and focused on the stranger standing in the doorway. The escaped bottle was trapped under one foot, and her arms were folded in disapproval. A foreigner, he guessed. Good-looking, too. But she looked like she had just been pulled through a hedge backways. She was also wearing one of Mulcahy's old jumpers. He looked again at the friend he had left outside Theo's cottage such a short time before, not even sure he wanted an explanation.

OLIVER USED A CHAIN-SAW to cut down the nearest roadside pole bringing a telephone line up the side of the mountain.

"Isn't that against the law?" Grace asked dumbfounded.

"It belongs to the gold mining company," Oliver said.

"But it's private property," she objected.

"They owe you that much," Mulcahy said.

The two men cut up the pole to make levers, which they cradled on the available rocks. Between them they heaved to right the car trapped in the bog. As they worked Oliver wiped away a trickle of sweat running down his temple, then leisurely tasted the tip of his finger.

"Neat *poitín*," he declared.

"Sweet Jesus, will you put your back into this," Mulcahy swore and grunted, his face purple and contorted with exertion.

"She's a fine thing," Oliver went on in his gentle, soft-spoken way.

"The car?"

"No, yer one. The Yank."

"She's crazy. Wired. Anyone can see that. And my whole

day will be wasted if you don't get a move on." Mulcahy heaved once more at the wooden lever, lost his footing, and fell on his knees in the wet ground.

"She's a fine catch," Oliver said and took the extra weight, while Mulcahy found a more secure footing. "The best in a long while."

"O Lord God, give me patience," Mulcahy pleaded and strained again to budge the car.

"There's something very appealing about her," Oliver speculated. "She has that vulnerable look."

"Vulnerable?" Mulcahy jumped on the word. "You didn't hear her yelling at me after the crash. It's not a voice you'd want calling you in the morning."

Oliver's shoulders shook in silent amusement, and with a deft pitch he raised the car. It rose in a slow arc, without assistance from Mulcahy, teetered at the top of the swing, and then landed on its wheels with a resounding squelch.

With the car back on its wheels Oliver began to uncoil the heavy loops of a steel tow-chain. Mulcahy made an impatient grab and took the chain from his hands. He marched to the front of the car and began to fumble, without success, for a place to secure the hook.

"It's time you started to look around," Oliver said and removed the plastic shield used to conceal the loop meant for towing the car.

"Let's just get this yoke back on the road," Mulcahy cut him short and clipped the chain in place.

"That other woman is gone. And she won't be back."

Mulcahy did not respond.

"You're not the first man, you know, whose wife left him."

"Thanks, Oliver."

"A man on his own is in bad company. That's what you told me."

"I was wrong," Mulcahy confessed. "You get used to being on your own. You develop your own routines. Your own way of doing things. I don't think I could go back to living with someone now. Not full-time, anyway."

"I'm just saying..." Oliver shrugged. "But you're the boss."

"Exactly," Mulcahy said. "That's what I like about the present arrangement. I am the boss."

GRACE STOOD ON the road beside Mulcahy's car and watched the rescue operation from a safe distance. Oliver took several long strides up the embankment and sat into his pickup truck. He eased the pickup into slow reverse. In the bog below, Mulcahy stood clear when the tension came on the tow-chain. The car gave a shudder, but seemed reluctant to move. The wheels of the pickup began to spin and skid up loose gravel, and the pickup truck skated about the road before settling into a steady haul. The crashed car began to crawl up the embankment. As the roar from the pickup's engine increased Grace was startled to hear raised voices, first on her left, then on her right.

"Keep her coming," one shouted. It was the old timer with the battered hat she had left standing with his bicycle in the middle of the road that morning.

"Easy... Easy does it," said another old timer, who might have been his double they were so similarly dressed.

"Now, give her the rev," a third arrival directed.

Where had they come from? Where had they been hiding? It was as if they had been spirited from the rock or risen like apparitions out of these tumbling mountain streams, ghosts brought back to life by the sounds of human activity in this lonely wilderness. Grace looked on bewildered at this sudden audience of old men, hunkering, signalling and calling out instructions.

"Steady."

"Steady."

"Lock her hard."

The left front wheel broke away from the axle, rolled down the embankment, toppled over and finished in the drain. Her car was a dreadful looking mess. Not a single panel had escaped without damage. The audience of old boys shook their heads knowingly, and passed around cigarettes.

Grace stood next to Mulcahy while he took a hammer and battered the fender roughly into shape. "A bit of filler in the wing and she'll be as good as new," he said. "The rental people won't even notice a scratch."

Oliver retrieved the lost wheel from the drain and tossed it into the back of the pickup. From his tool kit he produced a jemmy to force open the lock and rescue her luggage from the trunk. Then the front of the car was hoisted in the air and secured for towing.

Oliver sat in behind the wheel of the pickup and Mulcahy stood by the driver's window.

"Take her in to the workshop and see what you can do."

"It's a write off, another heap of junk to add to your collection," Grace called to Oliver over Mulcahy's shoulder.

"How soon can you have this yoke back on the road?" Mulcahy prompted.

"Tomorrow, or the day after," Oliver stated confidently.

"But I need a replacement car today!" she said.

Oliver smiled at Mulcahy. "I'll look after the car, if you look after the driver."

"I can't."

"That's the deal."

Mulcahy glared at Oliver.

"Excuse me," he said to Grace. He put his arm around her shoulder and ushered her along the road out of earshot.

When he got back to the pickup truck, he opened the driver's door and hissed between clenched teeth, "I don't need this, Oliver. I have to move the fish, see the bank manager, get back to Theo – "

"It's springtime. There's a great stretch in the days. You'll have plenty of time for all that," his friend laughed and started the engine. The truck with the car in tow moved off slowly. Mulcahy was forced to jog alongside the open door.

"What am I supposed to do with her?"

"Talk to her."

"I'm not interested."

"Go on out of that," Oliver said and accelerated harder.

"Will you slow down," Mulcahy puffed.

"Give her a chance. She might surprise you."

"Nothing a woman would do would surprise me," Mulcahy shouted back.

The driver's door closed. Mulcahy stumbled to a halt, gulped after air, cursed and turned wearily to walk back up the road to where Grace stood with her bags around her feet. The old-timers had melted back into the landscape and the mountain side was empty once more.

"I can look after myself," Grace said when he reached her. "Leave me here. I'll get by."

Mulcahy picked up her bags without a word and carried them to his car. She watched him load the bags roughly, but moved only when he sat into the car and started the engine. He pulled away before she had the passenger door closed. She secured the lock and fastened her seat-belt ready for a hard drive.

"Where to?" he barked.

"Strand Cottage," she said.

"Are you sure you have the right address?"

"Hey!" Grace objected.

"Okay, sorry. Only that place was sold not so long ago," he softened.

"Ever hear of Eleanor O'Connor? She was my mother. The cottage belonged to her family."

"I know the name. I've even seen a few of her films. But I didn't know the O'Connor family came from Strand Cottage."

"I've bought back the property," she said, and was delighted by the look of surprise on his face.

Mulcahy signalled to overtake Oliver's truck, with the car in tow. He beeped as they went past, and they began the drop towards the coast. Grace felt her spirits rise at the thought that she was leaving the problems of the morning behind. The paperwork could wait. A positive mental attitude would see her through this demanding day.

Mulcahy was now resigned to the new delay and his attitude had become more friendly and inquisitive at the news that Grace had bought property in the district. "Have you been to Ireland before?" he asked.

"No," she said. "When I started to look into my family history, all I had was the name of my grandmother, and what you guys call a parish in the West of Ireland. So I placed a notice in all the local papers. After a couple of editions these guys from the Ennismuck Town Improvement Committee – have I got that name right?"

"Emm-humhh," Mulcahy offered a non-committal hum to keep her story moving.

"They wrote to say they knew the house where Eleanor O'Connor's ancestors were born. They wrote again to let me know they could negotiate a sale, if I really wanted the property. They had photographs sent over. One look at the place and I knew I had to have it."

"It's – " Mulcahy tried to speak, but Grace cut across him. "It's beautiful, I know. The wild flower garden. The sea at the door. The thatched roof. Just like a postcard."

"It was signed over to a shopkeeper in the town a couple of years ago. It hasn't been lived in since – " Mulcahy started again, but she was not ready to listen.

"Mom always said we would visit Ireland together some day, but the trip never happened. There was always work to finish. Always another job in the pipe-line. And actors never turn down work, even when they don't need it. Next year, she used to say. Always next year."

The broken promise stirred a memory and she fell silent. Mulcahy left her to her thoughts. There was something she ought to know about Strand Cottage, but it was not really his job to break the news.

Once more they drove through the crossroads marked by the green mound, only this time Mulcahy took the remaining fork road. They were headed out on to a peninsula, but Grace lost track of the number of times they turned down further side roads, each one narrower than the last. Finally the car turned into a private lane covered over with grass, except for two narrow wheel-tracks along the sides. Mulcahy directed her attention to the view up ahead.

"This is it," he said. "Strand Cottage."

The car bounced in the rough track. At the end of a tunnel of arched shrubbery the cottage appeared. It was low and small and built along traditional lines, with a thatched roof, whitewashed walls, tiny windows and a simple wooden door. To Grace it had everything. Quaint, tranquil and idyllic, in a setting of tremendous beauty at the brink of the sea, it was surrounded by vivid patches of colour from the bushy garden plants grown wild out front. In the pasture fields at the back of the cottage a pre-historic ring fort stood like a low volcanic crater, mantled in short grass. The air had a sea-breeze freshness, but the heat of the sun would be trapped in the shelter of the walled yard.

Grace jumped from the car before Mulcahy had time to cut the engine. She spun around on tip-toes to take in the view.

"This is so beautiful," she cried. "It's exactly the way I imagined it... No. It's better."

She grabbed her travel bag and rushed to the front door. She rested the bag on the window ledge, opened a side pocket and found a key. Mulcahy brought up the other bags and waited at her shoulder.

"Okay, fingers crossed," she said. She fitted the key in the lock and jiggered it from side to side. Under rusty protest the key turned right around. The damp-swollen door swung open with a stiff creak.

Grace stood in the doorway and took in the interior with a new owner's pride. The front door opened directly into the kitchen. It was tiny and neat, with a bare stone floor, two wooden chairs, a massive open fireplace, a table and a traditional dresser stacked with old delf and a pair of antique oil lamps. The whole place struck her as a time-vault, undisturbed and steeped in atmosphere. A place preserved since her grandmother's era.

"Wow!" was all she could say.

Mulcahy came through with the bags. Excited, Grace set her precious travel bag on the kitchen table. "I'm going to love it here," she announced.

Mulcahy stood to watch while she produced a slim computer from an inside pocket of the bag and flipped open the top protective lid. A smooth screen and a keyboard were revealed.

"Nice," he said.

"I couldn't get along without it," she enthused. "I plan to work on the costumes for a new Irish play, and everything is going to be designed right here. These colours, this setting, the whole mood. It's perfect. But I hope my computer's not busted after the crash."

She unwound the power cord as she spoke and went in search of a power point. Mulcahy said nothing and watched her face grow more flushed and puzzled as she searched along the timber skirting and then behind the wooden dresser.

"I hope you brought a good supply of batteries," he relented.

Before she even looked up Grace knew what he was about to say.

"There's no power?" she guessed.

Mulcahy nodded.

"Fine," she said to mask her upset. She shoved the lap-top computer aside. He was not going to see her daunted.

She opened the bag again and fished out a sketch-pad, a miniature box of paints, and a selection of costly squirrel-hair water-colour brushes.

"I'll go back to pencil and water-colour," she said. "That's how I trained, and that's how I do all my finished artwork." She carried her things to the worktop nearest the kitchen window.

Her eyes darted anxiously about the hair-cracked enamelled basin.

"There's no faucet?" she asked, and found Mulcahy's eyes waiting for her.

"There's no running water?" she beat him to the answer.

"It's a very old cottage."

"There is a bathroom – tell me there's a bathroom," she panicked.

Mulcahy looked in the direction of the delf ewer and basin on the dresser.

"Toilet?" she screeched.

Mulcahy made a helpless face and jerked his thumb at the open door and the green fields beyond.

"No. No," she cried. "That can't be right. It's in the contract. The guy promised me – "

"Who promised?"

"Tuttle. Eugene Tuttle."

"The publican?"

"This guy is in real estate."

"And a lot of other things besides," Mulcahy said.

Grace snatched up a fistful of official documents from her bag and rummaged through them until she found the right one. Then she turned sharply and stalked out of the cottage, her face rigid with legal indignation. Mulcahy followed. He closed the door on the way out and removed the key from the lock. When he sat into the car she was already waiting in the passenger seat. He handed her the key.

"Tuttle's?" he guessed.

"**Y**OU'RE A CROOK! A cheap, lousy crook. And I'm going to let this whole town know it," Grace hollered, and used her bare fist to pound on the wooden door. The varnish came away in crisp little flakes, but the weathered doors remained securely bolted.

"Do you hear me? Open up."

There was no hint of life inside Tuttle's bar.

"He's not up yet," Mulcahy said. He looked around to see if they had attracted an audience.

Curtain corners stirred in the surrounding bedroom windows, but the white lace hems dropped back into place once the owners were spotted, and the town square remained empty.

"How could he be asleep at this hour? Doesn't he have a business to manage?" she raged.

"He takes tablets. His nerves are bad."

"What about his conscience?"

"Leave it," Mulcahy said.

IN HIS ATTIC bedroom above the bar a gangling and harrowed man, with a permanent worry frown – a frown so deep not even drugged sleep could press it from his forehead – gripped the cotton sheets with tense, bony fingers. The water jug and glass, and the stack of medications on his bedside locker, vibrated with the force of the pounding on the front door below. Low thuds shook the bedroom. Eugene Tuttle tossed restlessly as the muffled hammering echoed about the sleeping chambers of his brain.

He was a terrified and disobedient schoolboy again, racing for home in the dark, a plastic satchel full of bogus legal documents strapped to his back. Through the curtains of falling night came the pounding of monstrous hooves, and the blood-chilling squeals of a nightmare Black Pig. The noises were far off at first, but soon he could hear the pig's wuthering grunts, and the sound of the trees behind him splintering like matchwood, as the enormous creature broke through the undergrowth. Down the narrow, crescent-moonlit canyon he fled, with no hope of escape. He ran as fast as his poor, short legs could carry him, but the Black Pig kept closing. It could swallow a schoolboy in one awful gulp, and it was so close now he could feel the monster's hot, reeking breath on the back of his neck. The Black Pig issued one final, merciless and triumphant squeal.

"Ouuurreekre... "

Tuttle shot bolt upright in his bed, his eyes out on stalks, his face a mask of terror. Realising where he was, he climbed out of bed. He was unsteady when he put his feet into his slippers, and disorientated still as he went to the bedroom window to investigate the commotion in the street. He fingered the curtains open the merest crack, and was relieved to discover the drab, unchanging vista of the town square.

The only sign of life was Mulcahy. He was walking across the square with some tousled and wild-eyed gypsy girl, a brazen article, openly sporting one of Mulcahy's old sweaters – the fellow had the morals of a rabbit. And it was shocking to think that anyone needed a drink so badly, that they would come banging on the door of a public house long before decent people were up out of bed. Still, a publican had to make a living, and he had missed two early clients. It was time to get dressed. Time to get up and face the day. For the hours of light at least he would be free from these awful nightmares. And he had important news. News that could not wait. He was keen to be the first to break it to Mulcahy.

"I SAW THE bedroom curtains move," Mulcahy remarked after a glance back at Tuttle's premises. "We'll take a stroll around the town and come back in half an hour."

"Thirty minutes and no more," Grace warned. "I'm not letting him away with this."

"Settle yourself. This isn't downtown Manhattan. At the rate you're going you'll wind up in a strait-jacket."

"Are you kidding? I'm the only one who isn't nuts around here."

"That's what they all say."

Grace ought to have taken offence at the remark, but she saw Mulcahy was laughing at her, and there was some truth in what he said. She had over-reacted. She had inherited a quick temper from her mother, and her best efforts to curb this fiery trait, through meditation and Tai Chi, often let her down. She resolved not to lose her cool so quickly again. At the same time she meant to let these people know that nobody was going to make her look like an idiot, either as an American or as a woman.

She took several deep breaths and counted up to ten.

"Okay," she said. "I'm calmer now."

"Good."

"Tell me about this guy, Tuttle." She fell into step beside Mulcahy.

"He owns a bar. He's set up as an estate agent and he does a bit of auctioneering and property dealing on the side."

"Is he a crook?"

"They're all a shower of crooks; it's just a question of degree," Mulcahy said. "Estate agents are people who get to live in big houses by selling little houses to everyone else. Tuttle was brought to court one time for having two prices on the one property. The price the seller got and the price the buyer paid."

"He creamed off the difference?"

"It was alleged."

"It was never proven?"

"He collapsed in the witness box, and the story went around that he was dying of some unmentionable disorder."

"Was he?"

"That was fifteen years ago. He's still selling ancestral cottages to Americans."

"I get the picture."

"He's not the worst," Mulcahy added. "But when it comes to money he's tighter than the Vatican."

They went around by the newly restored stone plinth in the middle of the main square. Across from the empty plinth stood a cottage with a large but plain front yard and a thick growth of ivy around the windows. On each side of the open front door, and draped across the wall next the pavement, could be seen a series of posters on brightly coloured paper. They were crude but loud: GOLD DIGGERS GO HOME. FOOL'S GOLD. And STOP THE MINING NOW.

In the yard, a tall, wiry man in late middle-age was busy operating a home-made silk-screen printing press. He had a tight haircut, round glasses and a short moustache balanced like a hairy caterpillar on his upper lip. He wore a brown corduroy jacket and trousers, a boot-lace tie and a white shirt with the collar studs severely fastened. A collection of metal Trade Union badges flashed in his lapels. A gruff wire-haired terrier, with a face resembling its owner's, watched him turn out more posters on orange, pink and red fluorescent paper.

"Tom Giblin," Mulcahy explained. "He's the man leading the campaign against the gold mining company on the mountain."

"The guys who ran my car off the road?" Grace asked.

"'Morning, Tom," Mulcahy called.

Giblin raised his head. "Citizen Mulcahy," he saluted and went back to work.

"Every town has its social pecking order," Mulcahy whispered. "I have to warn you, Tom Giblin and myself are at the bottom. A socialist and a mad artist: you shouldn't really be seen talking to us."

Grace welcomed this confidence and the unexpected, wry smile that came with it.

"Who should I be seen with?"

"On the top roost is Councillor Oswald Archibald MacNabolla. Everyone finds it simpler to call him Councillor Oswald. Especially if you're trying to address an envelope. He's the chairman of the local political machine, Eugene Tuttle is the treasurer, and their tin god is John Charles Leddy, TD. If John Charles Leddy goes to the toilet, Coucillor Oswald is right behind him with the paper-work. "

"J. C. Leddy. I know that name," she said.

"Leddy is the town big-wig, a man with an unshakeable belief in his own importance. He's not a minister, thank God, but he is a government back-bencher. What we call a Deputy. You'll find him most Saturdays loitering by the plinth, shaking hands with the voters, firmly convinced there should be a statue of himself put there to fill in for the other days of the week, when he's away in Brussels or off on some other junket. He's also the town solicitor."

"We'd call him a lawyer," Grace laughed. "Street-walkers solicit."

"Solicitor is more accurate."

"You don't like him?"

"He doesn't have a badge or a gun, but our Deputy Leddy is a cowboy, all right. He tells the story himself about the time he was at a big function in Dublin, which was being broadcast live on television. This young lad comes up to him and says, 'You're the reason I had to emigrate to London to get a job.' Leddy kept smiling for the cameras, gave the lad a big hug and whispered in his ear, 'Why don't you piss off back there?'"

"J. C. Leddy is the guy who drew up the legal papers at this end when I bought the cottage," Grace said.

"That figures. He's stuck in everything that goes on around here. He pretends to be above all the skullduggery, but there's huge abuse of the regulations going on at the gold mine, and Leddy is the man covering it all up. Of course, you'd have a job trying to prove it, but all you have to do is take a look at Deputy Leddy's new all-en suite Bed and Breakfast emporium, to know there's funny money coming from somewhere." Mulcahy pointed across the square to an imposing three-storey town house of mixed architectural pedigree, with a black Mercedes parked on the asphalt drive, double-glazed windows and a wrought-iron notice hanging above gate posts topped with two enormous eagles.

"He's sure doing okay," Grace agreed.

"You can sing it. And straight in front of us is his sidekick, Councillor Oswald's, grocery and hardware." Mulcahy pointed to an old-time store-front, and a second entrance to a yard with a set of tall gates, and a sign above that read CEMENT STORE. "Together, Oswald, Tuttle and Leddy make up an unholy Trinity known as the Town Improvement Committee."

"Does everybody in this country have at least three jobs?" Grace marvelled.

"No," he said, "but there's an old Irish tradition known as greasing the fat hog's back."

They left the square and started down a hill street that sloped towards the harbour. Mulcahy led her down a flight of steps to the promenade. On the rocks before the sea there stood a building like a miniature castle, with turrets and towers and a solid cement roof sectioned out to make water tanks. One of the corner towers had crumbled away through storm damage and the windows were sealed up with cement blocks.

"The original seaweed baths," Mulcahy explained. "The new bath-house is further on."

"Are they open?"

"All summer, and weekends in the winter," he said. "You should try them some time. A long hot seaweed bath is the only cure I know for a murderous hangover."

"Does your friend Oliver go there often?" she teased.

"He keeps topping up all the time so he never really needs the cure."

Secure in his own territory Mulcahy was a much more attractive character. Grace let him talk on and point out landmarks as they walked the length of the promenade. A couple holding hands, dressed in honeymoon new clothes, approached and passed them with a smile. She glanced back and missed the last thing Mulcahy said.

They reached the harbour, where the orange and yellow lifebelts and the blue and black nylon netting of the home-made lobster pots added a touch of colour to the otherwise ugly cement pier. One old trawler in dry dock. No fishing boats. The single row-boat on the beach turned keel-up-wards to keep out the rain.

A mobile crane raised a great block of limestone high into the air. The boom swung about and deposited the stone block at the storm-damaged end of the breakwater.

"We've had a hard winter," Mulcahy explained.

A huddle of men stood watching the machine at work. They were a shabby but eye-catching crew, turned out in second-hand coats and worn out Sunday suits, with flat caps and woollen caps pulled down over their ears. Some stood smoking cigarettes. The remainder stood with their hands in their pockets, occasionally shifting their feet to stir a pebble or a sea-stone.

"The boys," Mulcahy said.

"Locals?" she asked.

Mulcahy shrugged. "Part-time fishermen, small farmers and *poitín* makers," he said. "Cliffmen, sheepmen, cornerboys. They get lifted off the dole and put on these government employment schemes to make local improvements. It can be argued what they do is of value to the community, but mending walls and cleaning up graveyards is hardly a career. On wet days a few of the boys bring their instruments to work and they all practise set dancing in the local hall. It's a lot of fun to see so many men dancing together and getting paid by the government to do it. The rest of the time it's a bit like the wall building projects the landlords organised for their starving tenants in Famine times. The notorious Famine walls."

"You don't approve?"

"To me it's just another bureaucratic ploy to demoralise the population."

At the end of the pier Grace noticed a solitary figure wearing a black bowler hat and a long black coat that reached down to his ankles. He was holding an open umbrella and reading a paperback book.

"Who's the dude with the umbrella?" she enquired.

"That's Sam," Mulcahy said fondly.

"A friend of yours?"

"He used to be a builder, and a gifted one at that. I had him with me when I was converting the workhouse. Then he discovered the plays of Samuel Beckett. What happened to Sam was a bit like what happened to Saint Paul on the road to Damascus. After reading Beckett he made a vow that he would never work in the rain again. And Sam reckons it rains all the time."

"Where do you guys come from?" Grace asked, looking between Sam and the town square, Mulcahy and the employment scheme boys.

Mulcahy glanced back at the town. "It was Thoreau who said, most people lead lives of quiet desperation. Here it's comic desperation. Some experts reckon all the smart ones got out of this country a long time ago on the emigration ships. We're descended from the idiots who stayed."

WHEN THEY GOT back to the square the sun was high above the rooftops, but there was still nobody moving in the seaside town. The awning over Oswald's shop-front stirred, restless for custom. The door to Tuttle's bar was finally open.

"Do you want me to talk to him first?" Mulcahy offered as they approached.

Grace went in the door ahead of Mulcahy. "You leave this guy to me," she said.

"Fair enough."

Sally Holmes was meant to be employed as Eugene Tuttle's secretary, her wages subsidised by a government job experience scheme. In truth she worked most of the time as a barmaid, for a few extra pounds paid under the counter, and the bonus of a rent-free room above the bar. Her skin had a pale, indoor complexion but her build was strong and athletic; she had large blue eyes, full lips and a loud voice, her thick dark hair cut in a short, no nonsense style. She was a resourceful and blunt-spoken girl who found most men dull and moody company, and a hindrance to the hopes she had for a bit more excitement in her life. She was trusted with a key to open up the front bar whenever Eugene Tuttle overslept, and she was at the sink with her employer, who was not long out of bed, when Grace and Mulcahy walked in to the bar.

Grace ignored Sally and moved directly to confront the tall, pale man wearing an old school-tie and a navy blazer two sizes too big for him, with an anchor badge embroidered on the pocket.

"Are you Tuttle?"

Eugene Tuttle stared at her blankly. He had the solemn and permanently concerned expression of an undertaker in the middle of a funeral service. He was also afflicted with a nervous stammer and entered most conversations like a small dog barking.

"Yeh-yeh-yeh-yeh... a minute, please," he pleaded.

Tuttle did not know who she was, this forceful hussy with the dirty face and Mulcahy's borrowed sweater, but she was not the kind of client he wanted on his books.

"Sally, will you look after this young lady," he said, eager to get talking to Mulcahy. He raised the hatch set in the marble bar counter, skirted expertly around Grace, and led Mulcahy away. "And, Sally, bring some coffee," he called back as an afterthought.

Sally Holmes looked to Grace. "Coffee?" she offered.

Grace O'Connor's eyes were like two knife blades planted between Tuttle's narrow shoulders. She was ready to explode, but she had business to settle with this starved and miserable individual, and it would be useless to start a screaming match too early in the deal. She bunched both hands in tight fists to control the rage.

"Mmm-Mmm-Mulcahy, I wish you wouldn't encourage these gypsies and New Age Traveller friends of yours to come in here," Tuttle said shaking his head sadly. "I have nothing against them but – "

Mulcahy did not wait for him to finish. "You have a problem, Eugene," he said. "I'd know by the look of you."

"No-no-no problem," Tuttle insisted. "I was fi-fi- fishing on the company estate – "

"You, Oswald and Leddy, no doubt," Mulcahy interrupted.

"In our official c-c-capacity. As members of the Town Improvement Committee – "

"Naturally," Mulcahy said.

There was an edge in his voice that threatened to cut through Tuttle's polite manner, but Eugene Tuttle had news for Mulcahy and he was not going to be put off.

"The mining company have agreed to pay for a new statue for the town square," he announced.

"A piece of sculpture?" Mulcahy corrected.

"Yeh-yeh. To go on the empty p-p-plinth," Tuttle said proudly.

Both men looked out of the bar-room window at the plinth. It was a prominent location and a focus for the town. In physical terms alone it would be an ambitious undertaking, regardless of the politics involved, and the memory that several pounds of rebel explosives had been used to remove the last monument put there.

"How much?" Mulcahy said finally.

"A substantial f-f-figure."

Mulcahy's eyes fixed on Tuttle and the publican twitched. He ran a finger in the gap between his thin neck and his stiff white collar.

"We didn't get down to the nitty gritty," he wriggled. "We thought we might talk to you first – to see if you were interested – in taking the co-co-commission."

Mulcahy ran a hand through his woolly hair and studied the bar-room floor to collect his thoughts. "What did you have in mind?" he asked.

"Deputy Leddy felt that we might c-c-commemorate a notable p-p-politician. The company suggested something co-co-connected with W. B. Yeats. The p-p-poet. For the visitors. The Continentals read a lot of Yeats."

"And the Americans," Mulcahy added.

"Americans? Yes. Americans, too," Tuttle said, puzzled but ready to agree.

"We could ask your client over there what she thinks of the idea," Mulcahy said. "She's an American."

"American!" Tuttle said, and he turned his head sharply to take a second look at Grace.

"Grace O'Connor," Mulcahy said. "You sold her a cottage by the sea."

"She's in the c-c-country? She's here?"

"What amazes me, Eugene, is how you could possibly remember that an old ruined cottage belonging to your friend Oswald was also the ancestral home of the late great actresss Eleanor O'Connor, and then you forget to mention that the place has no running water or electricity when you offer to sell it to her daughter."

Tuttle looked in panic between Grace and Mulcahy.

"You'd better talk to her. I'll get back to you about the ah... commission," Mulcahy said and he stood aside to allow Tuttle to face his seething client.

"Ah! M-m-m-Miss O'Connor. We meet at last," Tuttle started towards her bravely and held out a hand in greeting.

"Cut the crap, Tuttle. You promised me a bathroom." She waved the contract in front of his face.

Eugene Tuttle looked pained by her attitude and by her use of coarse language. He continued past Grace.

"Toilet facilities," he said.

"What?"

Tuttle raised the hatch and returned to the far side of the bar. "Toilet facilities, Miss O'Connor," he repeated and ducked out of sight beneath the counter. "If you read the description carefully, the wording on the contract was quite specific." The voice came from somewhere down below as he rummaged under the counter.

"Bathroom? Toilet facilities?" she snapped. "What's the difference?"

Tuttle reappeared clutching an odd-looking box. For a second Grace could not place its purpose. Then the penny dropped: a chemical toilet. Eugene Tuttle put down the crude antique on the marble counter. There was a spade with a short wooden handle and a bottle of disinfectant to go with it.

"I meant to leave it over to the cottage sooner," he said with a face as serious as a headstone.

Sally Holmes came through the alcove carrying a tray with three cups, a steaming hot coffee pot, stainless steel milkjug and sugar-bowl and a plate of custard cream biscuits. "Coffee?" she enquired of the company.

Grace's incredulous stare broke away from the squat and obscene contraption on the counter. "I've been suckered." She rounded on Mulcahy. "That old cottage is a baby weasel deal, and you knew all along." Before Mulcahy could answer she swung about hard, left the bar and slammed the door on her way out.

"Jesus! Eugene, you've hit a new low," Mulcahy said, studying the publican and his antiquated chemical toilet with mixed feelings of awe and disbelief.

"They're v-very efficient," Tuttle appealed.

SIX

COUNCILLOR OSWALD was not a happy man. He fitted the last of the groceries on the counter into the large brown cardboard box, and then reached for the ledger where the credit issued by his shop was recorded. He was, by nature, a penny-cautious and careful man. Since he had been elected to a position of influence he had whittled down and collected on the books his family had kept for three generations. There had been a steady calling in of old accounts through coin of the realm, a field surrendered here or a run-down cottage handed over there. "Fresh banknotes for fine produce," was his private motto, and all outstanding bills had to be settled at the end of the month, regardless of circumstance. Trade was slow but dependable, and he was a fine advertisement for the merchandise he sold: a barcode of oily hair combed across his white scalp, a pink meaty face and his substantial girth squeezed into a nylon shop-coat over a polyester shirt and tie and a one hundred per cent acrylic cardigan: a combination that crackled with static electricity. His belly rested on the rim of the counter as he delayed every client for news. The delay lasted only until the next customer walked in. Then the previous client was immediately dismissed and the new source of small talk and scandal beckoned to come forward.

Mulcahy cast his eye over the contents of the box of groceries on the counter. Enough to do his friend Theo for a week. The salmon had been passed on to a client up the street, but that money was owed to the bank. Oswald's bill would have to wait for another while.

"I think that's everything," he said. "I'll collect the cylinder of gas from the Cement Store on the way out."

"Is the gas on the... On the ah..?" Oswald could not bring himself to mention the ugly word.

"On the slate, yes," Mulcahy said.

Oswald opened the ledger and entered the purchase. His soft jowls dropped and the corners of his mouth turned down like a disappointed bloodhound. "You don't find it all adding up," he said as he turned back a leaf to read the previous page.

"I'll settle with you when I finish this commission."

"Ah! Grand. Grand. You were talking to Deputy Leddy," Oswald brightened.

"No. Eugene Tuttle."

"Yes... well... never mind. Did he mention we were all agreed the monument should be made out of cement? I'll be giving a special rate."

"He forgot that part."

"Ah, what would you expect?" Oswald sighed. "The poor man is a martyr to his nerves..."

Mulcahy longed for another customer to walk in to the shop, but he was not so lucky. Councillor Oswald's waist-line spread along the counter as he settled in for a long deliberation on a suitable public monument for the square.

Mulcahy hastily gathered up the box in his arms and began to back away towards the door. He reached a hand behind him to find the latch and fumbled his way in reverse out of the shop, still nodding in vigorous agreement with the owner as the bell over the door clattered above his head.

"I have all the details I need to start the commission," he said. "Leave it with me."

SAM SAT AT the end of the pier with an open book. Grace sat a short distance away on a cut-stone bollard looking down into the water. She listened to the waves as they broke against the stonework. The swell and suck of the water, the swishing coils of wrack and the wheeling cries of the white birds out skimming the breakers made a soothing, melancholy music to fit her mood.

She did not hear Mulcahy approach. After a minute she sensed him standing next to her. He did not speak but remained close, listening with her to the sea.

"Mom never made the journey back," she broke the silence between them. Her voice was tired and defeated. "One day, she promised. Now she's dead. I wanted to make the journey for her. The closer I got to Ireland the more I felt like I was coming home. I really believed something special was going to happen. But I was wrong. My mother was right. I should have stayed away. Left the dream alone. Dream! What am I saying? This whole trip has been a nightmare. The accident. The crummy cottage. That snake-oil salesman in the bar. The O'Connor family never lived in that cottage without any water, did they? Tuttle, Leddy, and Oswald, they read my notice in the paper and decided to sell that old shack to a gullible American looking for her ancestors."

"I really wasn't involved in any of that," he said.

"I know. I just lost my cool back there."

"I'm sorry, Grace."

His sympathy was genuine, but Grace could not bring herself to look at him. She felt cold, jet-lagged, sore and beaten. Her body was bruised all over. Every time she turned her head, she was struck by a stinging pain in her neck and shoulder. She needed a hot shower and a change of clothes. She needed to forget this had ever happened.

"I can take you to a good hotel," Mulcahy offered. "You can book in for a night, and I'll help you find a reputable agent to sell the cottage. The mining company are buying up a lot of property. I don't know what you paid for the cottage but you'd get some of your money back."

He looked at her closely and wondered if she was listening.

"I've wasted your day," she said.

"No sense making a start now on a bad day's work," he coaxed. "Tell me where you want to go and I'll take you there."

"How about the airport?"

"All right."

She turned to look at him, wondering if he really meant her to leave, and the pain struck.

"Hell!" she gasped.

"What is it?"

"My shoulder. It's really started to hurt."

"I should have brought you to a doctor earlier. It was selfish of me not to bother."

"No, it's okay. It's just a muscular thing."

"We don't have a full-time doctor in the town," he said. "But that old man you saw, Tom Giblin. He has a cure for strains. He's a faith healer."

Grace managed a weak smile. "Can he work miracles?"

TOM GIBLIN HAD washed the ink out of the fabric and was dismantling the home-made silk-screen printing press set up in his front garden. The boundary walls were draped with newly printed posters on fluorescent paper, hung out like fresh laundry. In the morning breeze the ink was already dry to the touch. The dog barked and Tom Giblin looked up.

"Hello, Citizen." Giblin's manner was abrupt, but the Citizen title seemed to be a long-standing joke between the two men.

"I have a friend with a sore shoulder," Mulcahy told him.

"Hi there," Grace said.

"An American," said Tom Giblin.

"New York."

"Never mind."

"Can you do anything for her?"

Behind the severe round glasses there was a fanatical light in Tom Giblin's eyes. The blunt, woolly moustache heightened the appearance of grim energy.

"Come in for a minute," he said. They left behind the chemical reek of cleaning fluids and followed him into the cottage with the dog sniffing at their heels.

It was a dark, traditional country kitchen with stacks of

socialist papers and journals left all around. The smell of turf smoke and old tea was overlaid with screen printing ink. Grace was struck by the three pictures on the walls: a bearded Jesus with a red bulb burning underneath, a dog-eared poster of Fidel Castro and a full length still portrait of John Wayne from *The Searchers*.

She was directed to sit in a kitchen chair. Tom Giblin stood over her and she heard him speak softly under his breath. She could not make out the words, but it sounded like a prayer. She had to contain a smile at the idea of a socialist cowboy faith healer, and she knew this amused attitude would prevent any cure. Out of politeness she sat still and allowed him to complete the ritual.

When he was through whispering the incantation or prayer over her head, Tom Giblin left the kitchen. "We don't see enough foreign visitors in these parts," he called from an upper room.

"Perhaps it's the way you treat them."

"She had a run-in with Tuttle this morning," Mulcahy explained.

"Oh!" said Giblin as he returned.

"That wasn't all," she said, and she gave her account of the accident on the mountain. While she told the story Tom Giblin looped a piece of cord around her neck and took a measurement. He took a second measurement by holding the cord over her head. With a quick jerk of his fingers he snapped the cord at the chosen length, tied a knot and hung the cord around her neck. Its pleated strands were cold and faintly greasy, but not unpleasant against her skin. There was no sense of healing warmth, or any kind of spectacular tingling sensation after the cord was fitted, but she found the searing pain had eased.

"I thought I'd got away without a scratch," she finished her story. "Then my shoulder began to hurt like hell."

"We'll do what we can for you," Giblin offered, "but if you're still worried you should see a doctor."

"It feels better all ready."

"Give it a couple of days," he said. "And leave the cord around your neck."

He turned to Mulcahy. "Were you a witness to this accident?"

"It would be hard to say who was at fault," Mulcahy hedged.

"I know who was at fault, and I wasn't even there," Giblin snapped. "That crowd on the mountain. They're full sure they can get away with anything. It's time someone put a stop to their gallop."

"What's to be done?" Mulcahy said. "They hold a legal mineral prospecting licence thanks to Councillor Oswald and his cronies."

"It would help if we got rid of that caucus on the Town Improvement Committee."

"You'll not shift them either," Mulcahy said.

"These are your friends Tuttle, Oswald and Leddy," Grace said.

"They're not my friends," Mulcahy said.

"But you side with them," Giblin insisted.

"I don't take sides."

"Doing nothing is the same as siding with them."

"It is not the same."

"Then why won't you come to our meetings? Help us to put pressure on the County Council for a full environmental and cost benefit analysis of the gold mine."

"What's a County Council?" Grace interrupted. "Is it a legal thing?"

"It's a form of local government," Mulcahy said.

"Government!" Tom Giblin exploded. "That crowd of nodding donkeys." He turned to Grace to appeal his case. "We have two very ignorant men in charge of this town and Councillor Oswald MacNabolla is both of them."

"I know, I know," Mulcahy tried to distance himself from this familiar dispute.

Grace noticed his discomfort. She stood up and flexed her shoulder. "It really does feel much better," she said. "I'd like to pay you, Sir, for your trouble."

"I don't accept money," Tom Giblin said shortly.

"But I would like to give you something."

"When you have your car back on the road, you can put up a few posters for me."

"I'll do anything I can to help your campaign, I promise."

"Good. I'll hold you to that."

"I thought you weren't going to stick around?" Mulcahy said.

"I've changed my mind. They tricked me and sold me the wrong cottage, but the records say my grandmother came from Ennismuck. I'd still like to know where she was born."

"What was your grandmother's name?" Tom Giblin asked.

"O'Connor. Sarah O'Connor."

Tom Giblin cradled his chin in the palm of his hand. His eyes turned inwards in an effort to recollect the name. He shook his head. "No. There are no O'Connor's left in this parish," he said. Again he thought hard and trawled his memory for any sprat of information. Nothing came.

"That's okay," she said. "It was a long time ago."

"Thanks, Tom," Mulcahy said, moving towards the door.

"You're welcome, Citizen," Giblin returned to more formal terms.

He walked with them to the end of the garden. At the open gate he stopped Grace. "You could ask Theo," he said. "Your friend, Mulcahy. He might remember something."

"I don't know, Tom. Theo isn't well. He's not well at all."

"I heard," Giblin nodded in sympathy.

Grace was ready to clutch at any straw.

"It would mean a great deal to me," she pleaded. "If I could talk to him for just five minutes."

"Theo would remember back further than me," Giblin said thoughtfully.

"He's not well enough for visitors," Mulcahy insisted.

Grace fixed her eyes on Mulcahy and willed him to say yes. "Please," she said.

Mulcahy's loyalties were turned upside down by that eager and imploring stare.

"All right," he said. "I have to leave a box of shopping and a cylinder of gas up to his house anyway. You can come along. But we have to go now. No more delays. And when we get there you stay in the car until I talk to him. If Theo doesn't want to talk to you that's as far as it goes. Have you got that?"

"Thank you so much," she said. "You don't know how important this is to me."

"And you don't know how important Theo is to me," he said, looking hard into her eyes.

Amazed that a man like Mulcahy had such intense, protective feelings towards anyone, Grace wondered if she had misjudged him. Drop it, an inner voice warned. That territory was already forsworn.

GRACE NOW LOOKED on the crossroads with the stone mound outside the town as a compass: the east branch for the workhouse where Mulcahy lived, west for the town of Ennismuck, north to her cottage on the peninsula and south for the mountains. They took the south fork and very soon passed the last farmhouse and the last flowering pasture field. The rocks broke from the ground in rough steps that led into the hills. Strong light bounced off the stones. One craggy rise rolled into the next. The scale of things was intimate and enclosing, and yet this landscape had an emptiness, a lonesome quality far beyond the great panoramas of the American north-west.

They entered a high valley with a lake in the centre, a bright circle of water like a powder compact mirror. After the lake she saw a middle-aged man wearing a white shirt and a dark waistcoat. He was slicing wheat-loaf sized parcels of peat from a cutting in the bog. A second man with a dark jacket stood over him, holding a fork with blunt prongs. Black and white figures isolated against a towering blue sky.

Mulcahy was enthusiastic about this traditional mountain craft of turf cutting. As they neared the men, he slowed the car for Grace to have a better look. The open black mouth in the side of the heather-covered embankment, he said, was the place where the winter fuel was cut. These turf-banks were handed down through generations of the one family.

Grace believed the tour was meant to compensate for imposing conditions on her visit to his friend, but she responded to the gesture. She liked the sound of his voice. The soft, slow, rolling vowels were very attractive.

"Take a good look," he said. "They're a dying breed, those hardy men with their white shirts and their *sléans* out there on the bog every spring."

Grace could see where each cut of the tool he called a *sléan* left behind a distinct wet gleam. The grooves made by the iron blade combined into a hound's-tooth pattern that stretched the length of the cutting. Layer upon layer of glistening peat, stripped away in benches like an archaeological dig. A journey back in time, past the limbs of Irish oak stained to ebony by the bog's pigment and juices.

The turf-cutters were beautiful to watch: the way one foot was used to sink the shaft of the *sléan* to slice a clean block of peat, which was raised immediately on the curved iron blade and tossed over the man's shoulder, a motion so fluid and regular the wet turf appeared weightless. Black motes sailed against the sky. His companion caught the flying turf and used the fork to load a wooden barrow. Then the barrow was hauled away and the wet turf scattered on the high parts of the bog to catch the drying breeze.

"Why is it always the oldest and the hardest ways of doing things that are most in harmony with nature?" Mulcahy pondered as the turf-cutters vanished from sight in the rear-view mirror. "There are machines up at the gold mine that tear-up acres of bog in an hour, and destroy generations of turf-banks in a single day."

Grace made no effort to reply. There were many answers she might have offered – progress, change, the powerful exploiting the poor, people not having the will to cry stop – but she preferred to follow this feeling of drowsy surrender closing over her head. Her eyes itched and burned. Her body-clock was upset. The day had been too long. Too hectic. Too demanding. She wanted to let go. To surrender to this exhaustion after the excitement. To be sucked down into dark and restful depths. To enter a more tranquil world, that moved at the mellow pace of Mulcahy's soft voice as it lulled her to sleep.

The car bounced over a pot-hole and her eyes sprang open. She could not say how long she had been asleep. Minutes only, she thought, five or ten at the most, but she couldn't be sure, and Mulcahy looked steadily ahead without speaking.

The bog road had become a cart-track bordered with uneven stone walls. At the end of the road they halted before a low stone cabin under a helmet of weathered iron. A ramshackle pig-sty extended from the gable. The cabin had been built in a sheltered hollow and the roof stood level with the hills at the back.

"Theo's place," he said.

"Someone lives here?" Grace was shocked.

"Why not?"

"It's so remote."

"That's the whole point," Mulcahy said. "I'm very fond of this old man. So even if Theo does agree to see you, I don't want you to delay. He'd talk all day, but he's not up to it. Is that clear?"

"Yes," Grace said, annoyed. She understood his concern for a friend who was ill, but she wished he would put a little more trust in her sensitivities. Just because she was from another country didn't mean to say she had no feelings.

Outside the cottage Mulcahy unloaded the box of

shopping from the car and told her to wait.

The house had a silent, unoccupied air. Mulcahy found the absence of life disconcerting. No smoke rose from the single chimney and the front door was closed. Theo always had a fire going, and like most of the old people who lived on the mountain, he left the front door open all day. Mulcahy dropped the box of shopping on the doorstep and hesitated for a split-second before he raised the latch.

In the half-dark kitchen he saw the body. Theo lay slumped over the table, his head pillowed in his arms. The carved wooden figure, on which he had been working until the last minute, had toppled over on its side. It lay close to his cold white face.

"Oh, no!"

Mulcahy grabbed the old man's shoulder. He shook him urgently and called his name. The frail body was still warm, and yes, mercifully, there was a stir of life, an unexpected return from this alarmingly dead sleep.

"Mulcahy!" the old man opened his eyes. His voice was hoarse and uncertain.

"You had me worried there for a minute," Mulcahy tried to make light of the heart-racing panic.

"I must have dozed off."

"I told you to go back to bed."

"No. I had work to finish. The final one," Theo said with a fond look at the carving on the table. He set the wooden figure up on its legs. When he rubbed his hands there was a strong aroma of wax.

"I don't like to hear that kind of talk," Mulcahy chided the old man. "You have several good years left yet, and dozens more carvings to finish." He returned to the front door to collect the box of groceries.

"There are three people you should never lie to, Mulcahy: your doctor, your lawyer and yourself."

The old saying woke in Mulcahy a buried dread. As he came forward with the box of shopping his legs began to wobble. The solid ground vanished suddenly from under his feet, and he was overpowered by a reeling sense of vertigo. He narrowly made it to the sink, and he leaned against the work-top for support.

"It's not right. You shouldn't be here on your own," he said choked by a feeling of helplessness. "If something happened..."

"Stop," Theo said. "I chose this life. I've always lived alone. Why should I be afraid to die alone?"

"I worry about you."

"I know. And I'm grateful," Theo said to close the matter.

The dizzy premonition of loss passed, and Mulcahy began to distribute the groceries around the kitchen. Wholemeal bread. Eggs. Milk. Porridge oat flakes. Dry leaf tea. He put the last of the things away, willing his old friend the strength and appetite to finish these humble provisions.

He turned to meet Theo: a forced effort at normality out of respect for the old man. "I would have been here sooner only I got held up this morning," he said.

"Trouble?" Theo asked.

"An American girl ditched her car on the mountain. I had to send for Oliver. He took the car in for repairs and I've been chauffeuring her around since."

"Where is she now?"

"She's outside. In my car."

"What's happened to your manners?" Theo's reaction was immediate. "Ask her in."

"Is that wise?"

"Stop fussing over me. You're worse than an old hen," Theo remarked. He put the carving away on the window-sill and began to straighten the chairs around the table. Then he used the edge of his hand to sweep the wood shavings from the top, his free hand cupped to gather and compact the debris.

"I'll do the tidying," Mulcahy offered.

"Dear God, I'm not that far through," Theo protested and

tipped the shavings on the open fire. They broke into flame over the dull embers and filled the air with the scent of applewood.

Theo cast his eyes about for aspects of his kitchen to which he had grown accustomed, but would be offensive to any visitor, especially a woman.

"It will have to do," he said finally, at a loss to know what last minute improvements could be made.

"You keep this place as neat as a convent."

"A celibate's retreat," the old man said. "It's so long since I laid eyes on a woman, I've forgotten what they look like."

"They still look like trouble," Mulcahy said.

He found Grace standing by the pig-sty at the gable. She was studying the two pigs there with interest. Her hand was at her throat and there was a remote but thoughtful expression on her face.

"Comical creatures," he said trying to fathom that look.

"Yeah. It's odd… " she said.

"What is?"

She reached around her neck and unhooked the gold chain. She held the chain out for him to see. A tiny gold pig was centred in the palm of her hand. "I brought it along as a lucky charm for my trip."

"You should look for a refund," he said after a token glance at the gold ornament. "Theo would like to see you."

Grace looked into his face. The expression there was both threatening and protective. She was not meant to accept this offer. But she had been through too much to get this far, and she was prepared to ignore his feelings this time.

She replaced the gold chain around her neck and started to walk towards the front door. Mulcahy followed a few steps behind her. Before the door he took her arm and pulled her up short.

"Go easy," he warned. "Theo will put on a show for you, but he doesn't have his old strength."

"Just how ill is he?" she asked outright.

"He could die at any time."

Grace froze and her insides twisted. Ugly memories threatened to surface. The private rooms. The hospital vigils. The silent waiting at her mother's bedside. That haunted period when she sat dry-eyed and terrified, not so much at the thought of her mother's death, but at the knowledge that one day she, too, would have to face this final ordeal alone.

"I didn't realise..." she stammered.

"If Theo dies, it's all over for me here. Finished. There will be nothing left to hold me. That's how important this time with Theo is to me," he said.

It was in this state of shock that Grace stumbled into Theo's kitchen. A room cluttered by broad interests. Fishing rods and cooking pans, old oil paintings on the walls, and incongruously fine bone china on the dresser. Chinese vases. Storm-lamps. Silver candle-sticks with a patina of great age. A wooden hand-carving in the kitchen window.

The stone walls were deep, and the light that entered through the little window was filtered through leafy ferns and flowering plants. It was a dim and shadow-packed room, but the atmosphere was cosy and immediately pleasant.

Theo was on his feet close to the door. When he spotted Grace he mustered a theatrical welcome. "My dear child, come in, come in..." He ushered her towards a big oak table in the middle of the kitchen.

"Theo, this is Grace. Grace O'Connor," Mulcahy made the formal introduction.

"Hi there," she said.

Theo looked pale and drained and Grace saw him reach for the support of his chair next the table.

"It's so corny," she apologised for the intrusion, "but I'm looking for my ancestors."

"Grace is a daughter of Eleanor O'Connor. She was a famous actress," Mulcahy explained, knowing Theo had not the slightest interest in American show-business celebrities, and had probably never heard the name before. "She was told her mother's family came from Strand Cottage."

"Or at least they may have been from this area," Grace added.

"There was an O'Connor family..." Theo said softly.

"I knew it," she blurted unable to contain her excitement.

"But the O'Connors never lived in Strand Cottage. And the whole family died of consumption."

"Consumption?" she quizzed.

"Tuberculosis," Mulcahy said.

"People talk about AIDS nowadays," Theo said, "back then we had TB. It was a terrible disease. People forget. Tuberculosis. Polio. Measles. Influenza. Even a simple thing like a toothache could kill. The past did not always have such a rosy glow before the discovery of antibiotics. The TB especially thrived in this damp climate. It began with a hard and constant cough. The stain of blood in the phlegm. Then the fever, and that fatal bloom of broken blood vessels on the cheeks. Whole families were wiped out. The better-off were confined to nursing homes where they simply wasted away. Many more died at home. Houses had to be fumigated with sulphur candles. Mattresses and furniture burned. Walls scoured with quicklime. Often these houses were closed up and abandoned, never to be lived in again. People were terrified."

"And the O'Connor family?" she asked.

"TB. The father. The mother. And finally the daughter."

"They all died?"

"Yes. The girl nursed both parents, and then she too caught the fever."

"You're sure about that?"

"I have very good reason to remember."

"I'm sorry," Grace said.

The old man accepted the apology with a curt nod of his head. "I wish I could tell you different."

She wasn't certain what he meant.

"Mulcahy, can you connect up that confounded gas cylinder, put on the kettle and make us a cup of tea, like a good man," Theo suggested.

"I really don't want to impose," Grace said with a quick but significant look at Mulcahy.

"Sit down, sit down," Theo signalled with his hand for her to take a seat at the table. "I'm curious. You do have the appearance of an O'Connor. Whatever led you to Ennismuck?"

"I traced my mother's mother, my maternal grandmother, back to Ellis Island and the date she arrived at the immigrant processing station there."

"Send these, the homeless, tempest-tost to me," Theo rhymed.

"The Emma Lazarus poem on the base of the Statue of Liberty," Mulcahy answered, bringing three bone China teacups to the table.

Theo smiled up at the younger man, and Grace recognised a compulsive and long established guessing game enacted by the two men and continuing now out of habit.

"I thought Ellis Island only processed the Famine generation Irish who left for America," Mulcahy turned to Grace.

"No, it was used right up until nineteen forty-three," she said. "Sixteen million people were processed there from the time it opened. But it was really only the poorest underclass that passed through Ellis Island. The steerage class passengers. The others were processed on board their ships. The ones who were off-loaded on the island were usually ragged, penniless and starving. They sailed up the Verrazanno Narrows full of hope, only to be unloaded on this tiny island, and then herded into an enormous brick building modelled after a French railroad station..."

She broke off. She realised she was talking too much. It was the first time she had really spoken to anyone about these vivid impressions she had of her family past, and of this emotional ghost hunt.

"I'm sorry, I'm going on," she said and looked to Mulcahy

to confirm her suspicion.

"No, please," Theo encouraged. "I want to hear."

"Are you sure?"

Mulcahy poured the tea but said nothing.

"Please do go on," Theo insisted.

"The processing on the island lasted four hours," she began again, aware of Mulcahy's disapproval. "There was a medical inspection for pink-eye, suspicious sores and fevers and then delousing. Those who failed the medical had a large white cross chalked on their backs. Then came an aptitude test of, like, forty questions, and you had to read from the Bible. If you passed you were ferried across to Manhattan. Most went directly from the Battery Pier to their own native ghettos. The ones who failed were put on the next boat back. The 'Anarchists' Boat' it was called. The rest were quarantined. Some tried to swim across and were drowned. More committed suicide rather than face the shame of being sent back."

"What about your grandmother?" Theo asked.

"She was one of those quarantined."

"Do you know why?"

"She was pregnant. She went into labour while she was waiting to be processed in the Grand Hall of the Ellis Island station."

"Jesus!" Mulcahy whispered.

"The records suggest my mother was born on the island."

"A flamboyant start to any career," Mulcahy said.

"And a difficult one," she said. "Her mother didn't survive the ordeal. She died, either in labour, or shortly afterwards. She never left the island."

"I'm sorry," Mulcahy said.

"The father?" Theo asked. "Was he present?"

"She seems to have been travelling alone. There is no name recorded in the space available for the father's signature. The baby was given over to a Catholic orphanage because the mother was Irish. From there my mother worked her way through a succession of awful homes and institutions until she found her way into the theatre."

"She went on to do a lot of big films. Musicals and Broadway shows," Mulcahy explained to Theo.

"She must have been an extraordinary woman," he said.

"She was. She died earlier this year."

"I'm sorry you had to come all this way for nothing," Theo sighed.

"But what made you think your grandmother came from Ennismuck?" Mulcahy asked.

"Ennismuck was the place of origin on her ticket when she arrived at Ellis."

Mulcahy waited for Theo to produce an explanation. The old man remained silent.

"The address was probably Louis J. Culkin's Draper shop," Mulcahy said. "Culkin was the local booking agent for the White Star and Cunard steamship companies. In those days you could book your passage, buy your suitcase, have a new outfit made and pick up your fine Irish linen presents for the relatives in America, all at the one shop. The train went from Ballisodare station to Queenstown, which was the name then for the port of Cobh in County Cork. You stayed in a guesthouse overnight and boarded your ocean liner from a tender in the morning."

"Hers was the RMS *Celtic*," Grace said.

"One of the largest ships in the world when she was built," Theo mumbled. "I believe she went down off Roches Point in 1928."

Grace was shocked to see how haggard, distracted and unwell the old man looked.

"Theo, you need your rest," Mulcahy intervened.

"You do look tired," Grace said. "Thank you so much for taking the trouble to see me. I really ought to go now."

Theo shook his head vaguely to suggest there was no need to leave, but Grace drained her cup.

Her spirits were sinking once more. It had seemed like the breakthrough she so desperately needed when the old man mentioned the O'Connor family by name, but the facts wouldn't fit. Now she had reached a conclusive dead end.

She stood up to go. While she waited for Mulcahy to leave the kitchen in proper order, her attention was drawn to the hand-carved figure on the window-sill. It was a kind of hog carved from the black timber found on the bog. Its back was arched and its legs were braced in an attack position. Two slivers of white applewood had been whittled down to make fierce twin tusks. Though ugly the creature had a sinister, compelling quality.

"Did you make this?" she asked Theo.

She took up the carving for a closer inspection.

"Something I do to pass the time," he said.

"It's very striking."

"You like him – he's yours," the old man offered.

"I couldn't."

"Why not?"

"He's too valuable."

"He's new-born and in need of a good home," Theo insisted. Some of his earlier animation had returned. "Consider it a small reward for all your troubles. Besides, I have others."

He stood up and beckoned Grace to follow him to the door leading to an upper bedroom. She drew level with his shoulder to look inside.

The room was fitted out as a carpenter's workshop. There was a bench and a rack of tools – rasps, spokeshaves, mallets and gouges – and a pervasive smell of linseed oil and wax. All four walls were equipped with shelving. More timber shelving reached from the floor to the ceiling, dividing the room in three. The shelves had been made to display a bizarre range of hand-carvings. There was just one subject. Pigs. Pigs of every description, size and posture. The carvings were made of oak and tropical hardwoods. More were carved out of dark and light timbers Grace could not identify. The effect varied according to the grain and colour of the wood, and each animal was brought to a waxed and loving finish before being put away.

"Theo?" Grace looked at the old man, not really sure what to say.

He was pleased with the effect this private and obsessive collection had on his visitor. Mulcahy, who stood looking on from the other side of the kitchen, was equally surprised. Very few people were privileged to view the contents of this inner chamber.

"The ancient Irish held the pig in high regard," Theo explained, and he allowed Grace to enter the room and move enthralled between the loaded shelves. As he spoke she lifted the smaller works in one hand and the larger works in both hands to admire the fine detail, running her fingers along the polished grain.

"The pig is a very potent image in Celtic mythology, found on coins and cauldrons and shields across the Continent," Theo enthused. "The fatted pig of plenty. And his twin brother, with razor-sharp tusks in the shape of the crescent moon. The bristled and ferocious black boar of death."

Grace could only marvel in silence at these fruits of a lifetime's obsession. She remembered the lucky chain around her neck and reached for the clip.

"Which kind of pig is this?" she asked showing the chain to Theo. "Is it death or plenty?"

Theo's reaction was immediate. He snatched the chain from her hand. "Where did you get this?"

"It belonged to my grandmother," Grace said and she looked to Mulcahy for an explanation. Mulcahy appeared equally astonished by Theo's behaviour.

"Sarah O'Connor?" the old man said.

Grace barely nodded, but the expression on her face gave Theo his answer.

"No. No. No. It's not possible," he said. "The girl who owned this chain died of consumption. I know. I've wept over her grave."

SEVEN

GRACE FOLLOWED THEO out of the workshop. He reached for a kitchen chair, pulled it towards him and sat down heavily, holding on tight to the gold chain.

"I was going through my mother's belongings when I found the chain in her jewellery case," Grace said. "She used to show it to me when I was a little girl. A nun told her it belonged to her mother."

"It can't be. It doesn't make any sense..." the old man mumbled, the knuckles of his fist bunched white as pebbles of hail.

Grace put a hand on his shoulder. Theo reached up and cupped his free hand lightly over hers. His touch was dry and frail and cold as an autumn leaf after frost. He looked up, shook his head and then turned to stare at Mulcahy in mute anguish.

"Talk to me, Theo. Say something," he appealed to bring his friend back from that shocked and faraway state where all thoughts spiral inwards.

"What are you playing at? What's going on?" he attacked Grace when he got no answer from Theo.

"I don't know. I honestly don't know."

"It's all right, Mulcahy," Theo whispered hoarsely. "I've had a terrible shock. I'll feel better in a minute."

"Do you want her to leave?" Mulcahy asked.

"No. Please. Both of you. Sit down," he ordered.

Grace sat at the table and reluctantly Mulcahy followed. They waited for the old man to recover. A magpie darted across the yard, a flurry of black and white in the airy space beyond the door. As the minutes passed in the dim kitchen Theo seemed to draw strength from staring at the gold chain in his hand.

He cleared his throat and leaned back in the chair. "I

95

knew a girl once, called Sarah O'Connor," he said, "but she wasn't from Strand Cottage. She was born in our gate lodge. It was a three room affair, carved from the limestone escarpment at the entrance to the family estate. A picturesque, romantic hovel. The gatekeeper was Pat O'Connor. His wife was called Bridie, and they had one daughter. Sarah. Bridie was in her forties and Pat well into his fifties when Sarah was born. A late addition to the household. It was a damp and unhealthy place to rear a child, but the O'Connors were glad of the position, and Sarah grew up healthy enough, or so it seemed. I was three years older than Sarah and I lived in the big house."

His voice had a dry rasp and he paused to swallow. Mulcahy brought him a glass of water. The old man drank, nodded in thanks and went on.

"I took no notice of Sarah. The child at the gate lodge was mentioned, of course, but only as the surprise she had been for the elderly couple. A gift was sent down to the lodge each Christmas. And then one day our car stopped at the main gates. This beautiful, dark-haired girl on the brink of womanhood came running out of the lodge with a message for my father. I never found out what the message was, or what took place, but my mother sent word the next day to have the girl's hair chopped off, and to dress her in less becoming clothes. Sarah had caught my father's eye. My mother was afraid of the consequences. For the girl, and for herself, no doubt. But it was I, and not my father, who was truly smitten. She was so lovely, so full of life." Theo swallowed hard several times, drank some more water, but finally, choked with emotion, he broke off.

Grace took his hand in her hand to encourage him to go on. She could feel every line in his palm and every bone under the skin. "Please," she said. "I know this must be painful for you. But it's why I came."

Theo lowered his head, going inwards again into the story and the source of pain.

"I visited the gate lodge every day," he said. "But we had an outbreak of TB in the district. Sarah's father fell ill. My parents were disturbed at the thought of this outbreak of consumption in the gate lodge spreading through the entire estate. Pat O'Connor died. And my father had no further interest in the girl. The gate lodge was placed out of bounds for the entire household. All traffic in and out of the house was instructed to use the back avenue. I brought medicines and any other comforts I could smuggle out of the house to Sarah's mother, who was by now also unwell. I had gifts too for Sarah. But there was no need for bribes. The attraction between us was immediate and deep. It was our first taste of that grand emotion called love. We were not sophisticated enough to be called lovers, but there was love between us."

Again the story faltered. Grace watched Theo closely. He alone had the power to reveal a life that had been closed to her by her mother's reluctance to consider her past.

"If the Sarah O'Connor you describe was the same Sarah O'Connor who went to America, she must have been very young when you met," she prompted. "Can you be absolutely certain we're talking about the same person?"

She squeezed his hand, wishing there was some way she could will to Theo the life energy in her own body. She would have made any sacrifice to give him the strength to go on. Theo returned the tender pressure of the hand in his, as if he had read her intention.

"At the time I speak of, I was Theodore Causeland, the son of the big house," he said. "I was eighteen years old and Sarah was fifteen. We were hopelessly in love and much too young for caution. We had the whole enclosed, magical world of the Causeland estate, the bluebell-drenched beech woods, the freedom of the boathouse, and the private lake, to play out our affair. And that blissful period continued until we had to accept that Sarah was pregnant."

Grace flinched but said nothing.

"I was not put out by this development." Theo had

noticed her reaction. "I could accept any complication as long as I had Sarah. I was brave and stupid. I told my parents. A Causeland involved with anyone as low-bred as a consumptive gate-keeper's daughter? It was unthinkable. We would have to be separated. That was the response I expected. But there was no argument. No blazing row. No big confrontation with my parents. They took a stern but common-sense approach, and came to me with an arrangement. Sarah would continue to look after her mother until the time of her confinement. I would travel to England, where I would be groomed for a position in my Uncle's law firm. We would be allowed to marry when I was twenty-one and able to support my own household."

Theo's voice dropped to a low whisper and his eyes brimmed with tears.

"They seem to have been very open-minded and liberal people, your parents," Grace said, at a loss to know how to comfort the old man.

"They were anything but liberal," Theo said bitterly. "Do you not understand what happened? The moment I left Sarah alone with them her passage to America was arranged. They lied. They waited until I went to England to get rid of her. And I have only this day realised what a cruel and terrible deception was perpetrated."

By saying it, the revelation hit the old man with the force of a physical pain. His drained and anguished appearance began to frighten Grace, but there was nothing she could do or say to stop him going on.

"I never suspected! The last night we were together, I gave Sarah this little fellow." He held the gold chain up to the light. "It was a love token. A symbol of plenty I told her. A symbol of all the happiness to come. She laughed when I tied the chain around her neck. She had such a pale, slender neck and such a bright laugh."

Grace felt his whole body tremble at the recollection. When she looked around frantically wondering what to do, she found Mulcahy's dark eyes burning into her. Blaming her for using up what remained of the old man's precious strength.

Theo leaned forward to look at Grace and he touched her face with his free hand. It was a token of a new intimacy between them, and Grace O'Connor's heart beat wildly. He was searching for traces of that other girl.

"You're upset," she comforted. "There's no need to go on."

"I want you to understand," he beseeched, and Grace was silenced. "They wrote to say Sarah's mother had died. It was the middle of winter. Snow across the country. And transport in those days was slow and unreliable. When I finally reached the estate they said that Sarah had exhausted herself looking after her mother. She took ill and died from the fever. They were buried together in a common grave. There was a wooden cross to mark the spot. I stood over Sarah's grave in the snow. I mourned. I blamed. I accused. But I believed."

Grace could not find any words. She would never have said outright she believed in ghosts, in a power remaining to dead generations to guide or influence the living. It was too bizarre, too close to the deep end to dwell on very long without being terrified. But this much she knew for certain: her journey was over. For once in her life she was exactly where she was meant to be. Here, holding this old man's hand, in a cottage on a mountain, in the wilds of Ireland. A sympathetic witness to his story. The unlikely means by which the threads of two lives, once so unfairly separated, had been knit again.

"You've never talked to anyone about this before, Theo?" Mulcahy said bewildered.

"Why mention it? Sarah O'Connor died when I was still in my teens. That's what I was told, and that's what I have always believed."

"She did die, Theo," Grace comforted.

"But not the way my parents said. And not before she had given birth to our daughter."

"Eleanor O'Connor," Grace said.

"But that would mean you're Theo's granddaughter?" Mulcahy stared at Grace.

"My God," Theo whispered, now the words had finally been spoken.

"If what he says is true, yes," she fought to subdue the tremor in her voice.

Mulcahy shook his head. It was all too new to fully comprehend or accept.

Grace tried to maintain the calm pose, but she could hardly get the words out past the lump in her throat. "You are sure, Theo? There isn't any doubt? Is there?"

Theo looked down at the gold chain in his hand and said: "I couldn't be more certain."

THE DUSK RANG with the twilight lament of the blackbirds. A crescent moon brightened over Theo's cottage. Luminous white vapours gathered over the flooded bog holes. The long half-dark of the spring evening thickened into night, and the lighted windows of the cottage became beacons in the wilderness of empty mountain. The snipe were mating over the wetlands, and as they cut the air in swoops their wing feathers made a quavering sound like the bleating of a goat.

Mulcahy returned to the cottage with his arms loaded with early potatoes, baby carrots and fresh herbs gathered in Theo's garden by the light of a hurricane lamp. In the kitchen he parcelled the wild salmon caught the night before in herbs. He used lemon rind, fresh parsley and thyme, half a bay leaf and a ring of onion for each steak, which he meant to steam on a tray in the oven. The timber rack on top of Theo's dresser was raided for old wine.

"Theo, are you sure you want to go ahead with this?" he

asked while Grace was out of the kitchen, using Theo's bathroom to freshen up.

"Where's your spirit of occasion?" Theo cut his friend short. "How often does a man learn he has an adult grand-daughter? I want her to feel welcome. More than welcome. I want her to feel loved," he said just as Grace stepped into the kitchen.

She wore Mulcahy's ragged old sweater for warmth. What remained of her make-up had been removed and her hair was simply tied back.

"I don't know why I didn't recognise you the minute you walked in the door. You have your grandmother's rare good looks," Theo complimented. "Now sit down and Mulcahy will do the cooking. I want you to tell me about your mother. What became of her. What she did with her life — there's so much I want to know."

"Really, Theo, there's no need to do it all in one day," she offered. "We can talk again. You've had one terrible shock already."

"Was your mother's life that shocking?"

"I meant, you should save your strength."

"No." Theo was adamant. "You were sent. Call it syn-chronicity. Coincidence. Serendipity. But you were sent. To heal a wound. To banish regret. To bring wisdom. You will stay to dinner, and we will break bread over Mulcahy's noble salmon."

Grace breathed in the smell of garden herbs, wood shavings, turfsmoke and tannin from her wool sweater. An unsayable feeling racing inside her.

The table was spread with a linen table-cloth, a silver service, delicate china plates and gleaming cut-crystal. Over the formal meal Grace sketched details of her mother's career. The stage and film parts that made her name. Their life together on Broadway and in Hollywood. Childhood summers out on Long Island. Grace's move into costume and production design with her mother's backing. The confession that even when they were both working on the same project, her mother was often absent or unavailable for long periods. Eleanor O'Connor had been a hardworking, remote figure; a professional actor first, a mother second. Grace steered the dinner talk back to her grandmother, Sarah O'Connor, and to Theo's youthful affair. They went over the whole story again, and still the conclusion remained: Eleanor O'Connor was Theo's daughter and Grace was the old man's grandchild. It was a discovery they were both prepared, and in Grace O'Connor's case, eager, to accept. Only Mulcahy remained sceptical.

"It seems odd that no one ever told you Sarah O'Connor had been packed off to America. Someone must have known the truth?" he suggested.

"Who was to know?" Theo returned the question. "Both her parents were dead. The estate was a private and controlled world. And no one knew of my relationship with the girl save my parents."

"But why did she not jump ship if she knew you were in England?" Mulcahy persisted.

It was a blunt and tactless remark. The old man shook his head in pained bewilderment. "Who knows what lure or deception they used to trick the poor girl. We had relatives in New England. Perhaps they promised her a job in service. To Sarah it would have been a welcome means to hide the pregnancy. Rear the child in secret while she waited for me to come of age. If she wrote to me her letters were stopped. All the mail leaving our house at that time was weighed in the kitchen before being taken to the post office. Easy enough to limit communication. For generations my family were a mean and cunning tribe. And we were young and inexperienced and easily fooled."

"What became of them, your parents?" Grace switched to save Theo's feelings. She was aware of the hurt caused by Mulcahy's line of questioning.

Theo considered the finery on the table. "I never forgave

them for Sarah's death," he said. "I left the house shortly afterwards and I never came back."

"And the estate with the gate lodge where Sarah O'Connor was born?"

"Those were troubled times. The house was looted and burned to the ground shortly after Sarah was said to have died. Perhaps someone did know the truth. The servants saved a few important heirlooms and carried off the rest to their own homes."

"The Causelands owned a big estate," Mulcahy offered cautiously. This was a topic which was rarely discussed.

But Theo went on without hesitation. "The estate was sunk in debt. There had been no real income for years. After the attack on the house my parents left for England. They died there in poor circumstances. I was out of the country for both funerals. And my feelings about the estate were entirely negative. I sold most of what remained after they died, and used the proceeds to continue with my travels through India and the Far East. The new Irish government had no love of those Ascendancy ruins. The house and the gate lodge were torn down, and the rubble used to build roads. You see before you on this dining table all that remains of that gracious and corrupt world."

By the end of the meal the flow of words had halted. Theo was drained. Physically and emotionally. He left the table to sit by the fire.

Grace and Mulcahy rose in unison and cleared the table. When they were through washing up, they moved to the hearth with their wine glasses to sit next to Theo. Together in the lull they watched the embers settle in the fire.

"Do you know why your mother never thought to follow the clues that led you to Ireland?" Theo asked after a long silence. "If she had we might have met."

Grace considered the question. "My mother's work often took her abroad. She liked being on the move, never having to stay too long in the one place. She wasn't one for permanent attachments. Of any kind. I'm not saying she was a bad mother. She was strict, and she had very strong opinions about most things. The only really grey area in her life was her past. Like a lot of great actors, she drew on the trauma and the strong emotions of her upbringing for her work, but her past was not something she considered or openly discussed with anyone. The interest in family history started with me."

Grace was worried by the effect her words were having on Theo. He stared blankly at the fire and then looked up with tears of distress in his eyes.

"I can't help asking a painful question," he said. "Why did fate deny me of my true role? I was meant to be Sarah's protector. I was meant to be a proper father to Eleanor. If I had been there when our child was born, perhaps young Sarah might have lived. If only I had known."

"If ifs and ands were pots and pans," Mulcahy repeated one of Theo's sayings.

The old man let the thought sink in. He rested his head on his chest to reflect. Grace gave Mulcahy a concerned look. He shrugged to suggest the best thing might be to let the old man deal with this emotional situation in his own way.

"You said your mother travelled a lot. Did she ever set foot in Ireland for any reason?" Theo stirred again after another long silence.

"She had friends in Dublin. Theatre and television people," Grace said. "They used to invite her over, but she always turned them down. 'I know the road to Córdoba, but I will never reach there,' she used to say to excuse the decision."

"Lorca," Mulcahy named the poet.

"Some places mean more to us by not going there," Theo said. "To go would only spoil the magic they have in our imagination."

"I guess that sums up how my mother felt about this

country," Grace agreed. "And I thought the same thing when I arrived. This trip seemed to go wrong from the start. But there was a purpose to it all. I know that now." She moved to sit on the edge of Theo's chair and she put her arm around him. "I've found a greater reward than I ever imagined," she said.

The old man did not shy from her gesture.

Mulcahy finished his wine and put aside the glass. The closeness between this odd, impulsive girl and his old friend had been immediate and binding. It was not the first time that night he felt like an outsider in their company.

"I grew up without a family. I grew up without this," Grace said to the two men sitting quietly beside her in the shifting light and dark of the fire. "I'm so glad I found you. I only hope you feel the same way."

The spontaneous embrace and her heart-felt remark coaxed a smile from Theo.

"It's a bit late in the day to start calling me Grandpa," he whispered, sad and fond in the one breath.

EIGHT

GRACE HAD NEVER seen a night sky so clear. A brilliant cloud of stardust floated in the middle of the sky. The brightest stars burned and shimmered with a fierce, remote intensity. The lesser stars hung in fine veils retreating to infinity. Such vastness. Such mystery. Such inconceivable distances between these far-flung points of light. There was so much empty space out there. Mysteries beyond the grasp of our puny minds. What tiny role had we to play in all of it? Why did it matter so much where we came from? Or what happened before we were born? The starlight striking her eye took so long to cross the universe. Not one star out there might exist at this moment in time. It was possible they were just memories travelling in space, the original stars long vanished and Grace the last living soul to inherit this light.

She blamed the drink and the change of time zones for these giddy notions, and noticed the stars were not standing still, but wheeling upwards, though never vanishing, beyond the rim of vision – a sign she ought to have gone easier on the red wine. Earlier she had felt the need for air. So many thoughts and emotions throbbed inside her head, she had stepped outside for a calm moment alone.

She went across to the dry-stone wall at the end of the garden and took hold. Her breathing came fast and hard. Her feelings had never been in such a churning turmoil. With every fresh surge a high ringing note invaded her ears. She held on tight to the cold stonework, seeking composure.

THEO LAY BACK in his armchair while Mulcahy added black turf to the fire. They were silent. The way men are silent when contemplating by an open fire with a drink to hand. On the far wall a clock ticked within its oakwood case. The restful swing of the pendulum set to measure the weighted, slow tempo of their thoughts.

Mulcahy could not bring himself to look into the old man's eyes. His attention remained with the fireplace.

"You've never spoken before about this girl, Sarah," he opened. "Was Grace O'Connor's grandmother the reason you turned your back on it all? The big house, the up-bringing, the career? Was she the real reason you came back here to live out your life alone? Carving wooden pigs for your own amusement."

Theo smiled at the notion. He looked at the young man hunched at his feet. Mulcahy had the shy, uncomfortable attitude of a small boy seeking a confidence.

"I was always an eccentric sort," he said. "Consider the parting gift I gave to Sarah. A gold pig. You're the romantic one, Mulcahy, not me."

"There's no romance in my life, Theo. Hasn't been for a long time." Mulcahy lifted the poker and began to riddle the fire. A burst of flames caught the dry turf.

"Don't allow what happened to sour you," Theo warned. "Marriage is like riding a bicycle or learning how to swim. Very few people get it right the first time."

Mulcahy listened to the flames flap like sailcloth and watched the sparks fly up the chimney.

"Time finds a lid for every saucepan," he said moodily. He drove the poker deep into the fire. "I'll not be caught out like a fool again."

"You have to live life as it arises, Mulcahy. No excuses. No explaining."

"I know. I know. But it's not easy."

"Follow your heart, man. I missed my chance. But not you. In the words of Joseph Campbell, follow your bliss."

"And where does my bliss lie?"

"With you it's a woman."

"No. Not any more."

"She is very beautiful," Theo urged the younger man.

"She's intelligent, independent, and just as spirited in her way as I remember her grandmother – "

"Theo!" Mulcahy rose slowly and stretched his limbs. A man reluctant to take a forward step.

"You'll need this," the old man said, passing him a fresh handkerchief.

"Thanks, Theo," Mulcahy said, and received a benign nod in return.

On his way out the door, he stopped. The old man was once more gazing with liquid bright eyes at the gold chain in his hand.

It took Mulcahy a minute to spot Grace standing at the top of the garden. He was struck by how still and how remote she seemed. Lost in a world of her own. He rattled a loose stone with his foot to signal his presence and came forward.

Her hair was drawn back, her face in profile. Tears rolled down her cheeks. He rested both hands on her shoulders.

"You're shaking," he said.

"I needed air."

He gave her the handkerchief and she wiped her eyes and the sides of her face.

"I never cry," she sniffed.

"There's no shame in tears."

She swung around very fast. "Did you see the way he held that silly little neck chain? Did you see the look in his eyes?" she begged Mulcahy to understand. "That was the way my mother looked sometimes. My God, the pain they shared. The emptiness they carried all their lives. In the last days – the closest I ever got to my mother – we talked about my childhood, her early days, all kinds of things we'd never got round to before. But we didn't have enough time. If she'd got better she might have come with me. She might have learned that her father was alive, that he was here all the time, and now it's too late."

She turned away but made no effort to conceal the sobs of

distress that shook her whole body.

Mulcahy pressed his fingers into the stiff neck muscles beneath the faith healer's cord, and in a half-way gesture began to massage away the pent-up tension.

Grace rolled her head slowly from side to side, glad of his touch, immediately responding to the tender pressure of his hands. She edged around slowly to face him again. Despite the professional remove of his touch, the sudden rise in emotional temperature threatened to make her do something stupid. She looked up into his face. There was only the smallest pool of air between their mouths. With every breath they shared that pool of air grew more intimate. She closed her eyes, but no kiss found her lips. She felt a stir of cold night air, and when she opened her eyes again he had taken a step back and away from her. He thrust his hands deep into his pockets, as if they held incriminating evidence.

"Let's just walk," he said.

THEY USED A narrow foot-style to cross the stone wall and followed a path across the mountain. The lighted windows of Theo's cottage fell away. In the distance a broad river unwound through the glen. White moths stumbled about the heather in search of some wild fragrance.

For a long time Grace said nothing. Private thoughts were being taken on board, emotional truths she was reluctant to face. Had she fallen for this man? Had she limped desperately into that trap again in all this other turmoil? She had just met him. She knew nothing about him. He seemed completely unsuitable. So what? That had always been the pattern before: sudden, intense, ill-matched affairs with the wrong man at the wrong time.

She was getting carried away. These feelings could not be genuine. They were the result of the raw and vulnerable emotional state she was in. She was confusing grief with passion. And what she took for love was really just a state of shock.

They kept on walking towards the pale radiance in the west. As they advanced Grace became aware of a strange, mechanical grinding noise. It was not just the grinding of her own thoughts inside her head: the night air throbbed with the sound. When she looked up she saw roving lights behind the hills. A black shape broke cover and moved in silhouette along the ridge.

"What's going on up there?" she asked, looking to the source of the noise.

"That's the gold mine," Mulcahy said.

"They work this late?"

"They work around the clock, tearing open the heart of the mountain," he said.

Over the steady rumble of big machines came a series of dull explosions and the thud of distant rockfall.

"It's frightening."

"Theo calls them the Black Pig," Mulcahy said.

"What's that?"

"It's a local legend," he said. "About a Black Pig that lived up in these mountains. It had been driven out of another part of the country on account of the havoc and destruction it caused. It was an enormous creature and it devoured everything in its path: crops, sheep, cattle, even people. Strangers crossing the mountain never reached home. Local people began to vanish. No one felt safe travelling the roads or walking the seashore, and a long time passed before the people learned about the monster hiding up in the mountains. When they finally found out that a Black Pig was responsible for all the people who disappeared, a group of warriors got together, tracked the Black Pig to its lair and laid siege. Eventually they drove the monster from its hiding place. They chased it all the way to the sea and forced the Black Pig to jump in off the pier at Easky. Normally, pigs can't swim, but this one could. It came ashore again and ran up the river outside Ennismuck killing all the fish as it went. To this day no one has ever caught a fish in that same stretch of river. The pig was so poisonous, in fact, that just one touch of its bristles could send the victim into convulsions. Several warriors lost their lives before they cornered the monster and killed it in the valley below." He pointed in the direction of the river valley. "You must have spotted the mound at the crossroads. That's the grave of the Black Pig. Legend has it, if the Black Pig ever returns, three days of darkness will fall on the town."

Grace did not like the story. Told in the dark over the alien sounds coming from the gold mine, it made her flesh creep.

"I don't think I want to hear any more," she said. "It's spooky enough out here already."

"The legend is meant to be frightening," he said. "When parents want to chastise their children, they threaten them with stories about the Black Pig. It stops them wandering about the fields at night. That's why Eugene Tuttle, the publican's, nerves are so bad. The Black Pig still comes after him in his nightmares when he knows he's done something wrong."

"So the monster isn't all bad," she said.

"He's probably not as black as he's painted," Mulcahy answered dryly.

There was another low rumble from the mines and a second earth-hauling truck crested the ridge.

The heather path remained faintly visible in the starlight and the continuing green-white glow out over the sea where the sun had set hours before, a thin band of rose-tinted fire on the western rim of the world.

"It's so beautiful and so full of atmosphere out here. Why were those guys allowed to start a mine?"

"There was nothing we could do to stop them," Mulcahy said.

"What about the sense of magic here? Don't you hate to see that destroyed?" she was puzzled by his attitude.

There was no answer.

"Or maybe you don't feel that magic any more?"

"So much has happened today, I don't know what I feel," he said, standing several paces off in the dark.

Grace might have guessed this was coming. The walk under the stars was just an excuse, a means to lure her away from the house for a private interrogation.

"You don't believe I'm Theo's granddaughter. Is that it?" she demanded. "Is that the reason you brought me out here?"

"No. Nothing like that," he said quickly. "Stranger things have happened. I'm just not sure how to handle it."

The admission surprised Grace: his uncertainty reflected her own.

When she caught up with him he was standing at the edge of the river. They could go no further. They stopped to listen to the river's smooth flow and the noise of the waterfall up stream. The clear water cresting and folding over the stones.

"I can't honestly call that old man Grandpa." she said, in an effort to put her feelings into words. "Not now. Like Theo said, it's too late. He'll always be a stranger to me. But knowing where I come from, knowing where I fit in, that's different. That's everything."

They heard a quick splash and glimpsed the gleaming scales of a salmon homing before the waterfall.

When Mulcahy spoke his voice was hoarse and emotional. "It's time we got back to the cottage," he said. "I don't think either one of us is going to have him for very much longer."

THEO HAD SWITCHED off the electric light and lit a host of candles. The effort of lighting the candles had exhausted him. He was asleep in his armchair, his head bent towards the fire. Mulcahy eased him back in the seat without waking him. Grace removed the empty wine glass on the floor beside his chair, and Mulcahy went to Theo's bedroom to collect a blanket. He passed the Foxford wool blanket across to Grace, who spread it gently over the old man. She was still fixing the blanket around him when he opened his eyes. He saw Grace bending over him and he smiled weakly.

"You should go to bed now," she coaxed.

"No. I'm past that," he said. "There's a bottle on the dresser over there. Open it. Stay with me. We can keep the Black Pig away for another few hours."

"What black pig?" Grace said alarmed.

"It's here. It's waiting for me," he said. "I heard it prowling around the house tonight and snuffling at the gap under the door. By morning it will have carried me away."

Grace wanted to believe the old man was still half-asleep and his mind wandering, but she had nursed her mother through the last days of her illness. She had witnessed this calm and resigned state of the very ill, a trance condition that prepared the living for extinction. It had come over her mother at the end. Then she had not grasped what was happening, but this time she recognised the signs. There was a tangible sense of death as a presence nearing. One might as well call it a creature from the other side, coming to take the living away. No earthly power could drive it off. Its quarry had been singled out and hypnotised by the far-off beat of approaching hooves. This was the Black Pig with the crescent tusks, a messenger from that darkness beyond our grasp.

She knew Mulcahy, too, felt this invisible presence. There was an element of quiet ceremony in the way he took the bottle of *poitín* from the top shelf of the pine dresser, and arranged the crystal glasses on the table. He used hot water to warm the glasses, measured three spoons of sugar, filled the glasses with hot water, and then added three big shots of the outlawed spirit.

He handed around the steaming drinks.

"A toast," Theo proposed and raised his glass to Grace. "*Uisce beatha* – the water of life," he said and he looked into the depths of her eyes.

Glass rang against glass and Grace knocked back the

scalding hot spirit. She felt the alcohol burn all the way down to her toes. A moment later she felt the glow.

"First you glow and then you blow," she murmured happily to both men.

She unlaced her shoes and curled up in the armchair opposite Theo. The kitchen was warm. A vellum-rich and drowsy light from the fire. A Persian rug beside the hearth to cover the cold flagstone floor. A whisper from the candles as the wax rolled down and nested on the sconce. A bamboo cane fly fishing rod over the mantle. A painted tea caddy with a shine of age. Light flaring on the copper pans and cast-iron pots, and the flame-cleaned iron hooks in the chimney. A mellow light on the oak furniture worn to the grain by the routines of a lifetime.

With each swallow of the hot *poitín*, Grace surrendered her grip a little more. Desire blunted by exhaustion. Pouches of fatigue under her eyes. The long freefall was over at last. The engine-heart thunder of New York city, Broadway and Times Square, now a distant memory. Replaced by soft candle and firelight. Turfsmell. Neat spirit. Low voices rising and falling to an unfamiliar music.

She wanted desperately to stay awake, to be with Theo, to protect and safeguard the old man through the night, but the early glow of the drink soon faded. Darkness crept along the edge of vision in the afterglow of day. By the time she lowered the second glass of hot spirits, her head was swimming and her vision blurred. She felt her eyelids being dragged shut by an overwhelming fatigue. She had lost track of the conversation. Thoughts went astray. Through the thickening vapours in her head she heard Theo recite:

"We who still labour by the cromlech
on the shore,
The grey cairn on the hill, when day
sinks drowned in dew,
Being weary of the world's empires
bow down to you,

Master of the still stars, and of
the flaming door."

The last thing she remembered was Mulcahy helping the
old man out of his armchair and guiding him towards the
bedroom. She wanted to help but she could barely open her
eyes. The weight of sleep would not let her speak or rise. No
cataclysm could bring her back to the waking world.

WHEN GRACE OPENED her eyes again, the turf fire had
settled into dust. A grey light entered between the plants
through the kitchen window. She was alone in a chair by
the fireside, a heavy wool blanket spread over her up to her
chin. She heard the cry of the dawn birds in the yard,
roused herself and instinctively moved to the front door.

The sky was overcast, but there was a bright morning dew
on the ground. The heather, the short grass, the stones, each
had a newly created gleam. Colours were intense, true
shades of moss, spring-bud and tree-bark green against
granite rock and umber bog. She was thirsty and light-
headed. She felt like a long-term patient just back on her
feet, ready to re-enter the rough bustle of life and meet the
world with new zest. Her body ached all over, her clothes
were stale rags, but she had never felt more sure of her own
worth, or more free from that life-long solitude and uncertainty. For the very first time in her life she felt blessed. She
loved this place, this view, this feeling of no longer being a
bystander in the wings. She had found continuity, history, a
ground of being.

She stood for some time drawing deep lung-fulls of that
pure mountain air. She promised never to forget this moment, to focus on this vivid and so alive feeling long enough
now to be able to summon it again in less certain times.

Then she turned and saw Mulcahy standing in the
doorway of the cottage. His face had the frozen pallor of
church marble. As he came forward she knew with certainty
what he was about to say.

"He just –" Mulcahy began. "Quietly. While we slept," he said trembling to control his feelings.

"Oh God!"

She threw her arms around him. Mulcahy's body stiffened. He seemed ready to draw back, but she laid her head along his shoulder, and his composure broke. The roar of grief rising inside him became a hard and frantic embrace.

PLENTY

THE FUNERAL TOOK place immediately after the church service. In the graveyard the rain beat down on the tight drumskins of the black umbrellas, the water streaming to the ground in bars between the spokes. Sam stood nearest the graveside. His bowler hat glistened above a face with the lined and craggy complexion of a peach-stone. The steel toe-caps of his boots were turned up. His long coat skirted the crushed grass, a ring of muddied, wet threads around the torn hem. He said nothing, but watched Mulcahy and Oliver shovel the clay into the grave. From the open gash in the ground there came a low thud of wet earth on wood.

With steady, silent purpose, the two men filled in the grave and then patted the mound of displaced earth to a smooth finish. When they were through they paused out of respect, an irregular guard of honour armed with muddy shovels.

Grace O'Connor moved to place a wreath on the grave. She stood with her head bowed over the bruised flowers in the downpour. Sally Holmes, from Tuttle's bar, followed with a smaller wreath.

Out of a vague sense of duty the brandy boys – Eugene Tuttle, Councillor Oswald and Deputy John Charles Leddy – lingered amongst the alien headstones of the Church of Ireland graveyard. They stood shoulder to shoulder under their dark umbrellas, close to the main gate. Deputy Leddy had driven from Dublin that morning in his black Mercedes. He never missed a funeral in his constituency, but he anticipated small support from the few broken-down big shots he saw standing around these old family plots.

A safety pin secured a black armband to the sleeve of his navy-blue top-coat. The coat was worn over a dark blue pin-stripe suit, a plain white shirt, shiny shoes and a bright polyester tie: the Roman toga of modern business, law, politics and crooked enterprise.

He was a stout, broadly built man with a flat, meaty face and woolly eyebrows with a life of their own. His hair was combed straight back from his forehead in corrugated strands, streaked black and white like the head of a badger. He smoked a pipe, the shank of which was often puffed at length, grasped between his teeth or waved in the air to emphasise his ponderous and authoritative gestures. He assumed rank over the other two men as an automatic birthright.

"Small turn-out," Oswald remarked.

"He-he-he was very eccentric," Tuttle stammered.

"A real odd-ball," Oswald agreed.

"What are you saying? The man was a lunatic," Deputy Leddy pronounced. "Pigs. That's all he ever thought about." For corroboration he directed their attention to Sam, with his broken umbrella, bowler hat and torn overcoat. "And will you look at the cut of the chief mourner."

The Reverend Minister Thomson and the hearse, both relics from another era, slipped away. Only a handful of townspeople remained. They stood inside the graveyard wall looking on, curious, thoughtful and circumspect.

Grace was unaware of the other people around her. She stared blankly at the fresh grave and listened to the rain drum steadily on the umbrellas. She felt dazed and abandoned. The death of Theo, or Theodore William Causeland, to give her grandfather his full name, was a terrible blow, but there had been no time to fathom the loss. From the moment the old man had passed away there had been a fixed order of duties to perform.

ON THAT TERRIBLE morning, after Mulcahy gave her the news, they had driven to a farmhouse at the foot of the mountain to make the necessary calls. Then they returned to Theo's cottage to wait for the doctor to arrive, and legally pronounce the old man dead from natural causes. They were pale and shaken, and spoke with hushed voices. They made funeral plans. They offered small comforts to each other. They tried to make themselves and the house of the dead man presentable.

With these chores done the moment came for Grace to enter the room where Theo lay dead. She had to face this ordeal, but she did not find the first steps easy. At a signal from Mulcahy she rose from the kitchen table and moved towards the bedroom.

She stalled on the threshold.

"You don't have to see him, but you'll feel better if you do," Mulcahy encouraged.

Grace nodded, tense and preoccupied. The air felt trapped inside her lungs. Her chest hard. She entered the upper bedroom with a soft and cautious tread, not really knowing how she would react.

It was a clean, sparsely furnished room. There was a wardrobe, a rosewood dresser with a delf jug and basin and a mirror on top, a bookcase and a bedside locker holding a water glass, pain-killers and her gold chain. She approached the antique brass bed and the corpse laid out by Mulcahy.

The body was a brittle, cold husk. Shrunken. Utterly still. She moved closer. Hesitated. Then reached out a hand. Just the faintest touch along the brow. To verify that the living person she had met so briefly was gone forever.

What it meant to die or what came after a person's final breath, she had no idea. She had never been the type to visit graveyards. She was not the kind who fussed over flowers and talked for hours to the departed. The thought that the dead might even wish to hang around their last resting place, waiting for the occasional visitor to bring scraps of news from the world of the living, was just too horrible to consider.

What surprised her most was how, having been through this business once already with her mother, she had hardened to the sight of death. Standing before Theo's corpse, she felt a familiar, frozen muscular anguish, but also a reluctance to feel anything as bitter as regret. You could not make terms or strike any bargains with death. Death was final. It allowed no conditions. What was once a living man was now an empty shell left behind in a bed awaiting burial. A life had passed away. Another loss. Another absence. Another emptiness forever in the world.

She lifted the gold chain from the locker and withdrew.

Mulcahy's friend Oliver arrived before the doctor. There was nothing she could usefully do at the cottage, and Oliver offered to drive her to her own place to pick up a change of clothes.

On the drive out on to the peninsula, Oliver wasn't sure what to say, and wisely stayed quiet. She was glad of the silence.

Wild branches brushed against the pickup truck when they drove through the tunnel of shrubbery before Strand Cottage. They stopped in the yard, and Oliver waited at the wheel while Grace went inside to pick up whatever she needed.

Her luggage was still there in the middle of the floor. Her abandoned travel bag lay open on the table with all her original documents and plans askew. Barely registering the strangeness of her surroundings, she tore open the airline tags and undid the fasteners on her luggage. She bent over her belongings to choose an outfit, then straightened to hold each garment up to the light, and several minutes later found that she had been staring off into space. She felt a strong temptation to linger. How lovely it would be to sidestep all the complications, to sit in the stillness and the shadows of this hideaway on the peninsula and just listen to the heave and backwash of the waves so close to the gable.

It took a great mental effort to go on. She broke the spell of the cottage only by making a promise to herself to return for a longer stay when circumstances allowed.

Eventually she selected a black polo-neck, a charcoal wool skirt and a matching jacket, dark tights and flat shoes. As she dressed her movements were automatic, remote from their real purpose. She might have been outfitting an actor for a funeral scene.

By the time they got back to Theo's place, Mulcahy was sharing a drink with two mountain farmers, men with fresh shaving cuts, even more hastily groomed than Grace and Mulcahy. Very soon more callers began to arrive at the cottage.

Theo's body remained in the house. There was no talk of a funeral parlour. Callers who came to the front door mumbled an expression of sympathy and went immediately to see the corpse laid out between fresh white sheets in the upper bedroom. On their return they accepted a drink and took a seat in the kitchen.

Following the first explosive release of emotion outside the cottage that morning, Mulcahy had become more self-possessed, and more distant. He had assumed the role of a friend of the deceased, there to meet the mourners, to put them at ease, to accept condolences and to talk about the dead man. Watching him move so deliberately through these duties, Grace could not gauge the true state of his feelings.

At one point Mulcahy took her aside to explain that under normal circumstances they could have relied on the help of the old women of the parish to organise the household for the wake. Neighbouring men, too, would have lent a hand.

"One thing about the Irish," he told her, "they have a great fondness for showing good will towards the dead. Dying is the only certain way to have anything good said about you."

But there was a problem. Theo's family had belonged to a different tradition and his existence on the mountain had been too wayward, and too eccentric, to invite close understanding. The callers to the house were mostly sheep farmers, turf-cutters, *poitín* makers and old bachelors who had stopped in Theo's kitchen on long winter nights over the years.

The men wore antiquated Sunday suits, white shirts and thin dark ties. They hung their hats on one knee when they sat down. The women wore tight-fitting skirts with contrasting floral print blouses and chunky hand-knit cardigans. They used talc and lipstick. Their features were hardened from work and the harsh coastal weather. The grip of their hands was welted and firm. Even the women's hands, Grace noticed, were strong and deeply wrinkled at the joints, the fingernails often broken.

While the women made tea, Grace had to keep up a supply of clean cups, saucers, and side plates. Oliver was put in charge of the drink. There were no short measures, and Grace noted an odd detail: when Oliver served whiskey to the mourners it was sipped and treated with respect. The home-made *poitín*, on the other hand, was swallowed in haste, with no regard for its lethal strength.

By nightfall the atmosphere in the house had become oddly merry. It was yet another contradiction, she reflected, that at this time of loss and grief the gathering in the house of the dead man should resemble a party. Grace thought this attitude both callous and disrespectful, and she hovered on the edges of the gathering, uncertain of her role.

With the passing hours Mulcahy became less uptight and dutiful. By midnight he seemed positively lit up. For a man who had just lost such an old and cherished friend, and treated Grace with such deep reserve all day, she was annoyed to find him so animated. Even euphoric.

He coaxed her to sit down beside him. He put his arm around her. He told her about a wakehouse he had visited where the widow woman had worn the clothes of the corpse all night; the jacket and the trousers of her dead husband, his shirt and waistcoat, even his boots with the laces open.

"I never saw anything like it," he said, confounded by the memory and too much whiskey. There followed a thoughtful pause after which he turned from Grace to confide to the man beside him.

"Seamus Heaney wrote somewhere that the human soul is the weight of a snipe."

"This is it," the old neighbour agreed.

Grace felt trapped and restless. She longed to rise and move amongst the gathering. She wanted to be acknowledged as a lost relative and to join in the low hum of voices coming from the next room, where the corpse was left out, but her connection with Theo was too recent and the discovery that he was her grandfather much too private to be mentioned. Everyone had presumed she was Mulcahy's friend. She remained detached, barely speaking. Excluded from everything going on around her.

"Relax," Mulcahy said and he filled up her glass. "We have a long night ahead of us yet."

She accepted the drink and forced a grim smile.

True to Mulcahy's prediction the wake continued into the small hours. Grace had no idea how much she was finally persuaded to drink in an effort to break the invisible wall she found between her and the other mourners.

She had been determined to remain awake and sober through the whole thing, but by the early hours of the morning the battle against physical and emotional exhaustion, and the still unfamiliar effects of the *poitín*, had brought her close to the borders of hallucination.

"God be good to him," the old people rhymed a litany of absence with each raised glass. Theo was remembered by all those who had settled in for the long haul to first light. Things Theo did. Stories told by Theo, and stories told about Theo. What happened the time Reverend Thomson came on a sick call and asked Theo to accept God, and to renounce the devil. 'This is no time to be making enemies,' Theo told him. 'God is good, and the devil isn't such a bad fellow either.'

Grace laughed with the rest, but three generations of grief went spinning around in her head as she heard these stories passed on like precious heirlooms to the careful listener.

Her throat tightened. Bitter tears wet her eyes. The strong spirits and this raw emotional state, the sleeplessness and the stirring up of old memories in the wakehouse, all combined to focus and heighten her feelings of loss and regret.

On the last drink she had a sudden, dizzy sense of revelation. The traditional Irish wake, far from being an unruly house-party, was the most profound and moving rite yet devised by which the living could not only surrender, but celebrate, their dead, a tribal sharing of intimate sorrows. Here was a ritual that took the living soul, the soul of the one who must endure, at its most tender, anguished and bewildered hour, and wrung it clean of grief.

She tried to explain this amazing insight to the old man sitting beside her.

"This is it," he answered and topped up her glass.

Grace lost all track of the night.

She woke in daylight in a familiar armchair to find Mulcahy standing over her. He presented her with a mug of hot tea, two aspirin and several thick slices of warm bacon between two slices of white bread. The hearse had arrived to ferry the body to the chapel.

IT WAS TIME to leave the graveyard, but Sally Holmes felt she had a duty to perform. She looked up from the inscribed wreaths at the American girl standing beside her.

"If it rains on the day of your funeral, they say your soul goes straight to heaven," she remarked.

"I guess Theo is taking the express elevator," Grace answered with her head bowed.

Sally leaned in close to whisper confidentially. "Wait till I tell you. I'm sorry about what happened in Tuttle's bar the other day. Really, I was mortified."

"It wasn't your fault," Grace said. "I should have been

more careful and read the small print before I signed the contract."

Sally was grateful for the kind word.

"What will you do with the place? Sell?"

"No. I'm going to spend some time there by myself."

"Are you serious?"

"Sure."

"It's a lovely spot, but it's not what you were used to."

"I'll miss my shower," she admitted, "but I'll get by."

Mulcahy and Oliver had laid down their shovels. They stood in silence an extra minute with their hands joined over the finished grave. Then they broke away, and came around to Grace and Sally.

"Come here to me for a minute," Sally signalled to Mulcahy. "Did you know this woman is moving into Strand Cottage?"

Mulcahy couldn't hide his surprise. "Are you really going through with it?"

"Why not?"

"The place needs a lot of work."

"I'll give you a hand to move in," Sally intervened. "I'd like to make up for Eugene Tuttle. He's so miserable. But we're not all that bad, really." She looked to Grace for consent.

"I'll take all the help I can get," she accepted.

"And Oliver, you'll help, won't you?" Sally added.

Grace couldn't imagine this big, awkward man being press-ganged into house cleaning. "Maybe you can find me a car," she suggested.

"He can do both," Sally answered for him.

Oliver was unable to look at Grace O'Connor, or string a full sentence together with Sally Holmes so near. He shuffled from one foot to another in a dumb-show of acceptance.

"And what about you?" Sally switched her attention to Mulcahy. "Are you going to help?"

"I have things to look after up at Theo's place," he avoided a direct answer. "When were you planning to move in?" he asked Grace.

"Today."

"You can't," he said.

"Why not?"

He had no answer.

"Okay. That's settled then," Sally said decisively. "Grace, you're moving in today. Oliver, you're helping. And, Mulcahy, you'll be along when you finish at Theo's."

With the arrangements finalised there was nothing to hold them in the wet graveyard, but they were reluctant to move on.

"We had such a short time together. I'm so sorry we didn't meet sooner," Grace said taking a last look at the grave.

"He was a lovely man," Sally said.

"We're all going to miss him," Mulcahy said.

"Poor Sam," Sally looked across the graveyard. "He's lost without his old friend."

Sam remained apart. A silent witness between the rain-streaked headstones.

"Theo used to say Sam's face was so full of creases it would hold a shower of rain," Mulcahy remembered fondly. "It was Theo who introduced all of us to the world of books. To poetry. To mythology and mysticism. And it was Theo who introduced our Sam to the plays of Samuel Beckett."

"He sure took them to heart," Grace said.

"One way or another, Theo changed all our lives," Mulcahy confided. "When we were young lads going to the dances, we used to call in to Theo's cottage on our way home. He had an open mind and a closed mouth about most things. We admired him for that. He took us on poaching expeditions and showed us how to make decent *poitín*. It was Theo who coaxed me to go on to art college. He always encouraged us to do our own thing. To express ourselves. 'Trust your talent', he used to say."

Hearing Theo's old phrase brought their attention back to the mound of earth and the plain wooden cross at the head of the grave. A sight as dismal as the weather that day.

"He deserves better," Mulcahy said.

"We can all chip in to buy a proper headstone," Sally suggested.

"We should put up a monument," Oliver said.

Mulcahy's head was downcast, but he looked up suddenly and stared with concentrated purpose at Eugene Tuttle, Councillor Oswald and Deputy Leddy.

"Oliver," he said. "If you had brains you'd be dangerous."

"What?"

"A public monument to Theo," he said, his voice brimming with enthusiasm, "and I know who's going to pay for it."

A dangerous gleam had entered Mulcahy's eyes. He had put the problem of a monument to furnish the plinth in the town square out of his mind. Although the commission was a rare opportunity to earn good money for his time and effort, he had been reluctant to take on any job financed by the mining company. But there would be a poetic justice in this. He could earn real money, pay off a debt of gratitude to his dead friend and satisfy his moral and creative integrity at the same time. The more he thought about it, the more excited he became. He edged away from the others, his mind already racing with possibilities.

"Grace, I'm sorry about this, but I'll see you tomorrow," he said.

"You go on. We'll look after this woman," Sally reassured.

"Hold your horses," Oliver called after Mulcahy.

"Sorry, Oliver, this won't wait." He was already striding towards the gate.

"What sort of monument do you have in mind?" Oliver wanted to know.

"What would Theo choose?" Mulcahy shouted back over his shoulder as he vaulted the iron railing.

EUGENE TUTTLE, COUNCILLOR Oswald, and Deputy Leddy watched Mulcahy's sudden departure and swapped puzzled looks. Oswald was outraged. Anyone with an ounce of respect would have the courtesy to shake Deputy Leddy's hand before leaving the graveyard. It was a deliberate insult to a man as prominent as the deputy not to put on a show of gratitude and make it "abundantly clear", to use the deputy's own expression, that the mourners were honoured by his presence.

"It's worse that fella is getting. Did you hear him shouting like a Baluba in a graveyard," Oswald said to boost Leddy's wounded sense of importance.

"He can be most unseemly," Tuttle agreed.

"It's the way he was brought up," the deputy said knowingly.

Mulcahy's green Wolseley car speed away from the church grounds, spraying up a hail of loose gravel as it went.

"Time to get you sorted out," Sally turned to Grace. "You won't recognise that old shack of yours when we're finished."

"Thank you," she said, distracted by the rush of disappointment she felt at knowing Mulcahy wouldn't be coming with them.

Invisible fumes of malted barley corn, spiced with cloves, teased Oliver's nostrils. He moved off discreetly with Tuttle's bar and a large hot whiskey in mind.

"Come here, you." Sally Holmes grabbed him by the sleeve of his coat and the anticipated drink vanished. "You're coming with us."

WHEN GRACE OPENED up the cottage, a fine light off the sea entered with her. The damp air after the rain carried into the house the smell of the wild growth invading the backyard, mingled with the scent of the rampant, flowering shrubbery competing for space in the front garden. The dim, damp atmosphere made her shiver. She baulked at the prospect of ever making this cottage habitable after so many years of neglect.

Sally Holmes was not put out. She ordered Grace to open up all the rooms while she wrestled open the sash windows. Oliver was told to light the open fireplace in the kitchen and the bedroom. A green straw broom was shoved into Grace's hands and sweeping instructions given. The furniture was moved. Rugs and mats were brought outside and the dust beaten free in clouds.

The day might have been lost in grief, but she found the work, and Sally's cheerful company, good therapy. Whenever she stood still to stare absently into space, Sally gave her a little prod and she went back to work. And as she moved from one job to the next, she felt a welcome warmth spread through her body. A sense of trust in life return.

When the fires were lit Oliver went to clear a path to the spring well. He cut back the nettles and briars with a slash-hook, and sheared the tufts of green rushes to a stubble using a scythe from one of the out-houses. He scooped out the silt from the bottom of the well, scrubbed away the green moss and the pondweeds, and dusted the original stone walls of the well with white powdered quicklime.

He was scattering the last handful of lime when Grace came out of the house to see how he was getting on.

"The old people were great believers in quicklime," he explained. "It's a powerful disinfectant."

She watched him skim the slick of excess powder from the eye of the well. Fresh water filtered up through the pebbles in the bottom. The water began to clear. It was an image she had called to mind often in an abstract way, but had never actually witnessed before this moment.

While they waited Oliver pointed towards a green, cactus-like plant growing high up on the gable of the cottage, a plant that appeared to live off air and rain alone.

"It's a house leek," he said.

"I have several of those in the roof already."

"It's not that kind of leak," he said. "It was put there to protect the thatch from fire."

"A magic charm?"

"Now you have it." he said. "And here's some extra protection for you." He handed her a neat, four-pronged cross made from the freshly cut and folded green rushes. "It's a Saint Bridget's cross. The Saint's day is over, but that won't stop it working."

"You made this?" she said, struck by the simple but delicate handiwork.

"Put it up in the rafters and the wee people in the fairy ring at the back of the house won't bother you," he said with a wide but tongue-in-cheek smile.

"Thank you so much," she said, touched by his kindness. She liked Mulcahy's friends.

When they got back to the kitchen with their buckets, she noticed an immediate change in Oliver. He had been easygoing and talkative before, but as soon as they reached the house the flow of words dried up. She pretended not to notice the change, and Sally ignored him.

The black, cast-iron pots and matching kettle that came with the cottage were hung on hooks over the kitchen fire to warm the water.

This business of transforming the cottage went on all day. Cupboards were emptied and the bare shelves washed down. The ornaments, cups and plates displayed on the dresser were carefully removed, soaked and scrubbed. Oliver was dispatched to carry more water and more fuel for both fires. All the time, while Sally and Grace worked as a team, Oliver came and went without saying a word.

"He's very nice, but is he always so quiet when you're near?" Grace asked.

"Not when he has drink taken, and then I won't talk to him," Sally said.

There was a lull while they returned a row of clean plates to the dresser.

"What about Mulcahy? What's the story there?" she probed.

Sally Holmes raised an eyebrow. "The story?" she said.

"You know. Where does he come from? Are his folks alive? What has he been doing all these years?"

Sally balanced the last willow pattern dinner plate on the top shelf. "Are you interested?"

"You two get along real well. I wouldn't like to interfere," Grace answered diplomatically.

"Mulcahy and me!" Sally was highly amused. "No way. He's away with the fairies."

"He's gay?"

"No, no," Sally laughed. "I mean he's too arty for me. I'd want someone more practical. Someone to boil the pot."

"Oh, I'm sorry." Grace laughed along with her at the misunderstanding.

Sally began to return the row of cups to their hooks on the next shelf down. "Mulcahy's parents died when he was a teenager," she said. "The homeplace was sold and he was supposed to move in with an aunt in the midlands. It didn't work out. She wasn't able to control him. He came back here to live in a caravan. People were good to him. They did all they could, but you could say he reared himself. There were wild parties. Mulcahy and Oliver used to race old cars about the roads, drink plenty and get stuck into gang fights at the dances. They had several run-ins with the law before Theo took them under his wing. Soon after, Mulcahy headed off to art college. He was gone a long time. Until he arrived back here a few years ago and built a float for the Saint Patrick's day parade. He's still doing that kind of thing."

"Is there a girlfriend?" she asked as she handed the last cup to Sally with deliberate care.

"Wait till I tell you. He's married."

"Oh!"

"They're separated," Sally added quickly.

"It didn't work out?"

"She was very political. A fierce woman, really. Always running off to meetings and organising rallies and campaigns around the country."

"What kind of stuff was she into?"

"Feminist stuff. The Environment. Greenpeace. CND. Amnesty International. Changes to the Constitution. Animal rights – it was a long list."

"I see."

"He got fed up," Sally said. She sounded very sure of her facts.

"Why do you say that?"

"He told me one time he didn't see how anyone could save the whole world when their own life was such a mess."

Grace could picture Mulcahy saying that. "And what about the workhouse?" she asked to bring the story up to date.

"I think he was hoping she might settle down and spend more time with him if he fixed up a proper place for them to live."

"A Famine workhouse!" she remarked.

"I know," Sally said sympathetically, but she was on the brink of laughter.

"Where is she now?"

"The poor thing is still out there on a rubber raft somewhere saving whales. Well, it was either that or a life in the workhouse." Sally burst out laughing.

When Oliver looked into the kitchen he could not imagine what the two women found so funny. The sight of him silently standing in the doorway set Sally off again. Puzzled, he bowed out, leaving them to enjoy their private joke.

NIGHT GATHERED IN dark pools behind the houses of Ennismuck. The yellow glow of sodium street lamps seeped past the curtains of the front bedroom windows, where tired heads lay settled on cotton pillows. Chores and cares, schemes and set-backs, all the events, moods, impressions and colours of the day were recalled, mulled and sifted in the dreaming memories of the population.

In the mountains beyond the town, ghostly fingers of light from the company yards stabbed the night-time sky. The mountains shuddered after every detonation. In Mulcahy's workshop an electric arc welder flashed into brilliance at the touch of metal. Great rays of light escaped from the high windows of the workhouse.

Sweat poured down Mulcahy's face behind the protective welding mask. It was hard work bending and fixing these steel rods, metal struts and supports to the shape held steady in his imagination. He worked by instinct at a furious pace. He had moved beyond the pencil drawing stage. Now the medium was a load of angle-iron, half-inch steel rods and wire mesh from Oswald's Cement Store. The arc-welder flashed again. Its lightning storm radiance streaked across the dark heavens.

He had forgotten how good it felt to be working with metal and welding rods without all the usual practical restrictions. He had the freedom to follow the whim and impulse of his creative imagination. To trust his talent, as Theo would say. Circumstance had not allowed him to indulge these gifts for a very long time. Now he had an original idea, and a gold mining company, for whom he had no respect, ready to pick up the bill when the job was done. He relished the possibility and the extravagance the arrangement allowed. This euphoria, and a good selection of music, would carry him through the entire night. "Dancing in the moonlight... it's got me in it's spotlight," he sang over an old Thin Lizzie tape from his art college days, and the lightning flash of the welder lit the sky above the workhouse.

LATE LIGHTS ALSO burned in Oliver's forge on the outskirts of town. He sat on a trolley with his head hunched low, his back supported by the dismantled shell of Grace O'Connor's car. The promise that it would be back on the road as good as new by tomorrow had been a little optimistic. Another deadline had gone by. He took a swig of *poitín* and held up a crinkled snapshot of Sally Holmes before the workshop bulb in its protective wire cage.

"Why couldn't you say something. Anything?" he cursed his shortcomings. "You were with her the whole live-long day and you couldn't open your mouth. Not once. You eejit." He blinked back the spirit-warmed flow of regret.

ALONE IN HER cottage by the sea Grace O'Connor prepared for bed. She sat on a low, padded stool in the bedroom looking into the dressing table mirror. Her reflection was tinted mild honey by the age of the glass. It would be her first night in a proper bed since she arrived in Ireland, but she did not imagine it would be easy to sleep. Her surroundings were too strange and new, and her mind working overtime to absorb the full consequences of all that had happened to her.

She was amused and pleased by the bold step she had taken; by this decision to stay on, and by this return to simpler things. She was stranded without a car on a remote peninsula with no electricity, dodgy toilet arrangements and a spring well outside the door for water. But she had the comfort of her personal belongings arranged around her, clean bed-linen in which to sleep, and the house was stocked with provisions for a week.

The stone walls were deep. The fire had been lit early and the bedroom was cosy and secure. Her silk nightdress gleamed in the candlelight against the umber shadows of the room. The fabric felt cool and gentle on the bruising after the crash.

She left the healing cord in place around her neck, but unhooked the gold chain and put it away. She picked up a hair-brush and the even strokes of its bristles through her hair had a pleasing sensual effect. One hundred strokes of the brush before bed, her mother had taught her as a child.

She wondered where Mulcahy had got to, and then put him out of her mind. This was her first night alone here, a time of special and private communion with the past. Many ghosts came to mind, but she had her Bridget's cross in the rafters for protection, and she felt both Theo and her grandmother would be too busy catching up for lost time to return this night. The shadows jumped in the candlelight when she moved to the bed. She climbed between the sheets, raised the candlestick, took a deep breath and blew out the flame. The air was suddenly full of candle fumes, a rich waxy aroma, and from the darkness beyond her window came the heart-beat of the sea, familiar, restful and evocative.

In his narrow, wainscoted bedroom above the bar and office – an office with a floor-safe full of documents that could land him back in the witness box – Eugene Tuttle's nerves were playing havoc. He washed down a second custard-yellow sleeping capsule and dragged the bed covers up under his chin. He screwed his eyelids shut and waited, but his body remained tense in a rigid state of guilt and dread. He could not forget that out there, past the flimsy protection of these four bedroom walls, that sinister display of lights in the sky raged on.

An hour before bedtime he had stood alone in his backyard, amongst the drink barrels and the empty bottles, to view that agitated sky. He could not explain those silent and ferocious bursts of lightning out over Mulcahy's workhouse. He felt the same kind of crawling fear that invades the brain before the first menacing flickers of a violent lightning storm, still out at sea, but closing steadily on the coastal town and his commercial property.

Any minute now the storm would break directly overhead, and he would be lifted out of his bed by cracking peals of thunder. Who was to say, then, what kind of black, warted monster could make its way to his bedroom under the covering rumpus of all that rain and thunder and lightning?

TEN

OLIVER'S PICKUP TRUCK bounced and rattled in the lane to Strand Cottage. He had an odd cargo of wooden posts, ropes, canvas, steel buckets and water vessels tied on the back. The pickup halted in front of the house and Oliver and Mulcahy jumped out. While Oliver unloaded the equipment from the back, Mulcahy went to find Grace.

He stuck his head around the jamb of the open front door. "Hello, where are you?" he called, but the new owner was not about. He went around by the gable, called out again and walked to the end of the backyard.

The sun was shining and the sea and the sky were the one bright shade of blue. He spotted Grace in the field next the shore. She was standing in the centre of the ancient ring fort, wearing a turquoise robe gathered in tight at the waist.

The ring fort was sheltered by flowering gorse. Past the opulent hedge of gorse, the Atlantic shimmered in the strong light. A family of seals basked on the sand-bars at low tide. On the far shore a limestone mountain, the shape of an Amazon warrior's breast, was nippled at the top with a Stone Age cairn – the mythical burial place of Queen Maeve of Connaught.

Mulcahy went to the edge of the ring fort. He stopped to study the look of serene concentration on Grace O'Connor's face. Her knees were bent and her bare arms enfolded the morning sky. Watching her practise her Tai Chi, he was struck by the simple beauty of her movements. He was high, high as a kite, after the long night's work, but the sensual configurations of her body brought to mind images of wonder; a deer crossing a high meadow, a flight of swans against a winter dawn.

When Grace spotted him standing at the edge of the fort she smiled and broke off. Mulcahy's eyes remained on her as she approached.

"How are you this morning?" she greeted him.

"Fine," he said.

Mulcahy's forthright stare made her feel uncomfortable.

"What is it? What's wrong?" she said.

"Nothing."

"You're laughing at me," she guessed.

"No."

"You think my exercises are ridiculous."

"No."

"You are laughing."

"I'm not."

"I know you are."

"I was struck by how beautiful you look this morning."

It was her turn to stare at Mulcahy. Why the sudden lack of discretion? She studied him closely. His eyes were bloodshot. The skin underneath looked puffed and tender, the dark rings exaggerated by his tired, pale face. He looked like someone pushed beyond the boundaries of exhaustion into a dangerous state of elation.

A careful reserve on her part might help to calm him down. She made small talk about the weather and the wonderful view from the peninsula on the walk back to the cottage. But his remark had shaken her. Did he really think she was beautiful?

When they came around the gable they met a peculiar sight. Oliver had mounted a rough wooden tripod in the front yard. He was making final adjustments to a set of ropes and pulleys fixed to a water tank on top.

"What's this?" she asked.

"Your car isn't ready," Mulcahy explained. "As a peace offering Oliver came up with this. What do you think?"

The tripod was screened from the lane by a hedge of green laurel shrubbery and surrounded by a canvas curtain for additional privacy. There was a rubber car floor-mat on the ground beneath what appeared to be the nozzle from a garden watering can. The two men stood back. She kicked off her sandals and went around behind the curtain. She reached out to hang her robe on the nail provided. Tentatively she tried the cord attached to the mechanism overhead. A fine stream of water came from the nozzle and fell about her shoulders. She pulled the cord hard and let out a shout as the force of the water hit.

"I think your shower is a success," Mulcahy turned to Oliver.

"Wait a minute," she called to Mulcahy. "No soap."

"Sorry, I forgot," he said. He reached into his pocket, tore the wrapper from a new bar of soap and came forward.

"Mulcahy... " she warned.

"Yeah?" he said halting.

"Pitch it to me."

Grace caught the flying soap between both hands. "Maybe you're the one who needs the cold shower?" she said.

Oliver's shoulders began to shake with big, boyish giggles. "Nothing a woman would do would surprise me," he mocked.

"Stop, stop!" Mulcahy said, but the warning had no effect.

OUT OF THE black mists of sleep there came a terrible hammering sound. A terror-stricken small boy ran for his life down a narrow canyon. He was followed by the sound of hooves hammering across the rough, stony ground. Then came the blood-chilling squeals of a nightmare Black Pig. More squeals echoed off the canyon walls. Lurid pink tongues of lightning licked at the surrounding trees. Young Eugene Tuttle ran for his life, but the pig continued to gain on him. He had cheated at his homework, and now the Black Pig was coming to get him. Soon, its snorting breath surrounded him. There was a final hungry and triumphant squeal as the monster's jaws snapped shut.

"Ouuurreekre... "

Tuttle jumped up in his bed, wide awake, his heart racing. It took him a full minute to come to his senses, and still the dreadful hammering sound continued. The noise bounced off the walls of his bedroom. He had not imagined it. The hammering came from outside his window. He climbed out of bed and nervously opened the curtains a crack.

Oswald had abandoned his shop counter and was clumsily fixing a wooden plaque in position at the base of the empty plinth in the square. The hammer hit close to flesh, and the councillor jerked back his thumb to suck the blood bruise. Bent steel nails lay at his feet like spent ammunition. Deputy Leddy stood a short distance away, offering directions with one hand, his pipe levelled in the other hand, to ensure the plaque was mounted straight.

The vague and misleading words on the plaque read: "In honour of John Charles Leddy, TD. Commissioned and financed by the Friends of the Town Improvement Committee: E. Tuttle & Oswald's Cement Store."

"How does that look now?" Oswald enquired, his face a dangerous burgundy colour.

"Lovely job, lovely," Leddy encouraged. He took a step back to consider the effect. In his mind's eye he could already picture his own imposing figure surmounting the plinth, his chin and chest thrust out to the town, a noble grip on the stem of his pipe, his brave and monumental forward stride set forever in cement. After a proud minute he concluded: "Of course this is just a rough model I had that shower of wasters on the employment scheme run up for me. The finished article will be made of the best quality brass."

"Brass... yes... naturally... engraved brass," Oswald agreed.

They were still admiring the plaque when a skinny, wire-haired terrier with a short tail strutted up to the plinth, raised its leg to the exact height of the painted board and let go three quick skites of piss.

"Good boy... You're a good boy," the owner encouraged and then called back the dog.

Oswald and Leddy swung around to identify the culprit. He stood in his front garden, offering the hound an approving pat on the head.

"Giblin!" Councillor Oswald blurted.

Deputy Leddy's face flushed with indignation, but he would not be provoked into a shouting match.

"Councillor Oswald. Deputy Leddy." Tom Giblin hailed the two men. "You're on important business as usual, I see. Are you sure your names are printed in big enough letters? How about a spotlight, two Grenadiers and a changing of the guard?"

"It'll have to be raised," Oswald said, contemplating the stained and dripping plaque. "He'll have every dog in the town at it next."

"Don't lower yourself talking to that rabble-rouser," Leddy warned his associate, but Tom Giblin's mocking voice followed them as they turned to make their escape.

"I was out at the workhouse last night to see what all the flashing lights were about. Mulcahy showed me the piece he's making for the square. You might want to take a look at what he has in mind for a public monument, Leddy, before you go putting your name under it."

"What's he talking about?" Leddy rounded on Oswald.

"Stirring up trouble as usual," the shopkeeper blustered. "Pay no heed."

SHORTLY AFTER THE incident in the square, a black Mercedes turned up the driveway to the workhouse and stopped in the courtyard. The black Mercedes was a car with political significance. A government minister's car, and as such, a symbol of power, influence and status amongst the loyal followers from all parties. A black Mercedes and a driver implied connections. They were a mark of special favour and rank within the floodlit mansions of power of the capital.

Deputy Leddy had never – and would never – reach the high political office of minister, or even junior minister. But he did own a black Mercedes. He had bought it from a used car dealer, hoping to improve his standing. But he had no grasp of the subtleties of these symbolic trappings, and the bygone appearance of his old Mercedes only increased the suspicion that the owner was a proper gangster. A small town mogul with a mini-empire secured through cronyism and jobbery.

For this show-down with Mulcahy he wore his broadest court-of-law pin-stripe suit and a fat polyester tie. He climbed out of the car on the driver's side trailing a thick rope of pipesmoke. He was closely followed by Oswald.

"You're wasting your time," Oswald protested. "It was only Giblin trying to rise us in public."

"I don't trust that Mulcahy," Leddy said going straight to the big door at the front of the workhouse. He had not forgotten, or forgiven, the show of disrespect in the graveyard. "I want to know what he plans to do with our good names."

He rapped several times on the plank door, but the sound was lost in the dark, empty chambers of the workhouse. The door was fitted with a heavy bolt that would not open to his fumbling. Then he spotted the key left in the latch of the smaller service door. He turned the key and the door creaked open.

The silence and the strangeness of his surroundings had knocked some of the wind out of the deputy's sails. He did not enter fully, but cautiously poked his head around the jamb to investigate. He waited for his eyes to adjust to the shadows, his ears keenly tuned for any threat. He bent further into the darkness.

In the courtyard Oswald consulted his watch, wishing he were someplace else. He did not relish having to squeeze through such a narrow opening. He did not want to have to go inside at all. The very thought of setting foot in the old workhouse spooked something deep in his Famine-haunted nature. Luckily, the deputy's wide and shiny rear end blocked the entire doorway.

Suddenly, as if a Famine ghost had jumped out at him, Deputy Leddy's whole body jerked backwards. The top of his head banged off the wooden lintel and the whole door-frame reverberated.

"I knew it!" he screamed.

"What... what? What is it?" Oswald panicked.

"Come here. Come here to me and see for yourself," the deputy insisted.

Oswald squeezed his head in under Leddy's armpit.

He could see nothing at first, only darkness and faint shafts of light. Then his bulging eyes found the object that had given Deputy Leddy such a shock.

"I don't believe it," he said.

"It's an insult," Leddy spluttered.

"It's a disgrace."

"It's a pig."

AFTER BREAKFAST GRACE O'Connor and Oliver sat on the wall outside the cottage, enjoying the sunshine. Mulcahy had taken up her offer of a shower, and while they waited for him to finish, Oliver described the public monument Mulcahy had in mind for the town square.

"It's wild, altogether," he concluded as Mulcahy returned from his shower, carrying his red boots in one hand, his socks stuffed in the tops.

"You look better," Grace said.

"I feel better."

Grace nodded. "Oliver tells me you've started work on the monument."

"I've made some headway," he said cautiously.

He began to thread the laces of his boots.

"Wait till you see it." Oliver was more enthusiastic.

"It's only a metal skeleton yet. It needs several more layers of wire mesh and then a skin of cement," Mulcahy explained. "I ran out of steam and raw materials last night."

"I'll motor you into town," Oliver proposed. "We'll load up at Oswald's, and I can give you a day at the workhouse. The quicker the job is done, the quicker you'll get paid."

"Amen to that," Mulcahy said.

Grace made up her mind not to mention Oliver's promise to have her car repaired. She recognised Mulcahy's urgent sense of purpose, and this monument to Theo mattered more to her than a junked rental car. If Mulcahy needed Oliver she was not going to take him away, but there was one condition.

"I want to help," she said.

Mulcahy had one knee tucked under his chin as he pulled the laces of his boots tight. He looked up. "You don't have to do this, Grace. It isn't necessary," he said with careful emphasis. "You understand?"

"I know."

"You've been through a lot already. Why don't you stay here today. Take it easy. Have a rest."

"I can't."

"Why not?"

She remembered the remark Mulcahy made the time he held her arm outside the front door of Theo's cottage. "Because it's not over for me here. Not yet," she said.

Mulcahy finished lacing up his boots. Nothing more was said.

WHEN THEY REACHED the town square Mulcahy jumped out at Oswald's Cement Store and tested the yard gates. They were chained and padlocked. Grace went to the grocery store. The notice inside the glass read: CLOSED.

"He must have taken an early lunch break," she said.

"How about an early pint?" Oliver suggested. "Before we get down to business."

"Only if you let me buy," Mulcahy said.

The two men started across the square.

"Hold it," Grace objected. "We've got work to do."

They pretended not to hear, and she was forced to go chasing after them. "How could anyone go drinking at this hour of the day?" she said dismayed.

When she stepped through the bar door she met a blue fog of cigarette smoke and the pungent smell of freshly drawn porter. Tom Giblin, Sam, and a full contingent of employment scheme workers from the harbour, were packed into the dim, wood-panelled bar. Sally Holmes looked up from the foaming taps and called hello to Grace. She went to the optic while the pints of stout settled on the marble counter and brought a tray loaded with double measures of brandy to Oswald, Deputy Leddy and Eugene Tuttle. They were huddled in private conference around a table at the opposite end of the room.

"Good men," Mulcahy approached the three committee members. "You'll be glad to hear the commission is well under way," he announced as soon as he reached the table. "I expect to have the job done inside a week." He turned to Oswald. "But I'm going to need more steel, and about twenty bags of cement."

The three men remained stone silent. Mulcahy noticed a sudden hush come over the bar. Oswald's face had turned the colour of pickled beetroot. The shopkeeper could not bring himself to speak and he looked to Deputy Leddy for an opening volley.

Leddy stabbed the shank of his pipe at Mulcahy's chest like an accusing finger. "You have a nerve coming in here."

"What!" said Mulcahy taken completely by surprise.

"Cement is it?" Oswald blurted, his voice trembling with outrage. "For that monstrosity?"

"Never!" Leddy was emphatic.

"What are you trying to do to us?" Oswald pleaded.

"Do you want to make a holy show out of us before the whole country?" Leddy reasoned.

"As if we weren't bad enough," said Oswald, and the deputy winced at the indelicacy.

"An-an-an- the company paying for it," Tuttle jumped in.

"What in the name of God were you thinking?" Oswald followed up quickly to save face.

The bar was now utterly silent. All ears were cocked to catch and record every word of the dispute. There would be no detail missing when the time came to report and embellish the day's events.

Out of the silence Tom Giblin called across the room.

"Citizen Mulcahy is an artist. I say he is entitled to freedom of expression."

"Keep out of this," Leddy warned.

"It's a public monument," Giblin insisted. "Every man, woman and child in this town has a right to their opinion."

Mulcahy stood frozen before the committee members, stunned by the vehemence of the attack. It had not occurred to him that his unlikely idea for a public monument would meet with such violent opposition.

"Don't go making an issue out of this, Tom," he said at last.

"Stand up for your rights, Citizen," Giblin prompted.

"That's enough, Tom," Mulcahy said.

But Tom Giblin was itching for a fight. "Let the people decide," he said. "We can take a vote on it here and now. Hands up all those who support Mulcahy?"

He looked around the room for a show of hands. There was not a stir.

"Oh, for Jasus sake, are ye ever going to wake up?" he roared at the employment scheme workers.

Immediately their hands shot into the air.

"And those against?"

The hands dropped.

"The people have decided," Giblin said with glee.

Deputy Leddy had put up with enough. "Are you finished the play-acting?" he said scornfully and jerked his pipe at the pub owner. "Now, Tuttle, say your piece."

Eugene Tuttle had the face of a frightened rabbit when he confronted Mulcahy. "M-m-much as I regret... And your f-f-friend too," he wandered off the words prepared for him by his fellow committee men. "As a co-consequence – "

"Spit it out, Tuttle," Leddy interrupted. "Mulcahy, Oliver," he took over. "You're barred. There's a bill on its way from Oswald's Cement Store for the hardware you've already wasted. If it's not paid in full this committee will instigate legal proceedings. Until such time you are not welcome in here, in Oswald's, or in my office or guest-house."

The deputy threw back his brandy. Tuttle and Oswald nodded to copper-fasten the decision.

Judgement had been delivered, and the honour of the committee satisfied, when the three members heard a dissenting voice.

"You have no right – " Grace came forward to defend Mulcahy.

"Now then, girlie," Deputy Leddy immediately cut across her. "You are a visitor to this country, and the committee extends a very warm and sincere Irish welcome to you, but keep your nib out of our affairs."

"That's democracy in action," Tom Giblin heckled from the floor. There was a rumble of agreement from the scheme workers.

"It's all right. Calm down everyone. We're leaving," Mulcahy said. He put his arm around Grace and led her away. "Come on," he said. "It's not worth it."

Uncertain of his next move Oliver followed them. He had not reached the door when Tom Giblin jumped up on a chair, threw his arms out wide and shouted.

"We will not stand idly by. Out! Everyone out. If Oliver and Mulcahy are barred, we're leaving in sympathy."

The confrontation had developed its own blind momentum. No one questioned the call. Cigarettes were decisively crushed out on the floor. Pints were grabbed and downed in frantic finishing gulps, the empties left in a neat row on the table nearest the door. Tuttle went as white as a sheet as he watched his best drinkers walk off the premises.

ELEVEN

THE MOOD BACK at the workhouse was depressed. Mulcahy had finished his search of the workshop and turned up only a few odd yards of wire mesh and less than half a bag of cement to complete the Black Pig monument for the town square. The job of converting the original workhouse into a studio and a living space had stretched his resources too far. The cupboards were bare and he was flat broke. The great current of euphoria that had carried him so far had ended in despondency.

"You can't give up," Grace urged.

"I don't have any choice."

"Another poaching expedition?" Oliver suggested.

Mulcahy shook his head. "The bailiffs are on to us. And my heart's not in it."

"So what happens next?" Grace asked.

"We forget it. That's what happens."

"No."

"What difference does it make whether we finish the monument or not? It's not wanted. Theo is dead, and I'm up to my neck in debt. It's time to move on. Time to get out of this backwater," Mulcahy decided gloomily.

"You can't leave," Grace objected.

Mulcahy was not in a mood to be told what to do. In a gesture meant to finish the argument he picked up what remained of the cement and went to the huge cast-iron weighing scales. He dumped the bag on one side. The scales tilted, and the right-hand pan banged hard against the floor, raising a cloud of cement dust. He threw a handful of nuts and bolts on top for good measure. Then he went to a corner table and gathered up a handful of bills.

"Let's see now," he said, leafing through the pink, yellow, blue and white counterfoils. "Overdraft, grocery, funeral expenses, electricity... " As he called out headings he went to the scales again and stepped up on to the raised left-hand pan, still clutching the fistful of bills. The cement and the loose nuts took off from the floor as the workhouse scales came down hard on Mulcahy's side.

"Now you show me how I'm supposed to balance both?"

Grace had watched his sullen performance long enough. If it was theatre Mulcahy wanted, he had chosen the wrong opponent. She crossed the workshop, grabbed hold of the chains attached to the arm of the scales, and found a footing along with the tattered bag of cement on the pan opposite Mulcahy. With the additional weight the scales tilted once more. There was a lurch towards her side before the arm swung back and the scales came into balance. Grace stood level with Mulcahy and looked him straight in the eye, holding out her credit card.

Mulcahy knew his stunt had backfired, but he turned in silent appeal to Oliver.

Oliver's shrug was impartial.

"I won't allow it," he called from his wobbly position.

"I'll pay the bills, if you stay on long enough to finish the monument," Grace bargained.

Mulcahy shook his head. "I said no."

"Maybe we could raise a bank loan and share the costs?" Oliver proposed.

Mulcahy looked at the metal skeleton of the pig, engineered on what he now considered a ridiculously grand scale. "It's too big. We'd need our own bank to pay for that monster," he said.

Having scored one over Mulcahy, Grace was feeling playful. "A piggy bank," she said. "You could put a slot in the top and use it to collect money. In a year you'd be able to pay back everything you owe."

"It wouldn't work," Mulcahy answered bitterly. "Leddy, Oswald and Tuttle would say the money belonged to the Town Improvement Committee and claim it for themselves."

"Not if we were the only people who knew how to get at

it," Oliver speculated. He reached for his box of cigarettes, found a pencil and began to sketch on the back of the packet. "Let's say we had a slot in the top, a collection box, some kind of a chute, and a hidden trap-door. If we used a basic electro-magnet, take a once-off shot of power from a car battery..." he planned the mechanism out loud. With his thumb ranged along the side of the pencil he measured up the pig. Then he walked away without saying goodbye. Grace and Mulcahy heard a diesel engine start, and the pickup truck pulled away from the workhouse.

"You've started something there," Mulcahy said.

"I was joking," she pleaded.

"Don't tell that to Oliver."

Getting off the weighing scales was not as easy as getting on. Mulcahy stepped off first and plucked Grace off the falling pan before it hit the floor. He swung her around to land her gently on her toes. Her hands were on his shoulders, his arms around her waist.

"Are you hungry?" he broke away quickly. "We could pick up something if you like."

"Can we bring it back here?"

"You buy the food, I'll do the cooking," he offered.

"Deal," she said.

Mulcahy went to switch off the lights in the workshop. Grace followed, but held back. She was upset, but she didn't want to show it. This morning Mulcahy had told her she was beautiful; now he couldn't wait to get away. She had revealed her real feelings a moment before, and he had pretended not to notice.

The lights went out one by one as they moved through the building. "I doubt if Oliver will be back this evening," Mulcahy said.

"You're very fond of Oliver." She made a fresh effort to understand him.

"He's a good friend and a good man," he said. "He's decent, loyal and obliging, but he can't stand routine. I call him the Leonardo da Vinci of useless inventions."

"Is that why you two get along so well?"

"I get a great buzz from people like Oliver," he said. "They add spice and colour to the grey soup of ordinary life. Everyone else is worried about rain, and income tax, and cancer, and there's Oliver, busy figuring out how to hide a money-box inside a cement pig. That's the kind of insanity I trust."

He reached for the last light switch inside the front door.

"Don't you think it makes a joke out of your work?" Grace hinted.

"What's so bad about that? The world is full of people who take themselves too seriously."

"Right, Mulcahy," she said, but he missed the insinuation.

THEY SAT ON the rug close to the massive open fire, propped up on dusty cushions with plates in their laps. The music in the background came from a paint-spattered tape-deck, while Mulcahy uncorked a second bottle of Spanish wine. Grace loved the airy feel of this enormous room, the heat on her face from the stone fireplace, the cool depths and heights behind her. It was like playing at lord and lady of the manor, though they were eating a spaghetti alla carbonara supper improvised from bacon, garlic, onions, Cheddar cheese and fresh cream, which they had to drive several extra miles to buy in a shop outside the town.

"This is good," she said, winding a forkful of spaghetti on a spoon and carefully raising it to her mouth.

"But not the perfect recipe for a romantic supper," Mulcahy said, and he wiped a spatter of sauce from his chin.

"You're a good cook."

"I like my food," he said. "New tastes have always been a big part of travelling for me."

"Have you travelled a lot?"

"After I finished art college I took off for a couple of years, to have a gawk at the world."

"And were you glad you went away?"

"I was young and giddy then. A pup. I'd do it differently if I went again."

He reached out and Grace held up her wine glass. She could feel the mellowing effects of the bottle they'd already drank. This feeling of safe seclusion was amplified by the deep stone walls and the massive oakwood beams of the workhouse roof, supporting the whole dark weight of night over their heads.

"I think it's wrong to look back and say you'd do things differently," she said. "What matters is that you did it once. And why would you leave now? You've put so much work into this place." She looked about at the beautiful art-work, the old furniture, the bric-à-brac antiques, the shelves loaded with books.

"I was mad to take on with this place on my own," he followed her eyes around the room. "It's too big for one person."

"Why did you choose an old workhouse?"

"At the time it was the right size for making and storing the big carnival figures I'd done for the annual parades. And the property belonged to Theo. He handed me the deeds one day and said, 'It's yours'. I said I couldn't accept, but he was very persuasive. When I told him I was worried about moving into a building with such an unhappy history, he laughed. What if there was a bad atmosphere? I said. Or ghosts? Theo said ghosts were all in people's heads. I could make the workhouse a happy or an unhappy place to live. The feeling here would depend entirely on me."

He stopped. The high ceiling gave the music in the background a distant, nostalgic tone.

"And are you happy?" Grace asked.

"Right now, yes. Usually, no."

"Why not?"

"Yeats said life is a preparation for something that never happens."

"How did he know?"

"Has it happened to you?"

"O, come on Mulcahy." Grace did not appreciate the evasion. "We're two people with opposite problems," she said. "You know who you are, but you don't know what you want. I know exactly what I want, but I don't know who I am."

"What does that mean? In plain English."

"I want to know where I belong in the world. Where I fit in," she said.

"Is that what brought you to Ireland?"

"I came here looking for..." she struggled to put the impulse, and all the uncertain feelings into words. "This may sound crazy to you," she said, "but I've always felt I'm not a whole person. It's like there are pieces of me still missing. My mother was the same. Only she never let it bother her. She was happy out there on Gatsby's lawn."

"Gatsby's lawn," Mulcahy said. "I like that."

"She was unreal, you know. One time our kitchen caught fire. My mother ran across the street and called from the neighbouring apartment to tell me to get out, the place was on fire. That was her way of coping."

Mulcahy watched the glow from the open fire light up the side of her face. Everything about this odd girl cried out for tenderness and understanding: the most natural of all our needs; a chance to love someone, and be loved in return. But he was not ready to accept that responsibility. Any closeness between them now was certain to be brief. He would not add to the hurt done already.

"You have a sad expression on your face. What are you thinking?" she coaxed.

"Don't ask."

"Tell me."

"No."

"Not even a hint?"

He shook his head.

"Okay," she said and signalled to Mulcahy to raise his

glass. "How about a toast?"

"To what?"

"To nameless feelings."

"Nameless feelings," their glasses touched.

They drank back the red wine. Their eyes connected.

"Mulcahy?" Grace said.

Against his better judgement Mulcahy moved closer.

Before their lips could meet, the dull throb of a diesel engine outside signalled the untimely return of Oliver's pickup truck. The moment escaped. They moved apart. Grace heard the scrape of metal wheels on rails and the rumble of the big door at the front of the workhouse being rolled back on castors. The pickup halted inside Mulcahy's workshop.

OLIVER'S FACE WAS black with smudges of soot from the forge, his hands caked with grease and coaldust as he moved with shambling speed to unload a new contraption from the back of the pickup. Grace and Mulcahy offered to help. Oliver said no. Only he knew how the various levers, metal pipes and struts, newly made in his forge, were meant to be fitted into the framework of the pig. Armed with a set of spanners and bolts, welding goggles and torch he began the transplant operation.

Mulcahy warned her not to look directly at the eye-scalding brightness of the welding flame. They stood back to watch while Oliver rushed back and forth, fixing, adjusting, hammering and welding. Finally, he cut the flame and raised the goggles. Setting his equipment aside, he collected a jam-jar full of washers, climbed up on to the pig and poured the washers into a slot created at the top.

"Grab the jump-leads," he called down to Mulcahy.

Mulcahy took the heavy-duty leads stashed under the driver's seat in the truck, raised the hood and fixed one set of the crocodile-jawed clips to the terminals of the battery.

"Start the engine," Oliver instructed Grace. She sat into the pickup, turned the ignition key and pumped the pedal.

"Now, fix the jump-leads to the tusks," he shouted to Mulcahy over the engine roar and the gathering black diesel smoke and fumes.

Mulcahy fixed the first metal clip to one silver-steel tusk and then, with some trepidation, brought the second clip into contact with the remaining tusk. There was a buzz of high voltage, and an explosion of hard white sparks that flaked and spat from the point of contact. He held on tight and Oliver's mechanical gadget began to rattle and click.

"Keep pumping that juice," Oliver shouted.

A lever dropped, a pulley turned and a trap-door wheezed open. Down an iron pipe the washers tumbled through to a spout, and from the mouth of the pig a cascade of metal washers spilled across the floor.

Grace eased her foot off the gas pedal and began to applaud. Oliver smiled proudly from his high perch at the money slot. Mulcahy punched the air.

"We're on the pig's back," he yelled.

"It's only a temporary arrangement," Oliver said. "When it's all bolted into place it will be our secret."

"Is there nothing we can do?" Grace offered again.

"Tom Giblin is looking for Mulcahy. The boycott on Tuttle's bar has spread. And the very mention of the word boycott is enough to keep even Leddy's cronies well clear of the place. A public meeting of the Town Improvement Committee has been called for nine o' clock on neutral territory in the Marine Bar. They want to settle the dispute. If you find out what's happening, I'll work on here."

"Jesus, I don't know, Oliver," Mulcahy stalled. "It might be better if I kept away from the place."

Grace looked at her watch and grabbed her coat. She searched around for another coat for Mulcahy. "Come on," she said. "You started this."

"Me!" Mulcahy protested while Grace pushed him out of the workshop past the skeleton frame of the Black Pig.

TWELVE

THE MARINE BAR was an extended fisherman's cottage and a turn of the century tea-rooms. Now, the timber windows were painted bright red and a newly thatched roof crouched under the Atlantic weather. On fine days plain wooden benches were left outside under the windows, and plastic chairs and tables with beer company umbrellas were spaced about the front yard that was also used as a car-park. Beyond the low boundary wall the strand started, a half-moon curve of stony beach, with Grace O'Connor's cottage tucked out of sight on the far headland. In summer the bar was peppered with tourists, day-trippers and Sunday coast road drivers. Only the hardy few stopped there in the winter.

By the time Grace and Mulcahy arrived there was an eye-catching collection of extravagantly unkempt motor vehicles parked outside. Motorcycles with multi-coloured plastic fertiliser bags used to make windshields and legshields. Tractors with homemade safety cabs, improvised from second-hand sheets of galvanised iron. Ageing imported Japanese cars, held together with nylon bailing twine. Battered jalopies and hen-hutch size, retired postal service vans. Salvaged technology washed up from the modern world and adapted for native use. Plus a good turnout of black bicycles walking with rust.

"Mind your head," Mulcahy warned Grace. He left his hand on the lintel-stone over the low doorway as they went in. A few customers looked around, but most were too involved with the meeting in progress, or too busy ordering drinks at the bar, to take any notice of the new arrivals.

Mulcahy was amazed at the turnout. A more serious affair would have raised only half that number of people. There were sheep farmers down from the mountain; fishermen who would have to rise in the perishing hours before dawn, to leave with the tide on the salmon boats; townspeople trawling for scandal; single men who were usually more interested in American pool, bar-room jokes and beer than in small-town politics; bemused regulars clinging bravely to their usual bar stools. The crew from the employment scheme were posted in strategic pairs around the room to stir up a proper row.

Extra seating had been set out in rows on the floor-space that was normally used for dancing. The plastic chairs faced a tiny stage with a makeshift high table, where Councillor Oswald sat between Deputy Leddy and Tom Giblin. A water jug, three glasses and a white bedsheet folded several times to make a table-cloth had been added to lend an air of formality.

The meeting had been under way for some time and Oswald, in his role as chairman, was having trouble keeping order. His sense of dignity prevented him from standing up to address the audience, and his voice was too soft to be heard over the noisy crowd and the electric buzz and chatter of the cash register. The atmosphere was primarily of ingrained cynicism and deep suspicion, directed at Oswald and Deputy Leddy, though Deputy Leddy was not without his supporters.

"Order, please. Order," Oswald shouted to be heard. He raised one hand in the air for attention. "Deputy Leddy has made it abundantly clear that he had no hand, act or part in agreeing to this monument..."

"It is a disgraceful abuse of our good names, our reputations and the good will of a major employer in this area," bellowed Deputy Leddy.

"What employment?" a scheme worker shouted towards the stage. "Not one person in this room was offered a job when that company started. They brought in their own people, and the rest is being done with machines."

"The mine is still at an exploratory stage," Leddy said reassuringly. "When the commercial development starts the company have promised two hundred-odd jobs."

"Very odd jobs," said the heckler.

"Jobs for a few outsiders," Tom Giblin told the crowd.

"Jobs for the boys," agreed a second heckler in the front row.

"This is a window of opportunity," Deputy Leddy pressed on, determined to be heard. "The gold in them mountains will make wealthy people out of every one of you here tonight."

"What about the cyanide in our river? What about the safety of our children?" a woman shouted.

"Certain trouble-making elements in this room have gone to great lengths to spread misinformation, rumours and lies. Yes, that's right, lies," Leddy implicated his rival at the table. "The gold is extracted by purely mechanical means. Read my lips. There is no cyanide."

"If you swore on the Bible it was raining outside, Leddy, I'd leave this room wearing sun-lotion," Tom Giblin said.

"Poverty or poison, is that the choice?" the woman protester shouted.

Tom Giblin sat visibly up-lifted by the barracking Leddy had suffered since the meeting started. Eugene Tuttle had backed out at the last minute claiming ill health. Councillor Oswald was out of his depth, and even Leddy had been caught off-guard by the large turn-out. When Giblin spotted Mulcahy standing by the door, he renewed the attack.

"Deputy Leddy, you still haven't explained to the people here tonight why a local artist has been denied permission by your committee to finish a public monument designed for the town square?"

"What person in their right mind would come here to look at... at... at... a pig?" Leddy could hardly bring himself to say the word.

"The Black Pig," Tom Giblin corrected. "I have it on good authority that Eugene Tuttle, a member of the said committee, gave specific instructions to the artist to take his inspiration from the work of the poet W. B. Yeats."

"I've spoken to Tuttle, and on mature recollection –" Leddy began, but Tom Giblin would not be interrupted.

"There is a poem entitled, 'The Valley of the Black Pig', on page eighty-three of my paperback edition of the collected poems of W. B. Yeats."

"I don't care if that old fool wrote about a pink, a blue or a Chinese pig," Leddy raged. "We are not going to be made the laughing stock of the entire nation!"

"It never bothered you before," the hecklers were quick to remark.

"Pig in the parlour. And pig-ignorant Irish?" Leddy roared. "Is that how you want to be known? Is that the way you see yourselves?"

There was a loud surge of agreement amongst the deputy's supporters.

"The legend of the Black Pig is part of our native folklore and the Irish storytelling tradition. It's part of our heritage and our birthright," Tom Giblin addressed the anti-monument lobby directly. "We have only a few resources here. Our wild salmon, our fine beaches and our beautiful scenery. And we have our legends."

"We've heard the same old Blarney out of you for years, Giblin. Where's the jobs?" Leddy demanded.

"Here, here," came a shout from the floor.

The meeting was starting to break up in separate arguments around the room.

Leddy put a match to his pipe and released a great drift of smoke in Tom Giblin's face. His opponent was playing a worn-out record, and the deputy could sense the mood of the crowd shifting.

"The jobs are in tourism," Giblin raised his voice to be heard above the dispute. "This is the last unspoilt wilderness in Europe."

"And how are you going to bring the people here? On the

back of your bicycle, is it?" Leddy mocked.

The jibe raised a cheer.

"Listen to the deputy," a supporter shouted. "We're in the arsehole of nowhere. We need the gold mine, and we need the jobs. We've listened to enough of your hogwash, Giblin."

"If we had a pig in the town square, we'd have a gimmick," Tom Giblin went on, unruffled by the abuse. "We could do like other towns around the country: start a festival to bring the people here. Let them laugh at us all they like, we'd still make money."

"Who in their right mind would come here to look at a pig?" Leddy shot down the suggestion.

"Who's going to come here and offer us work?" Giblin answered in return. "At the end of the day. A window of opportunity. Down to the wire," he mimicked the deputy. "Where have you and all your clichés got us?"

He wheeled about to confront his audience. "When will you get it into your thick skulls that nobody is going to come here to save your bacon. A third of the labour-force in this country is out of work, and that's the way it's going to stay. Nobody is going to come here and hand every one of you a job. There's no John Wayne, and no Fifth Cavalry, riding in to the rescue. We're on our own. Either we sit here doing nothing until we're starved out of existence, or we get up off our arses and make a go of it by ourselves. Now, Mulcahy has given us a gimmick. It's a pig. A Black Pig. It sounds daft, I know, but we have something the next lot down the road don't have. Why don't we use it? Are we afraid of what other people might think? Are we so terrified that people might laugh at us we can't grasp this opportunity? Are we that insecure as a people and as a nation?"

His passion surprised everyone, and the room had quietened to give him a proper hearing. "I have a plan," he said. "I need volunteers to get the thing started, but I know it can be done. We put that monument in the square, and we go the whole hog and start the first Ennismuck Festival of the Black Pig."

"Good man, Tom." There was a round of applause and calls of encouragement from the bar. The thought of some colour coming to an otherwise hum-drum existence in a monotonous seaside town had won support. And the idea was ridiculous enough for the assembled throng not to have to worry about it ever really happening.

"That's right, go on, drive the fool further," said Deputy Leddy.

Giblin would not be put off. "You've done this sort of thing before, Mulcahy," he called over the crowd. "Come up here to this table and tell us how to run a festival."

All eyes swung around towards Mulcahy, still standing at the door. Mulcahy shook his head forcefully and searched for a means of escape.

Grace prodded him with her elbow. "Go on, Mulcahy," she urged. "They're all waiting. Say something."

Mulcahy hedged and cleared his throat. He did not know where to begin or how to get out of this corner. "Running a festival is a lot of work," he said. "You need a lot of co-operation and good will. Everyone would have to be behind it one hundred per cent."

"Would it bring in tourists?" Giblin pressed.

"It might."

Grace could no longer contain her impatience at Mulcahy's blatant attempt to back out of the limelight.

"If your festival goes ahead, and you all agree, I'll make costumes for a parade," she announced.

"Someone buy that woman a pint," a Giblin supporter called. It was said to earn a laugh, but it was also a gesture of support for Grace, and a further annoyance to Deputy Leddy's supporters, who sat with their arms folded, furious that the joke was getting out of hand. Vigorous disagreement broke out around the room.

"No parades." Leddy began to shout down the conflict.

"The last thing we want is a horde of people invading the town."

"Have you something to hide?" came a shout from the front row.

"I'm not the kind of man to draw attention to all the hard and thankless work I've done over the years on your behalf as a politician," Leddy addressed the crowd in a voice quivering with wounded dignity. "But I'm telling you now, I have done everything in my power to play down this mining business."

"We know you have," said Tom Giblin.

"If it gets out that we have gold in them mountains, we'll have another Klondike on our hands," Leddy insisted. "Is that what you want? The riff-raff of every barrack town in the country camped on your doorstep. People who'd steal the washing off your line, the coal from your shed, the eye out of your head."

"Lies!" shouted Giblin. "All lies. And everyone in this room knows it."

"Is that what ye want?" Leddy hit the table with his fist.

The temperature in the room was rising all the time. Pints were being lowered at a fierce rate. Leddy had failed to strike the right chord. Tom Giblin's idea for a festival of the Black Pig had an irresistible element of madness. The crowd was falling in behind him.

"Mulcahy, are you with us?" Giblin followed the advantage.

Mulcahy could only press down the hair on his head with both hands and look around the room in horror. This was not what he wanted at all.

"We'll have music. A parade organised by Grace O'Connor. An official unveiling for the Black Pig," Giblin announced. "And we'll finish the night with a pig-roast on the beach. How about it?"

Grace leaned in close to prompt Mulcahy. "Come on, say yes. It sounds like fun."

Mulcahy's head shook forcefully from side to side.

"The whole thing is being hijacked." he said. "This has nothing to do with me, or Theo or the Black Pig. This is a political thing. You don't know what you're getting into."

Grace knew she would never get anywhere arguing with him. She took a deep breath and shouted up to the high table: "Mulcahy said yes to the festival."

Mulcahy stared at her in disbelief, but the cat-whistles from Giblin's supporters planted at the bar drowned out his objections.

Deputy Leddy stood up so fast he knocked over his chair. He signalled to Oswald to follow and stormed violently away from the table.

"Go on, have your laugh," he raged, "but don't come crying to me looking for work after you've disgraced your-selves, your town and your country for a few paltry coppers from the tourists."

"I'll take coppers in the bank before your cyanide in the river any day," Giblin countered.

He relished the empty high table, the fallen chair and the sight of his vanquished opponent. He got to his feet to make a further announcement: "The next meeting will be to appoint an organising committee for the Ennismuck Festival of the Black Pig!" His elated cry followed Oswald and Deputy Leddy out the door.

THE PLASTIC CHAIRS were stacked and pushed back against the walls and the stage given over to the musicians. There was a silver haired tin-whistle player from the employment scheme, who, though incoherent with drink, spoke straight from his heart through the whistle in his nimble fingers, while his head swam and reeled. A bodhrán player with a woodcock feather in his trilby, his pockets full of betting slips, maintained the pounding beat. A guitar player with a thin beard, one gold ear-ring and a strong voice led the ballads. A man with a finger missing blew on the harmonica for all he was worth. They were steered back to more traditional airs each time by an older man with a long, narrow jaw, his cap tilted back from his forehead, a white handkerchief on his shoulder to pillow his fiddle and mind the good suit.

Tom Giblin stood in front of the musicians calling out set dances.

Grace had been dragged on to the floor by friendly hands that led her through the steps and turns of the Siege of Ennis. People of all ages and levels of ability joined her: teenagers, grandparents, hefty farmers and matrons and a public health nurse. Grace was not a good dancer, but she could dance a basic four-hand reel. Her feet hammered out the count of one-two-three... one-two-three in time to the music. It was a great feeling to be asked to join the dance. The thump of synchronised feet pounding the floorboards, the smell of sweat under armpits and the concentrated air of the better dancers transported her to an earlier life. As she slipped from partner to partner, the dancing lessons she attended in the Irish-American clubs as a child came back. She was swept along by that part-learned and part-instinctive rhythm.

The plain set came next, and of all the sets it was the most difficult to dance. "Clear the floor and mind the dresser," Tom Giblin called, and the dancers locked arms and went into an exhilarating spin.

Grace improvised and floundered. She laughed. She got confused and lost her direction, but her feet kept time, one-two-three... one-two-three, and every time she went astray a hand grabbed her, and led her through the next set. All the dancers finished in their original position.

Mulcahy slipped in and out of view, but they had no chance to talk all night. Too many people wanted to meet Grace and welcome her to the parish. They offered fond memories of her mother's screen roles. They voiced their support for the festival, and said they would help Grace with the parade. The hours passed in well-meant banter and dancing, drinking and swopping names.

If the bar was supposed to close at a certain hour, no one seemed to remember. There was a slight falling off in numbers, a gathering of empty glasses on the counter, but inspired by more drink and elbow room, the musicians returned to earlier airs and sets with renewed uplift and gusto.

Grace needed a breather. She clapped her hands in farewell to the dancers before leaving the floor, and flopped down into a seat beside Mulcahy.

"Hi, stranger," she said. She was dizzy with the music and the names of so many new people going round in her head.

"You're having a good night," he said, lowering his pint.

"You didn't dance?"

"No."

"Are you mad at me?"

"No."

"Are you sure?"

He put his arm around her and gave her a warm hug. "You're some handful, all the same," he said.

"I think the festival is a really good idea," she was encouraged to go on. "It will help other people to accept your work."

"I doubt if the brandy boys will let Tom Giblin away with it," he said. "Politics, for some odd reason, attracts a very high percentage of petty, spiteful and self-important people. They don't like it when the humble electorate they're meant to serve start making accusations of incompetence, corruption and criminal stupidity. They take that kind of thing personally."

"But you do think the festival is a good idea?"

"Tom Giblin has his own agenda."

"So you're not going to help?"

"I'll finish the Black Pig for the town square, but I won't be a part of any festival committee."

"Why not? I've met some lovely people here tonight."

"It's like I used to tell Cathy. It's as easy for me not to get involved in these things, as it is for other people to be carried away by them."

THE BIRDS OUTSIDE had started to sing. The bar owner was making signs that she wanted to get to bed.

"Ye don't have to go home, but ye can't stay here," she announced.

Drinks were finished. There was a general movement towards the front door. Grace rose with Mulcahy and he helped her into her coat.

In the car-park they met the two men who had sat in the front row and heckled Deputy Leddy throughout the meeting. They were now very drunk, leaning on black bicycles and looking uncertainly at the sky.

"I'm telling you, that's the moon," one said.

"No. That's the sun," the other disagreed.

"It's the moon."

"The sun."

They called Grace over to settle the dispute. "Excuse me," one said. He pointed a finger at the heavens. "Is that the sun or the moon?"

"I don't know, boys. I'm not from around here."

Mulcahy dragged her away. "You're worse than they are," he said.

She was feeling reckless and brave. "Are you going to walk me home?"

"Across the beach?" He glanced quickly between Grace and the far headland. She waited with her head tilted to one side, her fingers snagged in the top pockets of her jeans.

"All right," he said. He looped an arm around her waist.

Winter storms had banked a ridge of stones against the fields and the gardens of the houses along the rim of the beach. They scrambled down the embankment of loose stones into a cove full of the sounds of the sea.

The sun had not yet climbed above the horizon, but all

the colours of a furnace burned in the east. They walked along the water's edge. Sand sizzled where the waves swept.

In the bar Mulcahy had mentioned his wife by her first name. Grace wondered what place she had in his life now? Was Cathy the reason Mulcahy was so reluctant to get involved with her? Were they still close? Did he still love her?

"Can I ask a personal question?" she opened.

The troughs and sudden reaches of foam and salt-water were hard to gauge, and she was forced to side-step an incoming wave.

"You don't have to answer," she said.

"What's the question?"

"Do you still see her – your wife – Cathy?"

"No. That's over."

"You sound very sure."

"I am."

"Were you hurt when she went away?"

"We were close once. We grew apart."

"And you're not bitter?"

Mulcahy looked up the beach at the wisps of sand being blown out to sea on the dawn breeze. Tucked in close to his shoulder, Grace watched his eyes. She gave him a full minute, convinced he would speak, but no answer came. She followed the direction of his gaze. A beacon light-house glimmered out in the channel.

They walked to the end of the beach. Sea-scoured driftwood and broken lobster pots lay amongst the stones. The sand finished and there was a terrace of weathered rock, with tails of seaweed in the fissures. They climbed up the rocks like a staircase to reach the fields.

"Landfall," he said.

Grace's cottage waited on the next rise. The low roof, the single chimney and the dark windows appeared cold and lonesome in the early dawn.

It was a decisive moment. They stood close and read the quick, intent look in each other's eyes. Two fully aware adults. Mulcahy bent to kiss her. Grace answered with a deeper kiss.

In the cottage they undressed quickly. Their needs were physical. Silent. After the rustle of clothes, they fell on to the bed, their limbs in a tangle. Pitched into lovemaking. Grace shivered with longing, and the cool of the linen. She needed warmth, the warmth of flesh against flesh, and in this body heat the melt-down of reason began. He kissed the cusp of her shoulders. He kissed her collarbone. His mouth began to explore her body. Her limbs were knowingly enfolded. Then a tremor close to pain and surprise. And in this giving she was equally caught up in her own need. Every muscle and sinew and nerve ending began to tremble. She tensed against this overpowering sensation. Her whole body shuddered in a prolonged agony. She wanted it to finish. She wanted it to go on. She clung to him with a desperate ferocity, but could not hold off the need any longer. There was a hovering spasm, when body and mind fused. Became one. Then her lungs emptied in a great unguarded moan. The tension broke. Little aftershocks darted through her belly and up her spine. She fell back. Emptied. Returned.

HOURS AFTER THEY had made love, Grace lay close to Mulcahy and thought about what had happened. At what point had she been overtaken by this unreasonable desire, this aching reliance on a man's love, or at least his approval? Mulcahy was asleep, his rumpled head turned away. She looked at the battered work-boots on the floor lying next to her sandals. Her hand travelled through the hairs on his chest. She raised herself up on one elbow to brush his cheek and feel the stubble of overnight beard. "How could I have let this happen?" she despaired. A sea breeze lifted the curtains. Daylight pounced on the room.

THIRTEEN

WHEN GRACE WOKE again, she got up and put on her robe. Mulcahy was still asleep, his first real sleep in days. She did not disturb him. Leaving the bedroom, she went outside. In the sunlight the sea was blue to the horizon. To judge from the strength of the light, it was late in the afternoon, but she was not interested in the exact time.

After organising warm water for a shower, she shampooed her hair, then patted her body all over with a soft flannel cloth dipped in warm water – it felt as good as a massage. Her injured shoulder was much better. She felt a surge of happiness. Life had its up side. She wondered how Mulcahy would react when he woke up in her bed.

Returning to the house, she heard him cough and stir in the upper bedroom. She took four oranges from the fruit bowl and cut them in half to squeeze out the juice.

Mulcahy did not recognise his surroundings immediately when he woke. He was naked under the eiderdown and his clothes lay in a heap on the floor. The sight of the discarded clothes brought back the night.

Grace came in carrying two glasses of orange juice. He sat up in the bed and rubbed the sleep out of his eyes.

"What time is it?"

"Who cares."

She handed him a glass of orange juice. He drank it back.

"Thanks," he said.

She sat on the edge of the bed. "How do you feel?"

"I could have done without that last pint."

"That's not what I meant."

He drew a lock of hair back behind her ear.

"You're really lovely," he said.

"But you love your wife, and you feel bad about what's happened," she said, anticipating the hurt.

"It's nothing like that."

"What then?"

"Come here," he coaxed. "I'm not at my best in the morning."

"You were okay last night," she let the evasion pass, and lay down beside him. They kissed. Less urgent than before, but more knowing.

THE SUN WAS dropping through broken cloud in the west. In the slanting rays of light they walked back along the beach they had crossed the night before. Grace wore trainers, a T-shirt, blue jeans and a short jacket. Mulcahy wore his usual baggy jumper and carried his coat over his shoulder pegged on one finger. Grace had put her camera in the pocket of her jacket, but she was not inclined to use it. She had abandoned any plan to record the day, aware of a growing flaw in the honeymoon mood.

The tension started the minute they left the cottage. Before they set out everything had been so simple. Hours of lovemaking. Breakfast. Coffee. Now Mulcahy walked the beach alongside her with the preoccupied and determined air of a man getting back to business that didn't include her.

They crossed the strand at a brisk pace. He had not spoken for several minutes.

"Is there something worrying you?" she asked.

He hesitated and half-smiled. A sad, resigned look. "You worry me."

"Me?" She was shocked. "Why?"

"I'm being practical, Grace. Sooner or later I know you're going to go away."

"Go where?" she demanded.

"I don't know."

"Then why did you say such a thing?"

"Because I can't see what future there is for you here. Not in the long term," he said frankly.

He looked straight ahead, walking hard. Grace fought to

keep up with his fast strides. The going had suddenly became tough where the beach was soft underfoot. Her feet sank in the damp sand. There was a painful drag on the muscles of her legs. She pressed on with her head bowed. Breathing hard. The rumble of wind in her ears.

They said nothing until they reached the Marine Bar and Mulcahy's car.

Grace had formed no definite plan crossing the beach, but this was a bad move. She could not sit into his car. Her mood was too volatile for that confined space.

Mulcahy also delayed. He recognised they were at a critical pass. He stood at the driver's door for a minute, and then shoved the keys back in his pocket.

"Forget the car," he said. "We'll walk."

"Walk where?"

"I want to show you something."

"Is it far?"

"Patience, grasshopper," he mimicked an Oriental accent.

He moved off, but waited for her to follow.

If she had any pride, she thought, any shred of self respect, she would tell him to go to hell. But she didn't. She shook the sand off her shoes and caught up with him.

Rainclouds were moving in from the sea, but the sun came through in broad patches. They walked inland, and the level fields on either side of the road shone bright green and manicured from regular harvest. Old ditches had been flattened, stone walls removed, the boundary hedgerows of the original narrow plots of land uprooted to increase the size of the fields.

They kept to the road and passed a prosperous new bungalow surrounded by large farm outbuildings. The cement yard was full of machinery. There was a sharp smell of straw and manure around the barns. Shortly after the farmyard they turned up a neglected laneway, where tumbling thickets of briar grew on either side of the stone walls. The brambles were more than head-high and enclosed the track in shade. Suddenly, they were in a much older world, closer to the past. A sigh of history in the still, green air.

A tiny village appeared up ahead. All the houses, seven or eight homesteads on either side of the road, were built of stone. Empty. Roofless. Abandoned. The pointed gables and the chimney stacks leaned dangerously off the vertical on the brink of collapse. Many had lost the lintel-stones over the doors.

"A Famine village?" Grace guessed.

"Famine. TB. Emigration," he said. "This place had it all."

It was a melancholy collection of hovels. Mulcahy called them a clachan. He drew her attention to the stone-craft of the original builders; the great cornerstones and the level rows of smaller stones arranged with such impressive skill and care. It was very beautiful, but the individual rooms were mouldering and cramped, the doorways low, the windows few and tiny. Saddest of all were the empty hearths and the chimney corners overgrown with brambles and the wild shrubbery that forced its way up through the gaps in the stone floors.

"God's judgement on an indolent and feckless people," Mulcahy quoted while Grace went from one empty room to the next.

"Does it upset you? The Famine and the thought of all those people who died?" She tried to fathom his intention.

"They call it the Great Irish Famine," he said. "I've often meant to ask the experts, what was so great about it?"

"Seriously?" she pressed him for a more considered answer.

Mulcahy reached into the undergrowth and lifted a cast-iron fragment belonging to a broken skillet pot.

"Some people have compared it to the Jewish Holocaust. To others it's an ecological disaster. The revisionists think of it as a massive social and political blunder, and say we only had ourselves to blame. The radicals, naturally, believe it was the means by which a whole unwanted social class of labourers and smallholders were wiped out, a ruthless re-ordering of power by native shopkeepers, big farmers and the clergy, creating a guilt-ridden, inward looking Catholic Ireland. The only thing they all agree on is that, whatever the cause, the Famine left a lasting trauma deep in our national psyche."

Across the fields came the sound of a tractor ploughing the headland.

"And what do you think?" Grace asked. "Personally?"

"I'm not qualified to say."

"But you must have some feelings about it?"

"It's all S.O.S. to me."

"What does that mean?"

"The Same Old Shit. Over a hundred and fifty years after the Famine, our lives are still being controlled by remote economic policies, gutless leadership, rampant bureaucracy, muddled and misguided social strategies, and the same use-less political in-fighting that was such a part of those Famine times. And people are too blind, too lazy or too stupid to notice, or do anything about it."

He spat the words out with open contempt, and looked away towards the elephant-hide wrinkled mountains capped with mist.

"But if life here upsets you so much, why do you stay?"

"I'm happy nowhere else," he said.

They crossed the road to look at a wooden cart amongst the brambles beside one of the larger homesteads.

"You know something, Mulcahy? You remind me of the Irish I knew in America."

He used one foot to tramp down the thorny stems around the cart, working with his back turned while she spoke.

"Talk to a Russian, a Polish or an Italian immigrant and they'll tell you the same story. Their families moved to the United States because life was hard where they came from. They wanted a better life and they believed that by working

174

hard they could make that better life. The Irish were different. Sure they worked. They worked as hard as anyone, sometimes harder, but they didn't want to be in America. They said they only came over because there were no jobs at home. They were full of resentment and frustration. It wasn't the life they wanted. It was something that had been forced on them. And they all believed when things got better they'd go back, back to the country they had walked out on. When I asked why they hadn't stayed and tried to change things, they had no answer."

"The work was near, but the job was far away," Mulcahy said.

He had made a path through to the cart in the brambles. On closer inspection the timber was badly damaged by the weather. The shafts had decayed beyond repair, and only one useless wheel remained, shrunken within an iron hoop.

"I knew a long time ago, doing what I do, I'd never be well-off living in this country," he confessed, "but it's important to dig in somewhere. That's where the sense of belonging comes from."

"You were the one threatening to leave," she reminded him.

"Don't get me wrong. Lots of things about this country depress me, but there are other things that I love."

"Name one. The important one. The big one."

Mulcahy was surprised by the direct challenge. Her eyes were searching and insistent. He had missed something important, but he had no idea what it was.

"I'd have to think about it," he said.

"Come on. The first thing that pops into your head."

He looked at the ground, at the delicate cream flowers growing under his feet. "Primroses," he said. "I love wild primroses. The flowers of May."

"And?"

"Lunatics like my friend Oliver."

"I know about Oliver already."

"The quality of the light," he said. "The amazing variety of skies and cloud formations you get here, especially in the west. The first mouthful of stout after a pint settles. Hearing Luke Kelly sing 'On Raglan Road'," he warmed to the theme. "Hot griddle-cake with the butter melted over it. Oh, man! And fresh mussels, straight out of the sea, and just steamed open."

"Go on."

"A good traditional *seisiún*. Making something with my hands. Getting it right. Walking the Burren in County Clare. A long seaweed bath after a hard week. And the freedom. I suppose that's what I love most. The tremendous freedom you have living here."

"Okay," Grace accepted.

"Now it's your turn," he said.

"You want to know what I love? Right now? This minute?" she said.

"Tell me."

"You, Mulcahy. I love you."

THEY WERE FAMISHED when they got back to the car. Mulcahy said they must have walked on Famine grass – the *féar gorta* – a spot in certain old fields where the living could be struck by the hunger pangs of its long dead tenants. They went into the Marine Bar to ask for food.

The owner, a mild-faced, heavily built woman stood behind the counter. The place was empty. She remained staring at a spot high up on the far wall and waited for Mulcahy to walk up to her to give his order. He asked if they could have toasted ham and cheese sandwiches with their drinks. The woman blinked and nodded. The drinks were served first. Then she went to the kitchen, which was just off the bar.

The pints of stout had a fresh, malt-cool flavour and sharpened their appetites. After a couple of minutes they heard the unmistakable sound of a knife blade scraping burnt toast in the kitchen.

Mulcahy looked at Grace over his drink. His eyes were merry. They listened and they heard the scraping sound again.

"Is that what I think it is?" she whispered.

"Not a great sign," he said.

They began to laugh. Comfortable. Much more in tune with each other, their feelings aired.

The toasted sandwiches were served in a little basket. They were crisp and brown and arranged on a paper napkin with slices of onion on top. They tasted surprisingly good.

"Strange," Mulcahy said, and glanced back at the kitchen. The woman had gone out, but they continued to speak with their voices lowered.

"What do you want to do next?" he asked. "We could try the seaweed baths."

"I'd like to see the mine. The gold mine."

"Why spoil a lovely day?" he said, raising the top slice of toast to spread mustard over his sandwich.

"I want to see what all the fuss is about. And I have my camera."

"I noticed you sneak it into your pocket."

"You don't miss much."

"Only the obvious things," he said.

Grace felt the happy, weightless feeling of the morning return.

"All right," he agreed. "We'll go to the mine. But let the record show I could think of a dozen better ways to spend an evening."

The sky had clouded over by the time they left the Marine Bar. The twilight was deepening fast under rain clouds when they arrived at the mountain. Mulcahy branched off the regular road and followed a rough, stony track through a pinewood plantation. It was darker still under the trees.

At last they came to a pair of locked gates blocking the road. Two large public notice boards had been bolted to the steel bars. One said: PRIVATE PROPERTY: TRES-PASSERS WILL BE PROSECUTED. The notice on the second gate had a black lightning stroke against a yellow triangle, and beneath it the words: DANGER: HIGH VOLTAGE. A barbed wire fence tensioned along cement posts extended across the mountain on either side of the gates.

Mulcahy turned the car around.

"Are we going back?" Grace asked surprised.

"It's an old poaching habit," he said. "Always leave the car ready for a speedy get-away."

"Could we get into trouble for this?"

"No, no," he made light of the idea.

But Grace began to have misgivings. "What about that electric fence?"

Mulcahy smiled at the worried expression on her face. "They do that to put people off," he said. "Pay no heed."

"Are you sure?"

"Come on. This was your idea."

Before getting out of the car he reached into the glove compartment and grabbed what appeared to be a large tube of artist's paint.

"I'll bring my camera," Grace offered.

"We'll have to hurry," he said. "The rain is on the way and the light is going fast."

They got out of the car and Mulcahy went directly to the big padlock securing the gates. Despite the warning notice he did not hesitate to take hold. He removed the cap from the tube, put the nozzle into the keyhole and squeezed.

"What are you doing?"

"It's plastic filler," he said. "It'll set rock hard in a couple of minutes."

Grace was annoyed by this act of petty vandalism. Mulcahy was only making trouble for both of them if they were caught trespassing.

"Did you have to do that?"

"I don't like people who use locks and put up fences," he said. "One day the mine owners might get the message. Oh give me land, lots of land, don't fence me in..." he hummed as the plastic paste in the lock began to harden.

She shook her head and walked up to the gates. She glanced at the warning notice again. Her hand hovered over the steel bars. Did she trust Mulcahy? She grabbed hold. There was no lethal shock.

She used the gate bars like the rungs of a ladder and together they climbed over the top.

Once inside the gates she had a distinct sensation of being in alien territory. The warning notices, the locked gates and the barbed wire had undermined her confidence. They walked up the rise in the failing light. Mulcahy stopped and used the toe of his boot to point out a motionless bird on the road. Grace immediately bent down to help the injured bird.

"Don't," he said.

"Why not?"

"It's dead. Poisoned."

"How?" she said and straightened up quickly.

"Cyanide from the mine."

"I don't understand?"

"Let me enlighten you. The company say they're mining gold here by mechanical means only. But mechanical extraction isn't very efficient, and what goes off to be smelted at the end of the process isn't very pure. You can get quicker and better results if you chemically extract the gold using cyanide."

"But they've told everyone they don't use cyanide."

"Remember the truck you met the morning of the crash? Why didn't the driver stop? Because he was carrying a load of vats. Steel vats from a closed-down creamery. Dead birds. Truck drivers who don't want anyone to know their business. They're using cyanide all right, and no one is supposed to know."

"What about safety and health regulations? How can they get away with it?"

"If the mine was classified as a commercial operation the owners couldn't fart sideways without the Environmental Protection Agency knowing about it and monitoring the emission. But this is called an exploratory mine, and for the time being at least, an exploratory mine comes under the jurisdiction of the County Council, and a certain –"

"Councillor Oswald," Grace finished for him.

"Exactly."

"The law isn't clear where final responsibility for an exploratory mine rests, and guess who is doing everything in his power to block Government agency involvement?"

"Deputy Leddy."

"You learn fast."

Grace shivered as she looked around the empty mountain. Under the gathering rain clouds, and with a dead bird at her feet, it had suddenly become a very sinister and threatening place.

"Mulcahy?" she said nervously as they moved on.

"Yes."

"No messing. No tampering with locks. We stop for a quick look around and then we leave."

"It changes your attitude, doesn't it?" he said pointedly. "When you know what you're up against."

The heather-covered rise screened the excavation site, but a throbbing vibration travelled through the ground under their feet. They could sense the mining operation before they could see it. When they crested the ridge it was difficult to believe the extent of the devastation that met their eyes.

"My God!" Grace breathed.

"It's some sight," Mulcahy said.

A huge tract of land had been furrowed open, leaving a labyrinth of canyons with terraced sides on which the excavating machines followed the seams of ore across the mountain. Shafts of light bristled from the machines and the pylons overhead. At the bottom of the canyon, enormous heaps of earth and rock rose between large ponds of foul, standing water. A fog of water came from the countless sprinklers mounted on rough hummocks between the tailings ponds. The spray agitated the bubbling ponds, making them appear even more poisonous to life. It was the sheer inhuman scale of the operation that sent a shiver down the spine. The mind reeled before the nightmare enormity of the forces polluting and tearing open this landscape.

"I'm convinced it's the Black Pig," Mulcahy said. "In the legends the Black Pig is a dark force that invades an area, roots up the ground, leaves behind deep trenches and earthworks and poisons the land. That's a pretty accurate description of how gold prospectors work, going back to Cromwellian times and earlier. They dig up trenches where the ore is close to the surface, and they leave behind spoil heaps of unwanted minerals and acids that poison the ground."

"Is that why Leddy and his pals objected to the monument for Theo? They didn't want anyone to make a connection between the gold mines and your Black Pig."

"I doubt it. Leddy is as thick as shit in a bucket, he wouldn't notice that kind of symbolism. But I had it in mind."

The mining operation was some distance further on, but down the vast canyons came the sound of iron teeth eating through stone, and other menacing rumbles and vibrations. Nameless machines and discarded machine parts, huge electric cables and coils of water-pipe had been left lying around a temporary workyard. The ground was criss-crossed with heavy wheel tracks that led to a collection of outbuildings and wooden portable cabins constructed about the edges of the yard, and left out in a row under a string of temporary floodlights mounted on leaning poles. The glow of the floodlights was steadily increasing in the deepening twilight.

"Give me your camera," Mulcahy said.

He slipped her camera out of its black vinyl case and looped his wrist through the safety cord. He plotted the shortest route to the yard and started down the road.

"Where are you going?" Grace panicked.

"Wait here for me."

"It's getting dark."

"I'll be back in a minute."

"Stop. Come back," she ordered, but he had broken away. He started at a run down the track. She was tempted to follow, but knowing her luck she would only get lost in the machine yard or fall down a mineshaft, and she held back.

With the passing minutes it became steadily darker. The spoil heaps changed to jagged silhouettes. The walls of the canyon disappeared. The yard below was now a livid pool of industrial light in the surrounding blackness. A cold wind ruffled her jacket and the first spatters of rain arrived.

Grace crouched down in the shelter of a rock and watched the lighted yard for Mulcahy. The eerie sounds and roving lights from the on-going mining operation in the canyons preyed on her imagination. Fear grew in proportion to the length of time Mulcahy was missing.

She saw a shadow cross the yard, and her nervous vigil was rewarded. It was Mulcahy, ducking between the machines, making steadily for one of the outbuildings. He did not appear entirely confident that the yard was deserted, and he was using the natural cover to get there. When he reached the first outbuilding he went from window to window, then moved to the next. At the third building he delayed.

"Come away from there," she pleaded under her breath. "Haven't you seen enough? I'm cold and I'm wet and I don't like it here."

Mulcahy continued to look the place over with great interest.

"No, please. Don't do this to me," she begged.

Mulcahy kicked in the door and disappeared inside. What was he playing at? Didn't he know he had crossed the line between curiosity and criminal behaviour? The mining company would have every right to press charges if they caught him. She was ready to run down there and haul him back.

There was a sudden bright explosion of light inside the building. Her heart hammered against her rib-cage. She remembered the warning notice with the lightning strike. Mulcahy had been electrocuted. Several more bursts of light followed. She knew what it was; he was using her camera. The light came from the automatic flash. It was a false alarm, but the fear in the pit of her stomach increased.

The rain was heavier now and she used the back of her hand to wipe the raindrops from her face. Her clothes and her hair were drenched, but she could not take her eyes off the broken door. She maintained such a close look-out on that one spot, willing Mulcahy to reappear, she failed to notice the approaching glare of headlights. A four-wheel drive jeep emerged from a side canyon.

"Oh no. No. No!" Grace cried helplessly when she saw the company jeep stop in the yard.

Several men climbed out and began to pull on raincoats and hats; two men went around to the back of the jeep. She inched forward in the darkness, desperately wondering what to do. It was too late to warn Mulcahy. He was cornered and certain to be caught.

The back door of the jeep slammed shut and something dark caught her eye. She didn't know what it was, but that one glance had produced an instinctive ripple of horror that made her skin crawl and her stomach muscles tighten with animal fear. Then she knew. Dogs. They had security dogs.

The men carried powerful torchlights. The beams travelled around the yard and went from building to building until the men spotted the broken door. They moved at a run towards the door. The dogs began to yelp. One man broke away and went around the back.

She grabbed her face with both hands. Her teeth ground tight and she squeezed her eyes three-quarter closed. She couldn't quite bring herself to watch, but she peered between her fingers with the rain streaming down her face.

The dogs went in first through the open door, followed by their handlers. Grace shook her head in despair, ready to sob with humiliation and defeat. She lowered her hands again when the men emerged without a prisoner. Mulcahy must have slipped out the moment they arrived, making use of the delay while they pulled on their raincoats.

The men spread out quickly and went to the edge of the yard where the illumination from the floodlights ended. The beams of their torches roved in a wide sweep, searching the rainy night. She stood without moving. She heard the jeep start up. It was leaving the yard and moving up the track headed straight for her. She could not abandon Mulcahy, and she could not be caught standing in the middle of the road. Sick with fear and indecision, she remained rooted to the spot. Run, you fool, an inner voice told her, but her legs were weak as water and she could not move.

The jeep was closing rapidly, and through the falling rain she heard a new sound. Stones rattled in the darkness. Then came the heavy panting. The dogs! The dogs were off the leash and almost on top of her. In utter terror she waited for the dogs to spring, but it was Mulcahy who burst out of the rainy night. He grabbed her arm as he ran past, jerked her around and hauled her after him.

"Come-on-come-on-come-on!" he hissed, desperate to get her moving.

They were not yet within the range of the headlights, but the jeep was now right behind them. She took off with Mulcahy and they dashed headlong for the gates. The beam of the headlights fell at their heels when the four-wheel drive bounced over the rise. In the next instant they were surrounded by light. They ran like dazed wildlife on the highway. The steel gates glimmered up ahead.

Grace threw herself at the gates. Her foot found the third bar up. The rattling gates were wet and slippery and she cracked her knee against metal. There was a scalding dart of pain. She almost fell back, but she was not going to allow these thugs to catch hold of her. Blindly determined, she tumbled over the top of the gates and half-clambered, half-fell down the other side. She pitched forward when she hit the ground, one leg numb and useless with the pain. Mulcahy caught her and helped her up and together they reached the car.

The company jeep skidded up to the gates. She heard doors opening and several outraged shouts. She fumbled for the door and dived into the relative security of the car. Mulcahy scrambled around to the driver's side and prayed the old Wolseley would start when he jerked the key in the ignition. She turned to see the men in their dripping raincoats on the other side of the gate wrestling with the damaged lock. This would give them vital minutes to make their escape, and she felt an instant surge of triumph. Then she screamed.

The car rocked under the muscular force of the blow. Two great splatters of saliva streamed down the glass in front of her face. Maddened animal eyes and a slavering mouth of razor teeth worked furiously to smash through the invisible barrier and tear away her face.

A second dog jumped up on the car as the engine started. Mulcahy skidded away and the dog was thrown clear. It went rolling across the road, but was immediately back on its feet and bounding after them. At the gates the dog handlers worked furiously to release the lock, but their jeep remained trapped on the opposite side.

The dogs fell back as the car picked up speed and entered the tunnel and shelter of the pine trees.

"Next time we're definitely going to the seaweed baths," Mulcahy said. He handed her the camera.

Weak with relief, and sick with the pain in her leg, she buried her face in the fold of his arm.

FOURTEEN

THE MEETING TO arrange the Festival of the Black Pig was held in the singing lounge of the Marine Bar, a week after the boisterous public meeting at which Tom Giblin had first put forward the idea. This time the turn-out was small. He waited on long after the official starting time, but even then only a handful of people had shown up when he called the meeting to order.

The town's people were conspicuously absent. Only one sea-front stall holder and a landlady with a guesthouse overlooking the beach had responded to the notice in the paper. However, the festival committee meeting did unearth another underground life, a normally invisible population who lived on the periphery of the town, people with no interest in local politics and the more traditional social gatherings. These were new arrivals who lived in old restored cottages and couples with young families, part of the community but also on the fringe, as they were never seen at Sunday mass, at monster Bingo nights or at club-level football matches.

There was an elderly actor who had appeared in a television advertisement for smoked salmon and never lost the accent: he adjudicated at amateur drama festivals. A retired German who made cheese from goats' milk, and hardly spoke at all. His wife, who was a follower of Bahai. A candlemaker with a goatee beard who thought most things in life had a comical twist. A stoneware potter, and his girlfriend who taught aromatherapy and practised as a healer. A sinewy organic vegetable grower in a tight jumper, with sallow skin, grey hair and a skinny lover half his age. A jewellery maker who also taught yoga and read the Tarot cards. A honey bee enthusiast. A teenage girl in a flowing black lace dress and boots with thick tyre-tread soles, who wrote poetry and wanted to work with her dreams.

Mulcahy knew all of them by name. He swapped hellos and dodged enquiries about his wife, Cathy, while Grace waited awkwardly for him to join her at a table.

"The biggest problem we have to face is a lack of interest in the town," Giblin announced after he had welcomed everyone along to the meeting. "A huge effort will be needed to make this festival work."

"We're all willing to do our bit," the sea-front stall holder said, "but don't come looking for money."

"We're not asking for a hand-out," Giblin insisted.

"Well, I'm glad to hear it. The Town Improvement Committee have everyone plagued for donations, and we still have nothing to show for it."

"That committee is about as much use to the town as tits on a boar," Giblin dismissed Deputy Leddy and his cronies.

"I think we should avoid politics," said the organic gardener.

"Agreed," said the Bahai.

"Why not start with a small event and build on it next year?" the beekeeper suggested.

"We need something that will hold people in the town overnight," said the owner of the guest-house. "Otherwise we're wasting our time."

"We could have the unveiling of the Black Pig at the stroke of midnight," said the girl in the black dress.

"With a procession of candles and coloured lanterns," added the candlemaker.

"And a barbecue on the beach," said the organic gardener.

"With cous-cous," the skinny lover added.

"No rehearsals. Improvisation and spontaneity. That's the thing," the drama adjudicator suggested.

"And costumes. Lovely flowing costumes," said the girl.

"That's my department," Grace interrupted. "But for a parade to happen, I'm going to need help."

"Have we any volunteers?" Giblin asked the meeting.

There was an enthusiastic response. Everyone felt they

had something to contribute to the town and to the quality of life in the area. This was their big chance to put on a show. A core group was formed. Contact telephone numbers were exchanged. People went to the bar and came back with drinks. Packets of roll-your-own tobacco and cigarette papers were shared, and while one person or another worked out the finer details of the parade, the unveiling and the barbecue, the rest talked amongst themselves. In this way a rough outline for a festival was agreed. The only one who refused to contribute was Mulcahy.

"What's wrong? Don't you want to help?" Grace asked him directly.

"Not this time," he said.

"But we can't do this without you."

"You can have the use of the workhouse, and if you freshen up the paint, you can take the mannequins and effigies I have there to bulk up your parade," he said. "That's as much as I can offer."

Oliver and Sam walked in on the meeting. They held back at the bar, ordered drinks as a priority, and Tom Giblin called everyone to order once more.

"We need to settle a date for the unveiling," he announced.

"Midsummer night," said the girl in black.

"Strike while the iron is hot," Tom Giblin said. "I say we aim for the coming bank holiday weekend."

"Too soon," Mulcahy objected.

"Why?"

"We'll have the barbecue organised," said the organic gardener.

"And we can promise you a parade," said Grace and her team of volunteers.

"But the monument will never be ready," Mulcahy said.

"Do you need help?" Tom asked, and he looked across at Sam and Oliver.

"No," Mulcahy was adamant. "I'll finish it in my own time. I won't be rushed."

Sam raised a hand to shield his lips. He whispered into Oliver's ear. Oliver nodded and laughed.

"Sam wants to know do you play draughts?" he called across the room to Mulcahy.

"I do," Mulcahy said baffled.

"Well, Sam says, if you don't make a move soon you're going to lose two men."

BACK AT THE cottage on the peninsula Mulcahy lay in bed with his arm around Grace. The shared danger of the episode up at the mine the week before had brought them closer. He had treated her leg, which had been badly bruised in the escape over the gates. He had made her rest in bed and brought her all her meals. He kept her company, and they made love often.

When she felt better they went to see a famous split rock in the fields near the coast road. They visited a hungry rock in the mountains, where a landlord was said to have left food to his tenants during the Famine. They took in the spectacular view from the Ladies' Brae. Grace made a wild dash along the rocks near the cliffs of Aughris to prove her leg was better. They visited remote haunts for a drink, and in the lingering light of the long spring evenings they returned to the cottage on the peninsula.

The touch of bare feet on the flagstone floor on the journey to the bathroom outdoors, the taste of well water drawn in an iron bucket from the spring, the re-kindling of the stove in the mornings before breakfast: these were just a few of the wondrous sensations of those perfect days she shared with Mulcahy.

She had found that other shore, with the clean strong light, the fresh Atlantic salt taste of the air, the brittle debris of sea-shells and fine sand grains between her toes, as she walked in the Valley of Diamonds, or crossed the empty strand below the cottage. Only this time, she was not alone. She had Mulcahy. They were never apart. Two lovers in a self-contained world. The meeting that night in the Marine Bar had been their first real contact with other people, and it had brought to light a problem she had evaded at the start.

Mulcahy idly teased up her hair, but she moved her head aside, and raised herself up on one elbow.

"You were very negative at the meeting, tonight," she said.

"I couldn't help it."

"Why, Mulcahy?"

"You see these?" he pointed to twin white scars on his upper forearm. "Vaccination marks," he said. "The birthmarks of a modern nation. I remember the day the nurse called to our school. We had to stand in line outside the headmaster's office. Word got out she was feeling our privates and giving injections – really to see if our testicles had dropped, and if we needed to be vaccinated against TB. She gave us sugar lumps, as well, to help us swallow our polio medicine. I look back on that day now and I think, what an amazing transformation. The first generation of ordinary Irish school children to be offered free education and health care. Go back a few years, and you had malnutrition and child hiring fairs, fine steel-tooth combs, to search your hair for head-lice. Then a choice of the boat to England or America, or the soul starvation of staying on in a country where only a Catholic bishop had the power to absolve the sin of staying out late after a dance. Then think what you have today. Young ones worrying about who they're going to 'shift', and the chances of infection if they don't use a condom? From headlice and polio, to a culture of instant gratification. CDs. Home Cinema. The Internet. Even the teenagers' socks have to carry a fashion brand label. And their headstones won't read Rest in Peace; they'll say Rest in Ecstasy."

"What brought this on?"

"I'm getting old and settled in my ways."

"You're kidding me?"

"Seriously. There's a new generation out there with totally different values. So why go to all the trouble to shake things up around here, when the whole world is changing faster than I can grasp?"

"You're part of that change, Mulcahy."

"Ten years ago maybe, but I'm tired trying to keep up. I prefer it here under a thatch roof out on a peninsula, with my candles and a bucket of spring water and a book of poems by Seamus Heaney."

"I don't want to set the world on fire... " Grace began a verse of the old song to answer this gloomy self-assessment and slowly eased her way on top of him.

"No, please," he wriggled.

"I just want to light a flame in your heart... "

"Not that. I hate that," he said, but she held down his shoulders with both hands and lowered her mouth to meet his.

"Trust your talent," she whispered as they kissed. "But you have to trust your feelings too."

THE WORKHOUSE BECAME the centre of the festival preparations, and Grace set about keeping her promise to the festival committee to devise a parade and design appropriate costumes. To stage a colourful and noisy parade would fulfil her earliest childhood ambition, but even a modest parade called for a staggering amount of work.

"Me and my big mouth," she said on the first day, as the scale of the job began to dawn on her.

"You'll be fine," Mulcahy said. "Don't worry."

"Will you help?"

"No."

But he did set up an easel in the living area of the workhouse, for her to sketch her ideas on paper, and a long bench where she and the festival volunteers could outline patterns, cut and arrange their costumes.

While her computer gathered dust back at the cottage,

Grace relied on broad, impulsive strokes of a brush loaded with water-colour to design robes, masks and headgear.

She decided to outfit a tribe of warriors, who would improvise the hunting and the slaying of the original Black Pig. Her inspiration for the warriors' costumes came from the colours of the shoreline, the dry-stone walls, the flowering thorn trees, the changing colours of the surrounding mountains in the morning, at noon and in the evening light. Her patterns were meant to echo the ring fort where she practised her Tai Chi, and the cairn-topped mountain behind it. The Black Pig would be conjured up with crescent tusks, earth colours, hints of poison vapour and all things associated with a blind greed for gold.

Mulcahy agreed to drive her to the neighbouring towns, where she scoured the fabric shops for materials. Her requirements were simple. The fabrics must be cheap, colourful and available in bulk. Coat and curtain lining, calico, muslin, cotton and polyester in as many colours as she could find. Remnants of printed silk and glitzy gold fabric and brightly dyed tweeds from Foxford were a bonus for special trimmings.

"I knew a long time ago, doing what I do, I'd never be well off living in this country, but it's important to dig in somewhere. That's where the sense of belonging comes from." Grace remembered Mulcahy's words as her workload increased and she met the bills out of her own pocket.

THOUGH MULCAHY KEPT away from the regular meetings and the festival preparations in the workhouse, he worked steadily to finish the Black Pig, with the help of Oliver and Sam. Oliver overhauled the hidden mechanism in the belly of the monument. Sam used his skill at mixing, shaping and smoothing the outer skin of cement. He worked tirelessly without any suggestion of payment, and when Grace poked her head into the workshop, to ask how the work was coming along, Sam always gave her the same answer.

"Making progress. Whatever that means."

Each day the festival organisers called to the workhouse, surrendering their spare time to make their costumes, repaint the mannequins and giant effigies loaned by Mulcahy, and take basic acting lessons from the adjudicator and stilt-walking lessons from Mulcahy. Tom Giblin badgered more volunteers from the town to lend a hand. There was a laughing woman in a print dress with pastry-damp hands, a shy freckle-faced young lad and his friend, both wearing white shirts and black leather biker jackets, and a young mother who bounced a baby on her knee and smoked cigarettes on the "QT". More volunteers took away paper patterns and parcels of fabric to make and finish their own outfits at home.

"I can't offer you payment for this," Grace had apologised on the first day.

"The poor will always be with us," said one caller, looking around the workhouse and laughing off the suggestion.

CLOSE TO THE DEADLINE for the parade and the unveiling of the monument, Grace and the core group of festival volunteers were sitting around the workhouse drinking coffee before they broke up for the night. Grace was exhausted, her confidence at a low ebb. When she picked up a roughly made costume with a crescent moon stitched on the back – an idea she had been proud of at the design stage – she felt a sudden sense of futility.

"You don't think my ideas are corny?" she asked the others.

"They're wonderful, love," the old actor said.

"Very Irish," agreed the German candlemaker.

"But what makes a thing Irish?" Grace wanted to know. "More to the point, what makes a person Irish?"

"Red hair and freckles," decided the candlemaker.

"It's where you live," said the organic gardener.

"I live in Ireland, but I will always be a German," said

193

the goats' cheesemaker.

"Being Irish is a state of mind," suggested the healer.

"I have an American accent. I think like an American. But I feel Irish," Grace said.

"You're not a native of a place if you can never relax there," the actor said. "If you can never drop your guard. All you do in that case is take on protective camouflage."

"Yes. I feel Irish because I have a such a good quality of life here," said the jewellery maker.

"I agree," added the Bahai.

"You're all a crowd of blow-ins," said the cheerful woman in the print dress. "Don't take it to heart, but that's how the town would look on you."

"What about Mulcahy?" Grace asked.

"Well, he's a bit odd, but he's still one of us."

"Who's a bit odd?" Mulcahy appeared in the door in a boilersuit spattered with cement.

"Good bless us! I didn't know you were standing there," the woman coloured.

"We're talking about what it means to be Irish," the healer said.

"To belong in a country you must adopt the principles of the people who live there," the organic gardener concluded.

"I certainly don't agree with the principles of a lot of my fellow citizens," Mulcahy said.

"So what do you have to do to belong?" Grace asked him.

"If you own a country you must belong there," said the young lad in the leather jacket.

"Not if you were a native whose country had been taken away from you," his friend pointed out.

"Well if you had to fight to get it back ... "

"I'm a passivist," said the girl in the black lace dress and Doc Martens.

"It's your lifestyle that makes you a native," said the woman who taught yoga and read the Tarot cards.

"I think not," the beekeeper doubted the assertion.

"There's a story about a local man," Mulcahy offered helpfully. "He was crossing the mountain one winter's evening. There was snow on the ground, and it was just starting to freeze. In the middle of nowhere he met a garda check-point. So he asked the guard on duty what was going on. 'Didn't you hear?' the guard said. 'A patient with no clothes escaped from the mental hospital. Maybe you saw something?' 'Come to think of it,' said the man, 'I did meet a fella with no clothes walking along in the snow.' The guard was outraged. 'You met a man with no clothes on top of the mountain in this weather. What did you say to him?' And the local answered, 'I said: hardy man.'"

Mulcahy found it difficult to finish the joke he was laughing so hard by the time he reached the punch-line.

"Hardy man!" he repeated. "Now, that's Irish!"

The others looked at him blankly.

WHILE THE WORKHOUSE was the place where Grace and Mulcahy met the demands and distractions of the forthcoming festival, the cottage on the peninsula remained their retreat from other people when the day's work was finished. Each evening they lit the candles, prepared and ate dinner together, then sat by the fire and went over all that had been said and had happened that day, and loosely planned for tomorrow. With so many things to do before the coming bank holiday deadline, they had fallen into the habit of going to bed early and rising early, and in the mornings Mulcahy made the breakfast while Grace went to shower and practise her exercises.

Mulcahy was enjoying this hard-working yet mentally tranquil time that made his head feel light and his body feel strong. He wrapped a piece of flannel around the handle of the cast-iron kettle on the hook over the open fire and brought it to the table. He poured the boiling water into a red enamel coffee pot and waited for the wake-up aroma of the coffee. Along with the coffee there was hot oatmeal, left to cool in the handmade bowls Grace had bought from the local potter. There was also a jar of heather-blossom honey to flavour the oatmeal: a present to Grace from the bee-keeper.

The sunlight flickered when Grace went by the window and Mulcahy began to pour the coffee.

"Smile!" she called from the doorway. He looked up with the coffee pot in his hand and the flash caught him in the eyes.

A whine of plastic spindles came from inside the camera as the film automatically wound back. "That's the last shot," she said, and removed the roll of film. "I'd like to see what's on this. Is there a one-hour photo place?"

"No, but you can leave it in to the post office."

"Why didn't I think of that?" Grace laughed, accustomed now to these fluid boundaries.

They sat down to breakfast and as they ate she toyed with the roll of film.

"Mulcahy," she said finally.

"Yeah."

"I need my car."

"I can give you a lift," he offered.

"What is Oliver doing? Why hasn't it been sorted out?"

"Tomorrow."

"Oliver said that yesterday."

"Or the day after at the latest."

"Some things are the same no matter where you go," she said exasperated. "Why do all repair men give women such a hard time? Is it because they feel threatened if they don't intimidate a woman client, leave dirty handprints all over her car, sulk or grunt if she asks a simple question, and then make her feel like an idiot if, after all the put-downs, she mentions that they haven't really fixed the problem?"

"Oliver's not like that."

"Men don't notice these things, but any woman can tell you, when it comes to painful dealings with the opposite sex, motor repair guys are right up there with your gynae-cologist."

"I have to go to Theo's place today," Mulcahy switched quickly. "Do you want to come with me?"

"No. Drop me off at the workhouse."

"Are you sure?"

"I have lovely memories of our last night there with Theo," she said. "I don't want to spoil that."

Mulcahy did not press her, but felt it necessary to explain what he had in mind. "The place has been empty since Theo died. I'm worried it could be robbed," he said. "I was thinking about moving Theo's stuff."

"It's your property now," she said.

"That's something we have to sort out. Theo didn't know he had a granddaughter when he made his last will and testament. He had no money, but all the bits and pieces he left to me in his will are rightfully yours. The house too. It's the nearest thing to the birthplace you came here to find."

"You said the gold mine company are buying up property on the mountain. You could sell that old place and use the money to clear your debts."

"I want you to have the house and everything in it," he said.

"I couldn't accept," she said immediately.

"Think of it as a gift from Theo and me to you."

"No."

"In lieu of what you've spent on the festival and the making of the Black Pig," he insisted.

She was moved by the sincerity and kindness of the gesture and didn't really know what to say.

"Can I have some time to think about it?"

"All the time you need."

She got up from the table, went to Mulcahy and put her arms around him. "Thank you," she said. "You're a good man," and she kissed his woolly head.

"I want to move the most valuable stuff to the workhouse

today, for safekeeping," he said, uncomfortable with any kind of flattery.

"And the animals?" Grace asked, remembering the pigs.

"Gone."

"Where?" she said surprised.

"Where do you think we're getting the pork for the barbecue on the beach the opening night of the festival?" he said in a matter-of-fact voice, and then saw the horrified expression on her face. "Now, don't look at me that way. Theo's pigs for Theo's banquet. Death and plenty, remember?"

Grace recovered quickly, but what he'd just told her disturbed her more that she wanted to admit. As a lover Mulcahy was capable of the most thoughtful and tender feelings, but there was also a barbaric trait in his personality. An inner threshold beyond which his better nature finished and a cruel, and callous, and separate self began.

"And the carvings?" she stammered. "The lovely hand-carved pigs?"

"Still there. There's so many I don't know what to do with them."

"Other people might like to see them."

"An exhibition?"

"As a part of the festival," she said. "Why not? It's a wonderful collection, and it shouldn't be broken up. Maybe a venue could be found in the town where Theo's pigs could go on permanent display."

"A kind of bequest from Theo to the town that loved him so well?" Mulcahy remarked drily.

"That is, if you have no objections," Grace said quickly.

"I think it's a great idea."

"I know you're a collector, and if you want to hold on to them – " she needed to be sure, but Mulcahy silenced her reservations.

"The more you own, the more problems you have. I'm beginning to agree with the Buddhists who say all things on the material plane are maya, illusion. You have to learn to let go. "

Grace was curious and surprised by this development. Perhaps their Spartan existence on the peninsula was having more of an effect on him than she thought.

"What about the workhouse? Have you changed your mind about all the lovely things you keep there?" she tested.

"Definitely."

"I don't believe I'm hearing this! You've spent your whole life collecting things."

"The more you try to hold on to things the more you suffer," Mulcahy concluded. "All attachments are a trap."

"Even the emotional ones?"

He looked at Grace and their eyes caught for a full second. "I walked myself into that," he said.

"Mom often said I should have been a lawyer," she said lightly, but she felt like someone who had just witnessed something she believed to be flawlessly mended tear again in the same place.

FIFTEEN

TO RELEASE ITS essential oils the seaweed gathered fresh from the shore that morning had been steamed bright green; when added to the tub the water became a rich amber colour. The seaweed oils and minerals gave the scalding water a pleasing sensual smoothness, without making it viscous or greasy to the touch. Grace scooped up a tangled shawl of the hot, slippery seaweed and wrapped it around her shoulders.

"God! this is decadent," she sighed.

"You've earned it," Mulcahy said.

There were two separate baths in the room, big Edwardian porcelain affairs on short legs, free-standing opposite each other. Mulcahy was submerged up to his neck in the other bathtub.

It was a clean, private room with tiles on the floor, slatted timber before each bath for the over-spill and a curved Italian marble trim along the walls, which were painted a fresh lime green. Decorated tiles ringed the baths, and the high ceiling was simply finished with pine. The top pane of the long window tilted open to the daylight, the larger glass pane below it opaque with steam.

Grace lay back and drew in the muscles of her stomach to relax like a swimmer treading water. There was so much room in the tub she felt her body rise up on the brink of buoyancy. She closed her eyes to soak in this floating sensation and allowed her mind to drift.

The Black Pig had been left in the workshop to allow the cement skin to dry. Her work had all been delegated. She was relying on people to show up on the day with their costumes made. Despite all the pressure, the festival arrangements were fractionally ahead of Tom Giblin's deadline. She might have allowed herself to believe things were going according to plan, except that deep down she knew there was no plan.

Low splashes echoed off the pinewood ceiling when Mulcahy shifted in the bath across from her. Their working days together were very good and their nights were still passionate, but she sensed a continuing remoteness, a lack of true involvement on his part. She had an idea he still clung to the notion that their relationship was not going to last, that they were working towards another harsh and inevitable deadline of the heart following the festival.

She did not know how to get this damaging notion out of his head, and the longer the problem continued the more hurtful she found his attitude.

She raised one leg above the water and massaged the last traces of the blue and purple bruise on her knee.

"Did I tell you I got the photographs back in the mail?"

"No." He sounded sleepy and uninterested.

"The vats in that outbuilding and the poison labels on the containers came out very clear. They are using cyanide."

"What do you plan to do?"

"Show the photographs to someone in authority," she said, annoyed by his attitude. "I thought you were going to help."

"I don't know," he said.

"Are you backing down?"

"Do we have any right?" he said.

"Right?" she demanded. "They have a building full of empty cyanide containers. They said they weren't going to use that stuff."

"I know."

"They set their dogs on us."

"I know that, too. But do we have any right to dash people's hopes of a job? God knows this place needs some kind of boost. What gives us the right to take that hope away?"

"What are you telling me?" Grace could hardly contain her anger.

"I'm not necessarily against the gold mine. Under strict

regulations and controls it might not be such a bad thing. It upsets me to see what's happening to the mountain, but should my romantic notions of the past be allowed to stand in the way of jobs and a hope of survival for this region? Sometimes the environmentalists can be just as unreasonable as the owners of the industries they want to outlaw. There's no balanced middle ground. Cathy had that ruthless streak and I didn't like it. So if you feel you have to act, do, but just think about the consequences."

Grace sat up in the bath. "Do you seriously believe what's going on at that mine is good for the people who live around here?"

"No," Mulcahy admitted. "But what happens if the mine is shut down? Have you anything to offer in its place?"

"I intend to expose what's going on."

"Think about it," Mulcahy said.

She was infuriated by his stance and the level of apathy it betrayed. All her unspoken resentment ignited.

"Christ, Mulcahy! What does it take to get you involved?"

Mulcahy sunk lower in the bathtub. The water was beginning to cool, but he pulled a fistful of seaweed up around his neck and shoulders.

"You can't bury your head forever," she said.

"I can try."

"It's not going to work out for us if you do."

THERE WAS A dim awareness in Eugene Tuttle's brain that he was a fully grown man, and if only he could wake up, he would find himself in the adult world of his bedroom above the bar. Still he ran, hampered by the short strides of a small schoolboy's legs, and the trapped weight and heat of the plastic satchel full of incriminating evidence strapped to his back. The Black Pig came thundering after him, delirious for the taste of warm blood. He could hear its horrible wet grunts and its filthy snorts, echoing off the walls of the canyon. He could feel its stinking hot breath closing on the back of his neck. In seconds the pig would snatch him up in its hungry jaws and swallow him whole. The pounding echo grew louder, and then came the Black Pig's triumphant squeal.

"Ouuurreekre... "

Tuttle sprang awake, terrified and drenched in sweat. From the town square came the steady pounding of hammers, and the delayed crack of their answering echoes off the surrounding walls.

He went to the window and nervously peered through the chink between the curtains. The employment scheme workers were out in force. They appeared unusually organised and busy. One group had tied strings of bunting from house to house across the main streets. Two men, up on separate ladders, were hammering home steel nails to secure a banner high over the start of the road to the harbour. Like a fall of snow the whole town seemed to have been covered overnight with posters for the FESTIVAL OF THE BLACK PIG.

Oliver's pickup truck went past carrying a cargo of canvas tarpaulin in the back, while Sam sat on top of the load. Along the sea-front iron barrels had been cut in half to line the promenade with make-shift braziers. Dozens of freshly cut pinewood shafts were being bandaged in rags which would be dipped in fuel-oil to make crude firebrands.

Oswald and Deputy Leddy crossed the square together, headed for the pub door at a brisk, embattled pace. They stopped briefly to look at Tom Giblin, who was bent over the home-made silk-screen printing press in his front garden, watched by his loyal dog, as he furiously churned out more posters.

Sally Holmes had opened up the bar and served Oswald and Leddy by the time Tuttle came downstairs, gaunt as a halyard in his navy blue blazer, old school tie and grey flannel slacks. When he came around to his usual place behind the counter, Sally found a sweeping brush and diplomatically moved to the far end of the bar. Trade had ceased following the boycott. If Tuttle were not in the habit of swallowing too many sleeping pills, there would be no need for her to show up for work in the mornings.

Leddy and Oswald sat with neat brandies on the table in front of them. A haze of smoke surrounded Leddy as he puffed steadily on his pipe: an old warship working up a head of steam.

He knew all about the van full of two-by-one timber laths, and a ladder on the roof, that went off each day to poster the surrounding countryside. There was a notice in the regional paper, and an ad running on the local radio station. The official parade and the unveiling of the Black Pig, were billed as the biggest entertainment in the region in a decade. And it was all going to happen this coming bank holiday weekend.

"They've been at that bloody racket for the last fortnight," Oswald complained. "That cute hoor, Giblin, has every cornerboy and lunatic in the town out working for him."

"The man would rise ructions in a graveyard," Leddy growled.

"Maybe if we just let them at it?" Oswald suggested. "It might all blow over."

"They're like a bunch of children. When the novelty wears off, they'll soon lose interest," Leddy agreed. "But we can't afford to wait that long."

Oswald stirred uneasily.

The deputy signalled to Tuttle to bring over another round of brandies.

"I don't expect you to grasp the subtleties of what's in-volved..." Leddy said.

"Certainly not, Deputy," Oswald agreed straight away.

"But I've been getting phone-calls. The company don't like all this commotion. They say they've had one break-in already. They want to know what we intend to do about it. What if more people start snooping around the mountain?

What if the likes of the Environmental Protection Agency get wind of the set-up there? They could pull the plug just like that... " the deputy snapped his fingers.

The councillor winced.

"No one ever said the mines would be viable without taking a few shortcuts," Leddy confided. "And even where a few fish get killed the concentrations of cyanide in the water are still no threat to human life. But who's going to be responsible if someone blows the whistle? You, Councillor, because you arranged the prospecting licence and the pollution emission licence. So, I'm telling you now, the last thing anyone wants is outside interference. No tourists. No news hounds. No pressure for public hearings, environmental impact reports or enquiries over property dealings."

"P-p-property?" Tuttle stammered, and spilled the round of drinks on his way to the table.

Leddy's eyes flashed in the publican's direction. "The company bought and dismantled that old creamery under your name, Tuttle. You're still the legal owner of those creamery vats full of cyanide and the pipes carrying waste product off to the sink-hole."

"What has to be done?" Oswald pleaded.

"If we stop Mulcahy's monument going in the square we can nip this thing in the bud," Leddy suggested.

"No pig, no festival, no busy-body visitors. Everything goes back to normal," Oswald fell in with the idea.

"They'll need planning permission to site that monstrosity in the square, but they won't get it. We'll have the documents objecting to the monument ready by this evening," Leddy said decisively. "We'll stitch them up nicely this time. And what's better, we'll have the law on our side."

They knocked back what little of the brandy had arrived safely at the table, and Tuttle walked the two men to the front door. After they left he stood on the threshold, watching all that thirsty work going on in the square, and he pondered the drop in his takings since the boycott. If only he could find some ploy to win back the sympathy of his best drinkers and still on keep the right side of Oswald and Leddy.

Sally Holmes slipped around past her employer while he stood there in a quandary, frowning and watching the street so hard she could almost hear his brain working overtime. She edged discreetly towards the alcove, grabbed her coat and went out through the kitchen.

SAM WAS SITTING outside the workhouse, slowly stirring a can of black paint with a stick in one hand, and reading a paperback edition of Beckett's plays in the other hand. A truck with the words CEMENT STORE stencilled on the doors rolled into the courtyard. Behind the truck a red tractor belched black smoke in a race to keep up. On the back of the truck there was a small crane, used to load and unload palates of cement blocks. Around the crane stood a group of volunteers from the employment scheme.

The truck stopped and Oliver jumped down from the driver's cabin.

"Where's Mulcahy?" he called to Sam.

"Gone to the seaweed baths with Grace."

"Is the pig finished?"

"It's ready for the first coat of paint."

"There's no time. It has to be moved."

The volunteers on the back of the truck jumped down and assembled in the yard.

"What's the panic?" Sam set aside the book.

"Sally ran across to Tom Giblin's house this morning. She said Deputy Leddy is going to have planning permission for the Black Pig denied. Once the Town Improvement Committee have the official paperwork they'll be legally entitled to stop the monument going in the square." As he gave Sam the story, Oliver drew back the bolt on the work-house door. "We have to site the pig before they get the documents signed. I've borrowed Oswald's truck for the job."

The door rolled back on its castors.

"Does Oswald know you have his truck?"

"What he doesn't know won't harm him. Say nothing."

The canvas cover from Oliver's workshop was thrown over the pig. Chains were fixed to the wooden frame underneath the legs, and the monument was slowly hauled from the darkness of the workhouse into the light of day. They used the red tractor to do the hauling, but there were several more steering ropes with tug-o'-war style teams in charge. The monstrous snout and head of the Black Pig poked through, and then the body appeared. To increase curiosity it had been decided at the outset that as few eyes as possible would be allowed to see the pig before the official unveiling ceremony. Only a vague outline of the monument could be seen under the canvas tarpaulin.

Oliver had anticipated the Black Pig would look a lot smaller once it was removed from the workshop, but it remained a commanding presence out in the open. If anything its impact had been increased with the scaffolding removed.

He went around to the back of the truck to operate the small crane. "All right, everyone stand back," he shouted. "I'm going to load the beast."

"This little piggy went to market," Sam said, and he replaced the lid on the can of black paint.

SIXTEEN

WHAT HAD BEEN intended as a relaxing and care-free day away from the workhouse had gone sour for Grace and Mulcahy. After the dispute in the seaweed bath-house, everything seemed forced. His lack of concern over the cyanide being used at the mines had upset Grace and forced her to take a hard look at other aspects of their relationship. They had never slept over at his place. Not once. Mulcahy said he preferred the neutral territory of her cottage out on the peninsula: it allowed them to escape the bustle and constant activity of the festival preparations at the workhouse. Now this preference struck Grace as a clever tactic to protect his privacy, another means to keep her at an emotional distance.

One look at her stiff, angry attitude, and Mulcahy guessed what was on her mind: commitment, or the lack of it. But even if Grace did not realize it, he knew she would be the one to leave when this festival madness was over. Sooner or later, reality would strike. What then? She would pack her bags, say, "guys, it was fun" and go back to the excitement and stimulation of New York. So why not enjoy the moment? Live it from to day, and forget the long-term stuff. No one knew better than he that even the big commitments didn't always work out.

They needed to get out of Ennismuck for a while. After the baths they went to Ballina for a drink and then opted for a Chinese meal. Conversation across the table was lim-ited. Polite talk. Wary glances. Evasions. They cut the meal short to catch a movie, where they could sit in the dark and not have to talk. On the pavement after the show there was no mention of a late drink. They headed straight home. Mulcahy silent. Grace brooding.

When they turned off for the workhouse, they saw a line of beat-up cars and motorbikes parked on either side of the driveway. A crowd had gathered in the courtyard. The crowd stood around the truck from Oswald's Cement Store, but the real centre of attention was lit by a spotlight mounted high up on the safety cabin of a farm tractor. There in the middle of the courtyard was the Black Pig. Several strong nylon ropes and wooden levers had been used in an effort to load the pig manually on to the back of the truck.

"I don't believe it," Mulcahy said.

"What's the matter?"

"I never paid the bill from the Cement Store. It looks like Oswald is repossessing the pig."

"Never!" she said and followed Mulcahy when he jumped out of the car.

Mulcahy pushed through the crowd. The tips of his ears had started to burn and his blood pressure was up. He searched the ring of faces and prepared for a bitter dispute, but there was no sign of Oswald, and he was unable to read any clear message from the expression on the faces of the onlookers. He spotted Sam.

"What are all these people doing here? Has there been an accident? Did something happen?"

"The crux of the matter," Sam replied, "is that nothing's happened."

The man standing beside Sam explained. "Oliver asked us to come over. The pig had to be moved right away, but we can't get it loaded on the truck. It's too heavy."

"Where's Oliver now?" Mulcahy asked, sizing up the situation.

"He looked fierce disappointed when things didn't work out. He left when it started to get dark."

"Gone to the pub, I'd hazard a guess," Sam said.

Mulcahy inspected the small crane and the lifting equipment attached to the pig. A few careful manoeuvres and it ought to work. He climbed up on to the back of the truck and sat into the operator's chair.

"Stand back everyone," he shouted.

"We've been trying all evening – you'll not lift it with that tackle," a scheme worker advised from the driver's cabin.

"Start the engine," Mulcahy ordered.

"It must weigh over two tons. You won't budge it."

The rear of the truck was raised and supported on twin steel legs to steady the crane. When the weight came on the outstretched boom the truck lurched awkwardly and the steel legs groaned, ready to buckle under the pressure. Mulcahy went from gently easing the levers and gear-sticks on a first attempt, to punishing jerks and tugs on the final attempt, but his best efforts could raise the monument only a few stubborn inches off the ground. The pig drifted left and right of the straining boom but it would not lift clean. If he pushed any harder he would cause permanent damage to the borrowed machinery.

"Unless that pig can fly, it ain't going nowhere," he heard the man in the driver's cabin say.

Mulcahy eased back the levers and the pig settled a miserable fraction away from its original position.

"Well?" Grace called up to him.

"Not a hope," he was forced to concede.

"So Oswald and Leddy are going to get their own way after all?"

"Looks like it," he said.

A rumbling vibration invaded the courtyard and a blinding shaft of light fell on the canvas-covered pig. The crowd parted to make way for the source of light. The walls reverberated with the thud of heavy machinery. Oliver entered, driving the mobile industrial crane from the harbour.

"Now we're sucking diesel!" he shouted.

Once the hooks and chains were fastened, the monument was lifted with ease by the powerful crane. Sam could not resist the insane spectacle of the moment. He sat up on the pig's back, his umbrella open for balance, while the pig rode high into the air. The truck sagged visibly under the weight as the monument and its passenger were lowered on to the trailer. The workhouse yard echoed with spontaneous cheers.

EUGENE TUTTLE STOOD by his silent cash register, a weighty antique with ornamented silver panels and a gaping money drawer, stiff elaborate keys and bright money flags that popped up into the window along the top with a crashing jangle every time the machine was pressed into action. It was the publican's equivalent of a Steinway grand-piano, silenced now for the want of customers. The bar-room clock on the far wall ticked away the empty minutes. Tuttle's fingers tapped a nervous rhythm to the dull metronome beat.

Sally Holmes loitered at the counter. Oswald and Deputy Leddy were the only customers on the premises. They had nursed the same two glasses of brandy all evening. In the silence their pens scratched as they added their signatures to a pile of official-looking documents.

"There," said Leddy with a final flourish of his pen. "All signed and sealed."

"We'll show them who's in charge around here," Oswald added confidently.

"Double brandies, Eugene," Leddy ordered generously. "And have a drink yourself."

For Tuttle, the order would bring the total to seven drinks sold all day, and two had been spilled by his own hands, which meant he couldn't charge for them. He balanced the glasses carefully on a tray. They shared a victory toast that soon faded to silence in the empty pub.

"It's quiet tonight," Oswald remarked.

Tuttle frowned and stared mournfully into his own glass of tap-water with a dash of cordial.

THE BLACK PIG thundered towards the town on the back of Oswald's truck. It was followed by the mobile crane from the harbour, and behind it came a cavalcade of second-hand cars, rusted jalopies, ramshackle vans and motorbikes, tractors and teenagers pedalling hard to catch up on bicycles. Roadside householders rushed to their front doors to view the spectacle. Small children in their night attire hid in their mother's aprons as the monster went past.

Eugene Tuttle bolted his front door for the night and climbed the stairs to his bedroom. It made no sense to keep the pub open, burning electricity and firestuff, when there was no trade. He closed the bedroom curtains and changed into his nightshirt. From the army of medications used to combat his nerves, he selected a brown bottle, and upped his regular dose of sleeping tablets by two further capsules. If this boycott continued he would be listed amongst the bankrupts in *Stubb's Gazette* by his next audit. He switched off the light, settled his narrow head on the pillow and waited for the medicines to take effect.

Deputy Leddy and Councillor Oswald stood under a street light in the town square to take the air. It was a mild, overcast night. A thick belt of cloud buckled over the rooftops. The square was deserted. The curtains drawn on the dark windows facing the street, and the empty plinth in the centre island. The town was sound asleep.

Leddy thumbed into place the stray fibres of tobacco hanging over the bowl of his pipe and struck a match. He took in several deep, restful puffs of mild Virginia and tossed away a cinder of matchstick.

With both thumbs hooked in the pockets of his acrylic-cardigan, Oswald waited for Leddy to complete the pipe-lighting ritual. "A good day's work, Deputy," he said breathing in the quiet.

"Aye," meditated Leddy, a satisfied man.

They were reluctant to part company, the mood of mellow authority over all they surveyed was so complete.

"Good night to you, now," Oswald said finally.

At that moment the convoy rolled into the square. Bangers and jalopies and tractors with toothless farmers at the wheel. Motorbikes with their exhausts missing.

Teenagers with an excuse to stay up late, clattering up gravel and mounting the pavement on mountain bikes. All swarmed in behind the truck.

The cavalcade divided in two to form a ring around the empty plinth.

Lights sprang on in every window – except Eugene Tuttle's bedroom. Dogs took off barking. Windows and doors were thrown open, and heads stuck out to view the hullabaloo. The square was suddenly full of people in their dressing gowns, slippers and pyjamas.

"That's my truck!" Oswald blurted.

Looking down from the back of the truck on the assembled townspeople was a motionless four-legged monster, wrapped in a dirty canvas shroud. Its exact contours were not easily distinguished, but everyone knew: the Black Pig had come back from its legendary grave.

Mulcahy broke away from the crowd gathered round the pig, and stood next the empty plinth. He waved instructions to Oliver in the cabin of the mobile crane.

Leddy stood dumbfounded until his thumb began to scorch on the bowl of his pipe. He jerked awake. No permission had been granted for the use of Oswald's truck, and as the chairman of the Town Improvement Committee, and chief trustee administering the employment scheme, he had not been consulted about the removal of the hired crane from the harbour.

"Stop. Stop right there," he shouted up at Oliver. "What do you think you're doing?"

"Out of the way, Leddy," Oliver said. "The pig is going on the plinth."

"Over my dead body," Leddy threatened.

The hydraulic boom began to unfold. A bright orange metal limb reached out for the monument. Sam fixed the lifting chains around the pig. With the chains secured he gave a thumbs up signal to Oliver to proceed. In the operator's cabin Oliver manipulated the various levers with confident precision. Slowly the pig began to rise.

Leddy prodded Oswald urgently in the back and bullied him in the direction of the plinth.

"Go on, man. Get up there. Don't let them away with this. Quick now before the thing goes any further."

Oswald's loyal attempt to clamber up the side of the plinth was awkward and painful. His shiny black shoes scuffed against the stonework as he scrambled for a secure toe-hold. He clawed the air. He heaved and he rolled over. Bright sparks of static electricity crackled in the folds of his acrylic cardigan as it rolled up his back, but he made it up on to the pedestal. He lay there to recover his breath, his arms and legs spreadeagled to take up as much room as possible.

Oliver was forced to jerk back the boom. Metal groaned under the pressure, and for a moment it seemed the Black Pig was about to break its tether for a straight and fatal drop on the councillor's head.

Oswald screwed his eyes shut to block out the sight of the enormous pig swaying perilously above him and tried to re-member how the prayer for the dying went.

The chains creaked and slipped a link. Bystanders covered their eyes. Even Grace was convinced they were on the brink of a terrible calamity, but the pig came to a standstill, miraculously suspended over its sacrificial victim.

"Go back to your beds," Leddy addressed the crowd.

He reached for an inside pocket, fished out a wad of offi-cial documents and waved them in the air.

"Any person who attempts to site that monstrosity on public property will suffer the full force of the law."

Oliver's face puckered in a look of disgusted frustration, and Mulcahy, too, looked across at Grace, heart-weary of these farcical manoeuvres. Most of the people in that square were out of work, yet all their political representatives could do was bicker over a public monument.

Leddy folded his arms, satisfied by the impasse.

A lot of unpaid bills would be written off if Oswald got

flattened under the monument, Mulcahy thought privately. The idiot would have to jump clear if the statue was slowly lowered into position, but there was an element of risk, and he was not going to endanger anyone's life over a cement pig.

"Load it back on the truck," he instructed Oliver.

"Are you sure?"

"I'm the boss, remember."

The pig began to rise once more. A deflated hiss issued from the assembled crowd. Oliver swung his cargo about to lower it on to the truck.

"Wait," shouted Tom Giblin from his gateway. "I'm giving you permission to leave the pig in my front garden."

"Hold it, Oliver," Mulcahy shouted.

The pig stopped in mid-air.

Mulcahy looked around at the crowd. All eyes were fixed on him, keen to witness his next move.

"Don't back down now," Grace urged him from the sideline. "Think of the festival. Think of all the hard work we've put into this. The only place for that monument is on the pedestal."

Mulcahy was a lot less certain. The issue of where to locate the Black Pig was now thoroughly ensnared in local politics. His work was being used like a football, kicked back and forth in a contest of wills between Tom Giblin and Deputy Leddy. He wanted no further part in their game. The quickest way out of this whole ludicrous episode was all he asked for.

"All right, Tom," he said. "We'll leave the pig in your garden, but if it leans too far to the left I'm moving it."

Grace could not catch Mulcahy's eye when he glanced in her direction for support, but Oliver needed no encouragement. He brought the levers back hard and raised the cement pig high over the town square.

At this renewed activity Oswald opened his eyes and raised his head from the cold stone plinth to look around the square. He was alone. The pig and the crowd had moved on.

The bystanders followed the mobile crane as it edged towards Tom Giblin's house. A street light stood directly in front of the cottage and twin power cables ran parallel above the garden wall. The boom had to be extended to its maximum length to gain clearance.

With the hydraulic arm at full reach Oliver had less control over his payload. The increasing pendulum swing of the two-ton pig swung dangerously close to the power cables. The boom groaned under the momentum, and the pig suddenly veered to one side. Cement collided with metal. The lamp-post was knocked out of kilter. Sparks jumped and showered. Oliver yanked at the controls. The pig swung clear and over the cables, but the light behind the glass began to flicker. This hiccup in the power supply spread to every light in the street. An explosion went off and glass showered on to the pavement. The town was plunged into blackness.

After a moment of hushed awe, there was an uproar of car and truck and tractor engines starting up. Headlight beams illuminated the scene.

Oswald scrambled down off the plinth. He collided with the deputy in the dark, grabbed the sleeve of Leddy's coat and looked fearfully about the town. "It was in the prophecies," he gasped. "Three days of darkness when the Black Pig returns."

"Oh, shut up!" yelled Leddy.

He was not going to be ridiculed by Tom Giblin, Mulcahy or this disruptive element of the town poor and country idle from the employment scheme. He shoved the councillor aside roughly and went after Mulcahy, determined to quash this blatant defiance of the rule of law.

Mulcahy stood in Tom Giblin's garden, signalling final directions, and deciding on the best aspect for the pig. The monument was so big it would block most of the light coming in the windows of the cottage. All he could do was make sure the owner could get in and out of his front door. With the pig safely situated Sam began to release the chains.

"Mulcahy," Leddy raged. "You've started something you're going to regret. Tomorrow I'm instigating legal proceedings." He stabbed his pipe at the leaning street light. "Riotous and tumultuous behaviour. Damage to public property. Endangering lives. Theft of privately owned machinery. Loss of income owing to power-cuts. By God you'll live to regret this night..."

"I don't believe this," Grace came forward to confront Leddy. "What is it with you guys? You allow thugs and gold-diggers to destroy your mountain and poison your river, but you take offence at a cement pig? The real enemy is out there." She pointed towards the mountains. "Tell him, Mulcahy."

She looked around but Mulcahy had walked away.

Grace was stunned into silence by this defection. Deputy Leddy said nothing, but he folded his arms and crushed her with a look of imperial scorn.

Grace was furious when she finally caught up with Mulcahy at the edge of the square.

"What the hell is the matter with you?" she demanded. "You'd better have an explanation, and a good one."

"For what?"

"You left me standing there like a fool."

The crowd in the square was breaking up, with the excitement over for the night. Mulcahy was headed for his car.

"The monument didn't reach its intended destination in the square," he said. "So what? If it's in Tom's front garden, it's part of the town furniture. I'm ready to leave it at that."

"You backed down."

"I'm tired and I want to get out of here," he said.

"You let those guys walk all over you. Didn't you even want to defend yourself?"

"No."

"Why?"

"It doesn't matter."

"It matters to me. The Black Pig was a monument to

Theo. That's what you said. That was the bargain we made."

"I think Theo would understand."

"Are you making excuses for them, or for yourself?"

"I'm fed up. I've had enough. Okay?"

"Fight back, Mulcahy. Show me some passion. Show me you care. "

"I've been down this road before," he said. "I'm not going to make the same mistake again."

"Your life is over because your wife left you. Boy, that's original," she accused loudly.

"Keep your voice down."

"Why? Are you afraid someone might find out how stubborn and selfish you are?"

"Don't push me, Grace. You don't know me well enough."

"Start again, Mulcahy. People do it all the time. Even when your whole life falls apart, you have to give yourself a second chance. Re-invent a life."

"What self-improvement book is that out of?"

"You're the one with the problem, Mulcahy. Face up to it."

"Right," he said.

She grabbed his arm.

"You can't go on hiding your feelings forever. It's hurtful to me. It's hurtful to yourself."

He broke free.

"Oliver will leave you back to the cottage," he said. "I'll see you tomorrow."

Grace froze. Sudden tears scalded her eyes.

"If you walk away now, you'll never see me again."

"I'll see you tomorrow."

"I mean it."

His step faltered, but he kept walking.

"Never," she cried. "Do you hear me?"

Mulcahy did not turn.

He left her standing on the pavement.

SEVENTEEN

OLIVER AND SAM sat at the end of the promenade near the old bath-house. They were propped up shoulder to shoulder, taking turns at a bottle. Only the dregs of clear spirit remained. It was late and both men were very drunk.

"It's a bad businessss, Sshham," Oliver said, surprised to find the spirits had the effect of a local anaesthetic on the end of his tongue.

"My best years are gone," Sam said to himself.

"I was supposed to give her a lift home. She ordered a taxi instead. I couldn't talk her out of it."

"But I wouldn't want them back," Sam rambled on.

"Two big red eyes. Crying her heart out."

"Not with the fire in me now," Sam said. He leaned back and tumbled off the wall.

"The poor thing was in bits. And you know who I blame?" Oliver accused. He looked around when he got no answer. Sam had mysteriously disappeared.

Oliver stood up, his partner in drink immediately forgotten. With no real destination in mind, he felt an impulse to head for the town square.

After a short somersault Sam was lucky enough to land on the soft sand. As he lay on his back looking up at the spinning stars, he deemed it prudent to remain there for the night.

The town square was deserted and the lights still out of order. Oliver flung away the useless empty bottle and then looked around in surprise at the sound of breaking glass. He staggered onwards until he spotted the cement pig in Tom Giblin's front garden. He lowered his head and met the shrouded monster with a level and forthright gaze.

"Nice piggy," he coaxed. "Would you like to go for a little trot with Oliver?"

He fumbled back the canvas cover and blindly fixed the lifting straps around the pig. Then he clambered on board the mobile crane parked before the house. The keys were in the ignition and the engine still warm. It started easily. The noise of the big diesel engine throbbed and echoed around the sleeping town. It would have been an awkward job for a sober man, but the drink had smothered all caution. The pig took flight from the cottage garden and rose in a graceful arc, swinging clear of the power cables and the leaning lamp-post.

EUGENE TUTTLE HAD tossed all night in drugged sleep. New and unfamiliar elements had entered his nightmare. There had been raised voices, crowds of faceless people and a dimly apprehended commotion. Only with the pounding vibration did the original nightmare begin once more. He was a small boy running for his life in a canyon with sheer cliff walls on either side. Over his shoulder came the sound of hooves and the snuffling grunts of the Black Pig, breaking through the undergrowth, ready to snatch him up and swallow him whole. He ran at breakneck speed, weighted down with a satchel full of bogus documents, the pig right behind him. Hot saliva from the Black Pig's snout drenched the back of his neck. He knew the monster was right on top of him.

Suddenly he was awake.

He blinked in astonishment. He was in his bed, labouring for breath after the chase. He could not believe his luck. For the first time since the nightmares began he had escaped the hungry jaws of the Black Pig. He had never in his life known such an enormous sense of relief and gratitude.

The feeling passed quickly when he looked around the bedroom. Something was terribly wrong. The room was dark. Black dark. It was night outside his window. That couldn't be true. He never woke during the night. Then he heard the sound. A vibration. A drumbeat of giant hooves rolling through the town square.

He turned back the eiderdown and crept towards the window. The noise was getting louder, coming nearer. He wanted to wake up a second time, to find that it was morning once more and all his terrors had evaporated in the daylight. But he couldn't wake up, and he couldn't hide. A cold sweat ringed his forehead. His hands trembled when he reached for the curtains. He told himself this was not real. Either his nightmare had taken a new and horrible twist, or his imagination was running riot.

"This is not happening," he whimpered. "This is all a bad dream."

Nobody was forcing him to open the curtains, but, like a bystander who cannot take their eyes away from the details of a grisly accident, he had to know the full horror. Compelled by this state of naked terror, he swept the curtains open with both hands.

A giant animal snout pressed against the window pane. A pig! A monstrous pig. Its tusks flashed like metal. Its baleful eyes were as cold as cement. His mother's dire warning had been right all along. The Black Pig had arrived finally to claim him for all his wrongdoing, his lies and his double-dealing. He could not say if the blood-curdling squeal that followed came from the Black Pig outside his window or from his own lips.

"Ouuurreekre... "

MULCAHY WOKE WITH a fright. His body seemed to have fallen from a terrifyingly dark height before it hit the mattress. When his eyes jerked open he felt an immediate sense of panic and foreboding. He rolled over in the bed and found the place beside him empty. He looked around the room. He was in the workhouse, not the cottage on the peninsula.

"Grace?" he said anxiously.

Every detail of the row the night before came back.

He dressed in a hurry.

He drove to the peninsula.

The front door of the cottage was locked, with no sign of life inside when he peered through the kitchen window. The ground under the temporary shower in the garden was wet. He went around to the back of the cottage, but she was not at her morning exercises in the centre of the ring fort next the sea. The sinking feeling in the pit of his stomach became a certainty. She had carried out her threat to leave.

"Shit, shit!" he swore rapidly.

He had driven her to this. Walking away in a sulk last night had been a bad move. He should have explained the way he felt. Instead, he had used her as a scapegoat for all his pent-up anger and frustration. He had been callous, stupid and selfish. And now Grace had left him.

If only there was some way to re-run the argument; to go back to that dark side-street again, to stop, turn around and beg her to stay.

Perhaps there was still time. He remembered her car. There was an outside chance he might find her at Oliver's.

He stopped in town, but Tuttle's bar was closed, and no one had met or seen Grace. Stories of an odd event in the night overshadowed her departure.

When he arrived at Oliver's forge, he found the front door wide open. A bad sign. It meant Oliver had been visited by a customer already. To Mulcahy's certain knowledge Oliver had only one client on his books: Grace.

He was reluctant to walk straight in. At the crucial moment he wanted to put off knowing the truth.

He was still standing in the yard when Oliver emerged. His arms were stretched out before him, his eyes squeezed tightly shut. He moved with the clumsy gait and uncertain reach of the newly blind, but there was a purpose and direction to his path. Soon his hands were fumbling along the rim of the water-barrel. He plunged his head into the barrel, held it submerged for a full minute and then stood up straight. He blew water from his mouth. More water gushed in torrents from his dark ringlets. He tossed his head from side to side and shook gleaming droplets in all directions.

"Buurwhoouurrrumuphhh," he half-roared and coughed as his eyes came open.

"Have you seen Grace?" Mulcahy began immediately.

Oliver could only muster a long groan and a bleary squint.

"I've been looking all over for her. Did you leave her home last night?"

Oliver rubbed the last of the water from his face. "I thought you knew," he said hoarsely. "She took a taxi home, and called here early this morning to collect her car. It wasn't fully ready but she drove off in it anyway."

"Did she say where she was headed?"

"No," Oliver said, sensing Mulcahy's panic.

"Nothing?" Mulcahy pleaded.

"When she saw the car, she got really mad. She said it was a simple problem to iron out with the rental people and I couldn't manage all that. She said she was fed up with the whole lot of us. We couldn't be trusted to do anything right. She said we'd never get our act together and she had wasted enough time hanging around with a bunch of useless deadbeats."

For the sake of his old friend Oliver tried very hard to remember her exact words. Everything that had happened between locating the monument in Tom Giblin's front garden and plunging his head in the water barrel a minute before was either vague or a complete blank. He imagined the night had been exactly like any other heavy drinking session, but along with the painful hangover he felt an unusually sharp and stabbing sense of guilt.

"I'm sorry, Mulcahy," he said. "I don't remember much more. But I know she was upset."

"How upset?"

Oliver pursed his lips in an expression that said it might

223

be better if his friend didn't know.

Mulcahy turned away and kicked an empty oil-can across the yard. "Well, that's it," he said. "She said she'd leave and she did."

"What happened?" Oliver asked.

"I made a pig's ear out of things as usual. That's what happened."

Oliver hitched up his trousers and brushed his hair back with his hands. Reality was returning at an alarming rate.

"For some reason I have this horrible, black guilty feeling myself this morning," he said.

"So you should." Mulcahy almost smiled.

"I'm not with you."

"Everyone in town is talking about it."

"About what?" Oliver said, alarmed.

"You really don't remember?"

Oliver shook his head and the contents of his skull rattled between his ears like broken crockery. "Bits of it are coming back to me," he said.

"The Black Pig broke out of Tom Giblin's front garden last night when everyone was asleep and took a peek in Eugene Tuttle's bedroom window. They say his screams woke the whole town. The crane driver had to be called out of his bed to move the pig away from the window before Tuttle could be calmed down."

"Where's Tuttle now?"

"Flat out in bed."

"And the pig?"

"Back where I left it in the first place."

Mulcahy was in no mood to laugh, but he couldn't help smiling at the expression on Oliver's face. Given the state of Eugene Tuttle's nerves, it had not been a very charitable joke, but it had been an inspired stunt all the same.

"How is Tuttle now?" Oliver asked.

"Sam told me he looks like something a crow shit in a famine."

"Do they know who's responsible?"

"There's a list of suspects, but it has only one name on it."

"Yours," Oliver suggested hopefully.

"No, yours. And Sam is unable to provide an alibi, on account of him being discovered unconscious behind the harbour wall."

"Don't tell me Sam is in bed sick as well."

"Sick. But not in bed. He went to the Marine Bar for a cure."

"I suppose I'll have to call round to Tuttle and apologise," Oliver said in a less than sincere mood of repentance.

"A doctor was called to examine poor old Eugene. They might have to send for a specialist," Mulcahy teased. "It could go to law if Oswald and Leddy have anything to do with it."

"Oh, God," Oliver moaned. "Sally will never forgive me for this."

It was agreed Oliver had better make his apology to Eugene Tuttle before Oswald and Leddy got in on the act. Oliver was prepared to meet the publican and make amends for what he'd done. He was a lot less ready to face Sally Holmes. He coaxed Mulcahy to come with him.

Mulcahy followed Oliver's pickup truck in his own car. They parked in the town square and saw the Black Pig in Tom Giblin's front garden, the monument hidden once more under its canvas cover until the official unveiling. Giblin's dog stood sentry on the garden wall and eyed Oliver with suspicion as he and Mulcahy approached. Oliver squinted at the dog, his eyes half closed by a murderous hangover.

"Bite," he whispered. "But don't bark."

News of Tuttle's misfortune had circulated around the town. Tuttle was the underdog again who needed his drinkers, and the breaking of the boycott by some parties was causing further upset in the town.

Sally Holmes was behind the counter when Oliver and

Mulcahy walked in. She looked up and rotated her head firmly before they reached the bar.

Mulcahy held up his hands in a gesture of surrender. "We don't want a drink," he said. "We're here to see Tuttle."

"He's not well," she said shortly.

"We heard."

"Why, Oliver?" Sally turned on Mulcahy's embarrassed partner. "What tempted you to do it?"

Oliver couldn't look at her; he simply bowed his head and offered no defence.

"You'd better go up," she relented. "Oswald and Leddy are with him."

"You go on," Mulcahy waved his friend ahead.

He moved nearer to Sally for a private word.

"Don't go making excuses for him," she warned.

"This isn't about Oliver," he said. He had known Grace O'Connor would eventually leave, but he never dreamt the break-up would happen so quickly or so bitterly. He was desperate for some parting message, anything to banish the memory of her sobs and that last terrible argument in the street.

"Did Grace talk to you before she left?"

Sally turned in her lips. "You really hurt her, Mulcahy."

"Grace said that?"

"She didn't have to."

"Where did she go?"

"Away – Dublin. She knows some people there."

"Did she leave any message?"

"She left this." Sally reached into the pocket of her cardigan and fished out a key. "It's the key to the front door of the cottage. She said she never wanted to set foot in the place again, but if Oliver wanted to fix up the house, it would make a cosy nest for the two of us."

A tearful brightness wet her eyes.

Mulcahy was stunned. He didn't know what to say. The break-up was even more final than he imagined, and now there was a rift between Oliver and Sally.

"You and Oliver, you're like two fekkin children," Sally attacked, but the tears began to tumble down her cheeks.

"Oliver would marry you in the morning," Mulcahy said in an attempt to limit the harm done. "You know that."

"Roaring drunk, he might," Sally sniffled. "I have some respect you know. I wouldn't marry someone who drinks as much as he does. How could I trust him? Look at the carry-on last night."

"I understand," Mulcahy said, floundering to redeem his friend.

"And you," the attack turned. "You should know better than to lose a girl like that. You were really suited. You looked well together. You were good for each other. I don't understand why you forced her to go."

"It's not easy, Sally," he said.

"It's not supposed to be easy," she said.

As the stair-boards creaked, Oswald and Deputy Leddy took up their positions on either side of Tuttle's bed. The curtains were drawn and the sick-room was dim and smelled of camphor and eucalyptus. Tuttle lay on his back gurgling low moans of distress. Leddy lifted the patient's hand from the bed and patted it gently to quieten him. Oswald squeezed out a damp flannel cloth into a basin and mopped Tuttle's brow.

"There, there," they babied the patient.

Oliver coughed from the doorway and shambled into the bedroom, stooping his shoulders as he came through the low door-frame. His whole manner was subdued and apologetic and his eyes locked on the rug under his feet.

He waited for someone to speak, and Oswald and Leddy gave him plenty of time to consider the full extent of the injury he had caused. Euge Tuttle looked like death warmed up, and they were going to milk this incident for all it was worth. Tuttle was set to get a lot worse before he got better.

At last, Leddy spoke. "This is your doing," he accused. "You and Mulcahy and that upstart, Giblin."

"Eugene, I'm sorry," Oliver said ignoring the other two.

Tuttle's eyes remained closed and the low moans continued.

"Let this be a lesson to you," said Leddy.

Oliver backed out of the room. Sally Holmes kept her back turned as he left the premises with Mulcahy, utterly mortified by the consequences of his prank.

OLIVER WENT IMMEDIATELY to the Marine Bar. Mulcahy went home to the workhouse, opened a bottle of wine and ate reheated left-overs. The day passed in a state of listless frustration.

He sat in the workhouse kitchen. He moved to the big room. With every minute the workhouse became more unbearably empty. He had lost his parents a long time ago. He had lost Theo. His wife had left him. Grace had left him. The whole dark legacy of the past began to press in around him. The workhouse felt like a vast mausoleum, with nothing but sad tokens of lost lives interred there. The abandoned bench where Grace had worked on the costumes for the parade, still scattered with remnants of coloured fabric. Vases and lamps and the hand-carved pigs salvaged from Theo's cottage.

What was it they said about people who collected things, especially antiques? They didn't trust the future.

The summer was coming. There would be a demand for his work on the streets at the arts festivals and the heritage days. For a few months he would be busy. Then what? Another winter here?

A flock of starlings perched along the eaves of the workhouse. Their screeches mimicked the monkey chatter, jungle insect noise and tropical bird calls of the warmer climates from which they had migrated. This eerie impersonation of the jungle brought to mind his first impression of Grace: an exotic creature blown off course on to a strange shore. Now she was gone.

He sat into the car, crossed the broad hump of the hill of Dromore West, and parked at a farm gate. He walked across the fields and stopped at the edge of the cliffs. The rocks were intricately formed in perfect triangles, arranged like sharp teeth sawing the waves. To prove her injured leg was better Grace had run down those treacherous rocks, dragging him with her in a wild freefall, finding their footing instinctively as they gathered speed, racing towards the sea. A blind plunge, intuitive but sure-footed.

He went to the highest part of the cliff where a big sea churned in the cave, the Cora Dún, cut deep in the headland at Aughris. Great waves crashed against the rocks and broke into white spray. He stepped up to the edge. What now? Jump? End it. But he was not a man who believed in extremes. He left the headland and tramped the fields of delicate wild flowers, headed on foot for the Marine Bar.

Sam had left, but Oliver was there, slumped and despondent at the bar. When the door opened Oliver looked around slowly, red-eyed and dishevelled.

"Jasus! You're a shook looking outfit," he said when he spotted Mulcahy.

Mulcahy called for two pints and two half-ones of whiskey while they waited for the pints to settle. They leaned together with their elbows on the counter and peered at their reflections through the rows of bottles in the mirror behind the bar, two men set for a day of hard, wordless drinking.

BY THREE O'CLOCK in the morning they were back at Oliver's forge, passing around a bottle of *poitín*. Both men were now anxious to talk, but neither was ready to listen. They began to broadcast their remorse on separate wavelengths.

"Oh, Sally, Sally, I didn't mean any harm," Oliver was repentant.

"She might have told me where she was going," Mulcahy said.

"She'll never look at me again," Oliver went on.

"No note, no message."

"Never."

"Not a word. Nothing."

"I love that girl," Oliver declared boldly.

"Who? Grace?" Mulcahy turned.

"No. Sally."

"Right. Right." Mulcahy raised the bottle and drank. The home-brewed spirit scalded his throat the way swallowed disappointment burned. "She's gone for good this time," he said.

"Sally's gone?" Oliver said surprised.

"No, Grace. Grace is the one who left."

"I know," Oliver gave his friend a supportive pat on the shoulder.

"I should have done more," Mulcahy realised.

"I should have drank less," Oliver said.

Through the open door they could see the mountains on the horizon. Alien lights prowled along the rim. There was a far-off rumble like thunder, or a large animal digging in to the side of the mountain for a long occupation.

IN TOM GIBLIN's front garden Sam paused when he heard the rumble in the mountains. The canvas tarpaulin used to cover the monument lay at his feet. The town was in darkness. The power had not yet been restored. It was rumoured that Councillor Oswald and Deputy Leddy had intervened to have the repairs delayed, to increase public unease over the Black Pig and to sabotage the festival. Grace was missing. Oliver and Mulcahy were off somewhere on a batter. Tom Giblin was prowling the town like a maniac with his dog, tearing out the smalls hair of his moustache and pasting up more posters. It was rumoured Eugene Tuttle might never recover. Sam took up his paint brush. As he circled the pig each broad stroke of black paint glistened in the flames. "I can't go on, I must go on, I will go on," he recited under his breath.

EIGHTEEN

MULCAHY CARRIED THE first of the boxes from the workhouse into the old Church of Ireland hall, now used by the town of Ennismuck Credit Union as a part-time branch office, and loaned for the weekend to the festival organisers. The stoneware potter, the jewellery maker and the aromatherapist had just arrived. The German cheesemaker and the candlemaker had already set up their stalls. It was nine o'clock and the exhibition and crafts fair were meant to open to the public at ten-thirty for day one of the first Festival of the Black Pig.

"Am I late for the flower show?" Mulcahy called as he arrived.

He put the box down on the floor and took the first wooden pig out of its newspaper wrapping. Oliver was at the side of the hall, driving home the last screw in the shelving he had removed from Theo's cottage and adapted for use in the exhibition. Mulcahy settled the hand-carved pig on the new shelf. It was the last one Theo had carved: the bog oak pig with applewood tusks he had offered to Grace: a gift she had left behind. Mulcahy had chosen the box at random and he considered this an unlucky first dip.

Everyone in the hall abandoned their stalls to help bring in the other boxes, unwrap the carvings and arrange the display. It was the first public appearance of the intricately carved wooden pigs: an eerie unfolding of a lifetime obsession, and while there were little gasps of wonder and admiration at the number of carvings and the quality of the work as each pig was revealed, an overall silent fascination held sway.

"Remarkable... incredible... amazing," were the words spoken in a kind of hushed fascination.

The wood smells, the teak oil and wax, the scents and traces of his old friend Theo clung to the carvings as the exhibition took shape and had a strange and unwanted affect on Mulcahy. What the hell had it all been for? Why had Theo chosen such a ludicrous and futile pastime? Art, mythology, philosophy: what were they only sidelines, distractions, means of forgetting the constantly passing seconds that brought an old man closer to death, having missed the real purpose of his life.

Mulcahy was honouring a commitment to Grace O'Connor by mounting this exhibition, but he would not have gone ahead with it if he had known how hard it would hit him. The whole thing made him feel utterly betrayed: by Grace, because she had left him in such a painful lurch, by Theo for not having lived a more fulfilled life, and by the terrible pointlessness and stupidity of his own behaviour.

"Any word from Grace?" Oliver asked, sensing what was on his mind.

"None," Mulcahy said, and the sore, terse edge in his voice quashed further enquiries.

TOM GIBLIN STRETCHED the blue nylon rope tight and tied a rough knot on the end. He was perched at the top of an extended aluminium ladder, and he leaned back to admire his handiwork. TORCHLIGHT PARADE AND UN-VEILING OF THE BLACK PIG – TONIGHT, the banner read. Below him, in the square of trampled lawn, the pig was loosely shrouded under canvas.

Mulcahy and Oliver had left the Credit Union building as soon as the doors opened to the public, and the first callers arrived to view the exhibition. They crossed the square together and stood on the pavement outside Tom Giblin's house.

"I think you should call off the parade," Mulcahy shouted up.

"It's too late," Giblin said. "All the arrangements are made. And if we don't do the unveiling tonight, it'll never happen."

"Who's in charge of the parade?"

"No one, but we're going ahead with it anyway."

"It's not going to work without Grace."

"You could make it work, Mulcahy."

"You know my answer to that."

"Do what you like, but the parade and the unveiling are set for tonight."

The two men walked away.

"What does he expect?" Mulcahy pleaded with Oliver, knowing it was useless to argue with Tom Giblin. "Everyone loved the way Grace fussed over them. She made them feel important. She got them motivated. That was her gift. There's no way I can take her place."

Oliver looked back over his shoulder at the cement pig under the paint-splattered canvas, and the home-made banner already starting to sag in the middle.

"I wouldn't fret too much," he said. "It's not exactly the Pope's visit."

The bunting along the route from the square to the harbour flapped in a fresh sea-breeze. It gave the town a festival atmosphere. But the employment scheme workers, the team from the workhouse, and the volunteers from the town, who had brought along their own costumes for the parade all stood about the harbour in aimless groups.

The sight produced in Mulcahy a sensation of sorry dread. Without Grace the parade had no chance. Her reputation, her energy and her enthusiasm had brought along the confidence of these outsiders and blow-ins to the point where they were willing to dress up and march in a public parade. The props and effigies from the workhouse had been brought to the harbour in advance. The papier-mâché- and bamboo-built mannequins, the carnival heads, the disconnected limbs of the larger figures, the warrior costumes, the lanterns and the torches lay there like the scattered elements of a jig-saw puzzle with the big picture missing.

The first Festival of the Black Pig, like so many things before it, would end up a victim of that unique Irish talent for farce and fiasco.

"The only thing you could start around here is a fight," Mulcahy summed up the debacle.

They joined Sam, seated at the start of the pier.

"What's the story, Sam?" Mulcahy cast his eye about the jumble.

"Still waiting," he quipped.

Mulcahy wished he had stayed away. His only reason for being there was to collect his street performance costume, which had been brought to the harbour by mistake with the other props.

He was ready to do his bit, to dress up for the festival and entertain any visitors to the town in the early part of the day. He had supplied the parade organisers with props and mannequins. That was his trade, but he was not going to take overall responsibility. He had said no all along. Why should he feel guilty now? It was Grace O'Connor who had let them down.

He thrust his hands deep in his pockets and sat on a bollard, looking at the slipway and the murky water. He wanted the whole sorry day over and done with. He would sooner a visit to the dentist than this.

Sam passed around a packet of tobacco, and they rolled up cigarettes. Mulcahy had been off the cigarettes for years. The first puff of smoke made him feel even worse. He tossed the butt-end out into the water and returned his hands to his pockets.

"It was a nice idea," Oliver said. No one took up the thought.

Mulcahy's costume waited. He ought to be getting ready. But the last thing he wanted to do was dress up and act the clown.

The brooding silence continued until they heard a sharp gunshot or a small explosion in the town.

"Jesus! What was that?" The sound rattled Oliver's tender nerves. The three men looked up at once in the direction of the square.

"They must have called in a vet to put down Eugene Tuttle," Mulcahy suggested.

"Or blown up the monument," Sam said. "You know they never got the boys who blew up the last one."

It was intended as a joke, but they all craned their necks to search for a plume of tell-tale black smoke.

A motor-car appeared at the top of the road and back-fired a second time to alert everyone at the harbour.

The district had a fair quota of old bangers and broken-down wrecks on the road, but this new arrival stood out from the competition. The radiator grill was missing. The front fender had been hastily secured with string. Most of the original paintwork had been stripped away and the crumpled shell crudely repaired with a dozen different brands of filler. Between the patches of filler there were ring-spots of rust primer and grey undercoat. Several shades of paint had been tested in spray blots and stripes along the sides.

A gleaming commercial van with a satellite dish on the roof chased close behind the wrecked car. Both vehicles came to a stand-still opposite Sam, Oliver and Mulcahy.

They heard metal grind against metal as the battered driver's door of the car was forced open.

"Hi, guys!" Grace called.

Mulcahy gaped at her in amazement and then looked askance at Oliver.

"I told you the car wasn't ready when she took it." Oliver's face burned.

"Why are you sitting around here with your hands in your pockets?" Grace demanded.

"We thought you'd left us," Mulcahy stammered.

He might have said more, but he was distracted by the sight of the stainless-steel flight-cases being unloaded from the side door of the van with Satellite News Gathering team stickers on the lids.

Men in faded denims and a girl wearing tight black ski-pants began to fuss over light meters, microphones and sound recording equipment. The legs of a metal tripod were extended and secured and a camera mounted on top.

"I had people to see," she said with the confidence of someone whose plans had worked out even better than anticipated.

A reporter with a ginger beard stood next the film crew. Mulcahy had seen the same reporter many nights on the television news, wading heroically through winter flooding in the west of Ireland. He had started the bulletins in a pair of green Wellington boots, which he swopped for thigh-high waders and then a dry platform on the back of a tractor trailer as the flood waters kept rising.

"These guys have offered us a spot on the news. So get your asses in gear," Grace said. "It's showtime."

"I thought I'd never see you again," Mulcahy said.

Grace averted her eyes and looked around the harbour, giddy and anxious to get things moving. She was back in a familiar element, amongst lights and microphones, cameras and costumes.

"We haven't got time for this," she warned Mulcahy and began to walk towards the reporter.

"Grace, wait."

"Not now," she said.

"I really missed you."

She stopped and turned.

"Is that true?"

The girl in the ski-pants approached. "We're ready for you now," she told Grace.

"I was heart-broken when you left," he said.

It was as much as he could bring himself to declare in front of so many people.

"I know it's going to be like a madhouse here today," he said. "I just wanted you to know. That's all."

He turned to leave, his stomach in knots and his head reeling.

"Mulcahy, come back."

"They're all waiting for you." He gathered up the costume he planned to use for the street entertainments in the town. "Oliver, can you help me get into this?"

The employment scheme workers had spotted the television people, and began busily picking up costumes and fitting face-masks to avoid being caught by the camera. The actor had moved centre stage, while the others looked to Grace for guidance. The girl in the ski-pants cut in before Grace could follow Mulcahy.

"I'm sorry," she said, "but there is a strict deadline if we're going to make the evening news."

MULCAHY WAS TRAPPED. A crushed and anxious figure behind iron bars, his legs gathered up tight against his chest in the confined space. The cage was strapped to the back of a giant witch. She had a long, wizened face, a beak nose and a hooked chin. She wore a shiny black crinoline cloak, long skirts and a pointed hat. She roved the town square in search of other prisoners, and bent in the middle to peer into doorways or lunge at bystanders.

Children ran around the witch, exhilarated and terrified. The more boisterous youngsters plucked at her skirts. Some even ran at the witch to kick her shins. Oliver walked a short distance behind the witch. He moved in quickly when the children's antics threatened to get out of control and knock Mulcahy off his stilts underneath the costume.

The witch was a popular piece for street events. The illusion allowed the upper half of Mulcahy's body to remain in the cage, with two fake padded legs gathered up in front of his chest. He wore a brightly coloured costume and his face was made-up with grease-paint. He was barely recognisable, except for his distinctive wild hair. His gloved hands grasped at the bars of the cage, or waved and pleaded for help, as he circled the square on stilts, strapped in to the costume in a harness of his own devising. It was an athletic and demanding job, and he had to keep his concentration focused to operate the witch, to stay up on the wooden stilts and to mime his awful predicament.

At one point he saw Grace and the camera crew recording his performance.

He did not see her again, but she never left his thoughts all day. Her sudden and unexpected return had made everything clear. The instant reflex from despair to pure joy at the sight of her climbing out of that battered car had left him in no doubt. How could he have been so stupid? How could he have missed what had been so blindingly obvious all along? He was crazy about the girl. And to think that he had caused her even a fraction of the heartbreak he felt right now was unbearable.

THE SEA-FRONT STALLS and the amusements had opened ahead of season. The promenade and the beach were populated with strollers. In the town square the local musicians were grouped around the empty plinth. The regular Friday shoppers delayed in the doorways, wondering what all the commotion was about. There was a steady flow of visitors to see Theo's hand-carving pigs, and people emerged from the Credit Union building carrying the bits and pieces they'd bought at the crafts fair. The posters, the newspaper, the local radio advertisements, Mulcahy's performance and the music in the square all focused interest for the early part of the day, but it was the evening news on the television that caused the greatest stir.

The town was still without electricity when the broadcast was aired, but the idea all along had been to send the news further than the last house in the borough and to boost the Festival Committee's efforts from the level of parish endeavour to national news. After the headline news of political scandals, factory closures, industrial disputes, drug seizures and gangland shootings, foreign wars and fragile ceasefires, the reporter with the ginger beard appeared. He was standing at the harbour – without his green Wellington boots. Grace could be seen in the background, making last minute adjustments to the hem of the actor's warrior costume.

"A visit to the west of Ireland," the reporter began, "has resulted in an unusual collaboration between Broadway and Hollywood costume designer, Grace O'Connor, and the people of Ennismuck."

A line of brightly costumed figures paraded past the camera. The pagan masks and rich, natural colours were caught in close-up.

"Better known for her work for the stage and screen, Grace has returned to her Irish roots for this carnival production."

The scene shifted quickly and the local beauty spots were highlighted. The camera pulled back on a mountain panorama. The reporter appeared, strategically posted beside a bend in the river.

"Worried by the actions of a gold-mining operation in the area, Grace and her friends hope to make the natural beauty of this richly historic region known to more people."

A quick montage of shots of the crafts fair and Theo's collection of pigs. Then a close up of the Black Pig under its cover in Tom Giblin's front garden.

"The highlight of tonight's activities will be the unveiling of the Black Pig of the ancient Celtic myth."

The camera tightened on the banner and the posters for the Festival of the Black Pig pasted up around Tom Giblin's front door. The reporter's head popped up in the frame.

"The entire event was put together at the last minute in what organiser Tom Giblin calls one of his 'rasher decisions'. The townspeople are appealing for support for what they promise will be a remarkable spectacle."

The entire item lasted only a minute and a half, but no event was finally believed to take place unless it could be witnessed, however briefly, on the television. The Festival of the Black Pig, and a two-ton concrete monument, only became real by going out on invisible airwaves, in a quick radiation flash on screens across the country.

When the festival item wound up, the blonde newscaster in the studio returned, with a blown-up version of one of Mulcahy's photographs hovering over her shoulder. Then the reporter appeared. He was back in his green Wellington boots, amongst the spoil heaps and canyons of the gold mine on the mountain.

"Coming up next," the newscaster announced, "fears increase over the environmental impact of gold-mining in the west. Calls for government action, and an enquiry into alleged breaches of environmental legislation."

DEPUTY LEDDY KNEW all about the television crew going around the town and snooping about the mountain with their satellite news van and their awkward questions. He had gone to a loyal party member's house, beyond the range of the blackout, to see the evening news. It was as revealing as he feared.

Immediately after the broadcast, he rushed home to a dark house to find his telephone jumping out of the cradle. He lit the bottled gas light and fought bravely to restore calm through a barrage of upset phonecalls. The Dublin crowd had closed ranks against him. The grass roots were hinting he might have to be put out to pasture. He swore the minister would be kept out of it. He was a loyal party man. "Deny everything," was the rule of his career. People had short memories. He had soldiered through worse scandals and never lost a vote, but he could not hide his agitation when the final call came from the mining company.

"I know. I know," he blustered into the mouthpiece. "I know I promised... No publicity... That's correct... But it's not my fault. I did try. The power is out. No one here in the town saw a thing... Now, hold your horses. I won't be threatened in my own constituency. I'm a democratically elected representative of the people. What about the public money? The grant aid? The tax concessions? The private investments? You can't pull the plug... "

The line went dead.

"Hello, hello," he pleaded over the static dial tone and the steady hiss from the portable butane gas light on his mahogany desk.

Beyond the town the roving lights on the mountain stopped. The industrial grinding noise faded. The animal breathing sound became shallow and died away. The lights winked out.

Deputy Leddy returned the telephone to its cradle. It was incredible how much damage a little bit of truth could do. Numbed by the speed at which his plans had collapsed he stood frozen on the spot, deaf to the increasing noise in the street.

NINETEEN

ALL DAY PEOPLE had been drifting into the town. Now, as the daylight faded, the individual strollers, the couples holding hands, the loose groups going around together began to merge. A crowd took shape. The route from the harbour to the town square was lined with bystanders. The more trustworthy were given flaming torches or coloured crêpe paper lanterns lit up inside with candles to hold. A necklace of bonfires glimmered on the beach. Two fatted pigs had been roasting for hours on metal spits over charcoal. There were cut-off oil barrels full of glowing coals set about the square. The flaming torches threw long shadows on the house fronts. A smell of burning coals, pork and wood-smoke spiced the air.

The residents had thrown open the windows of the houses facing the square. Children in their pyjamas jostled for space with their elbows on the sills. Bolder teenagers went higher, and could be seen sitting along the ridge-tiles or perched against the chimneys of the attic roofs.

The carnival parade was under way. A pipe band dressed in white stockings, red and black tartan skirts, brass-buttoned jackets and plumed hats led the march. Then came the giant mannequin of the poet W. B. Yeats. He was followed by a band of warriors with flashing spears and a troop of mock horsemen, giant salmon, a glowing moon and spinning stars, imitation boulders. The children were dressed as moths and caterpillars, glow-bugs and fairy lantern carriers. New Age Travellers beat tom-toms, tin drums, maracas, bodhráns and home-made percussion instruments. Whistles pierced the night. The lines of flaming torches burned like those of a search-party on the side of a mountain as the piecemeal parade came up the incline from the harbour and entered the main square.

Grace ran alongside the parade, seeing that no papier-mâché figure came into contact with a naked flame from a torch. After a full circuit of the town square, the whole noisy and eye-catching spectacle stopped outside the wall of Tom Giblin's front garden before the shrouded Black Pig.

Oliver stood in the front row, strapped into the giant figure of W. B. Yeats, working the mouth while the poet appeared to read from his book. Grace pressed her face up close to the tiny slit, cut in the front of the paper effigy, through which Oliver peered.

"Where's Mulcahy?" she shouted.

"I don't know."

"He should be here for the unveiling," she said, upset.

"I doubt if he'll show up. He said the whole thing is too personal. He doesn't want the attention."

Grace looked all around.

"Can you find him for me?" she pleaded.

Oliver settled the mannequin on the pavement and wrestled out of the harness. He used the lull between the end of the parade and the official unveiling ceremony to get out from under the effigy.

"I won't promise anything," he said.

"Just bring him back to me, please."

Oliver vanished into the crowd, and Grace was left alone to wonder if Mulcahy had any idea how confused her feelings about him were right now. She had blamed him and she had tried to understand him. She had cursed him and then forgiven him. She had gone through so many changes of heart she didn't know any more how she felt, but Mulcahy was the one person who might understand why she came back.

After the row in the square that night she had made up her mind to rescue what self-esteem she had left and bring the affair to an end. She rose early the next morning, and, as arranged, the taxi driver collected her at the start of the lane. She dropped a key off with Sally Holmes and was sorry to say goodbye. She would be copping out on the parade and the friends she had made, but on that final morning, everything about that crummy seaside resort – including the mess Oliver had made of her car – reinforced her decision to leave. She drove away with the clear intention never again to set eyes on that squabbling little backwater town.

Travelling the coast road, two things overturned that decision.

The first was a promise she had given Tom Giblin, after he treated her injured shoulder, to help with his campaign against the gold mine. As she sat behind the wheel of the battered car, in which she had been so nearly killed, and flexed her shoulder muscle without any pain, she knew it would be wrong to break that promise. She determined then to show the photographs Mulcahy had taken at the mine to her mother's friends in Dublin, and use their influence to alert the right people.

The second reason was less easy to define. As she looked across at the retreating mountains in the early morning light, she remembered Theo's cottage. A vision came back, a vision she had experienced moments before she knew her grandfather was dead. The newly created gleam of the world that morning. The incredible sense of release from solitude and uncertainty. A feeling of passionate well-being. An absolute conviction that despite all the pain, life was a high and wonderful adventure. She would not go so far as to call this a mystical or a religious experience – there had been no grand answers to anything – but she had never felt more intensely alive. She could not separate that rapture from the place where it had first gripped her. And suddenly she knew very clearly that it would be impossible to leave the only place on earth her life had ever felt truly centred.

THE PARADE WAS at a stand-still, and the crowd had become restless, waiting for something more to happen. Grace had no idea what had been planned for this part of the evening.

Her part was done, but it seemed that neither Tom Giblin nor Mulcahy was willing to face the public for the official unveiling of the controversial monument.

It galled her to think she would have to take the initiative once more. They really were a hopeless crowd. She was still wondering what to do or say to save the situation when Tom Giblin stepped out of his front door.

The usual brown corduroy jacket and trousers had been discarded. In their place he wore a bright red dinner-jacket, a red-and-white-striped waistcoat, white butterfly-collar shirt and a red dicky-bow. A straw hat, tight black breeches and a pair of red boots, borrowed from Mulcahy, completed the get-up. The look fell somewhere between a singer in a barbershop quartet and an old-time music-hall master of ceremonies.

In one hand he carried a set of lightweight wooden steps. In the other hand he held a cone-shaped megaphone, or hog-caller. Sam darted around Giblin like a conjurer's assistant, took the wooden steps and placed them beside the monument. Tom Giblin climbed up on to the top step.

"Ladies and gentlemen," he announced through the hog-caller. "Welcome to the very first Festival of the Black Pig."

Good-humoured cheers drowned the hollow, booming voice.

"We have gathered tonight for the official unveiling of a new public monument, created by our native artist, Mulcahy, and dedicated to a noble scholar, local historian, and on the evidence of a posthumous exhibition that opened today, a great artist: Theodore William Causeland."

More cheers and applause, and a pause for Mulcahy to come forward to acknowledge the good will of the crowd. Grace looked around with the others, but there was no sign of Mulcahy.

"This is an important moment," Giblin improvised quickly. "It is not just a turning-point in the life of a small Irish town, it is a turning-point in the life of a nation. We have gathered here to celebrate the achievement of a local artist, and to commemorate the passing of a remarkable man, known to many of us simply as Theo. And we have gathered here as a community. We have endured hardship, we have pulled together, we have come through. This bold representation of the Black Pig of Ennismuck must be regarded as a final triumph. A triumph over pig-ignorant and pig-in-the-parlour Ireland, and all the sorry associations those terms have had for us in the past. The Black Pig of Ennismuck is, in the words of our American friend, a pig with attitude. A figurehead for a new, and proud, and self-confident nation. A symbol for a people with the capacity to laugh at themselves; to enjoy themselves; to be themselves."

"Don't rupture a blood vessel, now, Tom," someone shouted from the crowd.

Giblin accepted the laughter and lowered the hog-caller. He reached for the watch pocket of his red waistcoat and produced a pair of scissors.

"Without further ceremony," he shouted. "I give you... the Black Pig."

He snipped a rope, and Sam plucked away the canvas cover.

The first sight of the monument sent a ripple of unease through the crowd. Instinctively, those in the front row took a step back. This was no playful little piglet from the pages of a nursery book, or a ready symbol for a new Ireland. It was a black boar, moulded from ancient nightmare. A warted monster with enough poison in its bristles to cause the strongest warrior to fall in convulsions; a physical embodiment of the darkest of all forces, that which destroys life for gain.

"Janey Mac!" gasped a young girl with a head of tumbling red curls.

Tom Giblin signalled for Sam to come forward. Sam carried a red plastic bucket and a sack. He left the plastic bucket under the pig's snout and emptied the contents of the sack. Golden flakes of Indian meal tumbled out.

"Sooiee... Sooieee..." Giblin shrieked through the hog caller.

The tension broke. Children rushed forward, and climbed up on the garden wall to touch the Black Pig's rough snout, the ugliness rendered lovable. The crowd clapped their hands.

"Drop a pound in the slot to make a wish," Giblin petitioned the adult bystanders.

A line of well-wishers formed along the garden path for a closer inspection of the Black Pig and to drop luck-money in the slot.

EUGENE TUTTLE GROANED pitifully in his candle-lit sick-room, but Oswald and Leddy no longer heard the suspect moans and the broken mumbling. They were at the open window, watching Tom Giblin encourage the crowd to shove money in the pig.

"He's making a mockery out of the town," Oswald complained.

"There should be a law against making that kind of spectacle out of yourself," Leddy threatened.

Eugene Tuttle gurgled his consent.

Their threats rang hollow. The brandy boys were cornered men working up a false bravado. Leddy had told Oswald and Tuttle about the last phone call. Nothing was openly discussed, but they each privately knew the bubble had burst. The gold rush was over, the whole crooked enterprise scuppered. The best they could do now was save their own hides.

They were still watching the square from the upper window when Sally Holmes burst into the room.

"Councillor Oswald, you're needed at the shop," she announced breathlessly.

"What's up?"

"The place is mobbed. The girl behind the counter can't cope on her own. And you're needed at the guest-house," she told Deputy Leddy. "The town is full of people who want to go to the party on the beach. They're all looking for a place to stay overnight."

"What do they look like?" Leddy hesitated.

"If you think tourists' money isn't good enough for you, forget it," Sally snapped and turned to leave.

Oswald and Leddy collided with each other in their hurry to get out of the bedroom.

"Get some rest," Leddy shouted back to Eugene Tuttle as he took the stairs two at a time.

After the pounding of feet on the timber stairs the bedroom became very quiet. Eugene Tuttle held his breath and heard the ring of the antique cash register below in the public bar. He knew from the high trilling note that someone had parted with a wad of money. His eyes sprang open.

Sam stood in the bedroom doorway.

"How's the patient?" he enquired.

"Poorly, Sam. Poorly," Tuttle croaked.

In the silence that followed the cash register rang again. Eugene Tuttle could not contain his curiosity.

"Are there many clients downstairs?" he asked weakly.

"Enough to fill a telephone book."

"Are they buying much?"

"You'd think they were never going to taste another drop between now and Judgement Day."

Tuttle threw back the eiderdown. "Pass me my trousers, Sam," he said. "I'll get up for an hour."

THE LIGHT FROM the coloured lanterns and the burning firebrands about the harbour shivered on the water. Mulcahy sat in Sam's regular spot at the end of the pier. After the official unveiling of the Black Pig, the carnival parade had moved to the beach. The pig-roast was ready to be served. He listened to the far-off shouts and the laughter of the figures queuing for food. He watched the couples move off together to sit around the bonfires.

He turned when he heard footsteps on the pier. For a long time Oliver said nothing and stood behind Mulcahy looking off in the direction of the beach and the party.

"How did the unveiling go?" Mulcahy asked.

"Giblin gave us one of his state of the nation speeches."

"But apart from that, it was okay?"

"Everyone loved the Black Pig."

Mulcahy looked back towards the town square. Deputy Leddy was at the open door of his bed and breakfast, ushering in guests with a flashlight. Councillor Oswald had extended his opening hours. There was a steady flow of customers passing in and out of the shop, which was lit up with paraffin oil lamps.

"Oswald and Leddy are happy, anyhow," he remarked.

"Why wouldn't they be happy, they're raking in money."

"It's ironic, isn't it?" Mulcahy said. "They do everything in their power to block the festival, and they're the ones who end up making all the money. I'm sitting here without the price of a pint in my pocket."

"Same as that."

"Pity. I could do with a drink."

"Grace is looking for you," Oliver said.

"How is she?"

"She sent me to get you."

"I can't face her, Oliver. I'm ashamed of the way I treated her. I was such a bollix. And even if I could face her, I'm not crawling back with one hand as long as the other."

"If you're stuck for the price of pint, we'll raid the piggy-bank."

"Forget it," Mulcahy said.

"Come on. We'll try it for the *craic*."

"No, Oliver. Sally said we were like two children. She was right. It's time we grew up. Shouldered a few responsibilities."

"You're the one who says, trust your talent. Have you no faith in mine?" Oliver coaxed. "We're the only two people in this town who know how to get at the money in the Black Pig. And feck the rest if they can't take a joke."

DOZENS OF PEOPLE were still wandering around the town square when Oliver's pickup truck skidded to a halt outside Tom Giblin's front garden. Two furtive commando-style characters, wearing black woollen hats pulled down over their ears and waxed cotton coats with the collars turned up, jumped out of the truck. One man raced around the front to raise the hood and clip a set of jump-leads to the battery. The second man vaulted the low wall and ran across to the Black Pig. He fixed the other end of the jump-leads to the steel tusks. The pickup engine revved loudly. Blue, white and crimson sparks showered about the garden.

"Nothing," Mulcahy hissed.

"Try it again," Oliver urged.

The engine revved hard and Mulcahy jiggled the clips. More sparks leaped from the tusks and strange sounds came from inside the belly of the pig, but nothing happened.

Mulcahy shook his head. The mechanism was jammed. Bystanders were starting to move in their direction to intervene.

"Again!" cried Oliver.

EUGENE TUTTLE'S CANDLE-LIT bar was packed when Grace pushed in to look for Mulcahy. It was mostly visitors from out of town, but she did find Sam at the bar, wiping a moustache of froth from his top lip.

"Is the boycott over?" she asked.

"Not officially, but we're being generous in victory," he explained.

Grace searched over the heads of the crowd.

"Have you seen Mulcahy?" she called when she spotted Sally.

"No. Have you seen Oliver?"

Grace shook her head. She was wondering where to look next when Tom Giblin came up to her with two pints of stout.

"Do you know what happened to Mulcahy? Why wasn't he there for the unveiling?"

"Have a drink," he said, handing her a pint. "Did you know the mining crowd are pulling out, lock stock and barrel?" he announced happily. "The word is, their assets could be frozen until there's an official investigation. They're high-tailing it off the mountain with all their stuff before that happens." He raised his glass. "We'd never have done it without you. *Sláinte*!"

"*Sláinte*," Grace answered the toast mechanically.

Her eyes searched all about the bar. She wondered if she should drive out to the Marine Bar to look for them there. They were probably too proud to ask Eugene Tuttle if the barring order was still in force. She rushed back her drink and was ready to leave when there was a commotion at the front door.

The employment scheme workers and all her friends from the workhouse piled into the bar behind Mulcahy and Oliver. Both men were dressed in old coats and woollen hats, but the festival volunteers still wore their warrior costumes and painted faces from the parade. The crowd cleared a way to the bar.

"A good, old-fashioned show-down," Tom Giblin whispered with glee.

Mulcahy stopped short of the counter and faced Eugene Tuttle.

"Drinks for all the festival workers," he ordered.

"M-m-money on the marble, please," Tuttle responded cautiously.

"Pull the pints," Mulcahy said.

The silence around the room deepened as the line of pints took shape along the marble counter. Eugene Tuttle worked with steady application at the tap. Oswald and Deputy Leddy entered. They had the upright and authoritative appearance of men with money in their pockets, but they stopped short and stood quietly near the door when they saw what was going on.

Sally topped off the pints and Eugene Tuttle began to do a total on the antique cash register. The stiff clang of mechanical keys finished on a high, dramatic note. Tuttle turned to announce the total.

"One hundred and forty-eight pounds and three pennies, please," he chirped.

Grace was convinced Mulcahy had arranged this showdown as an act of public humiliation. A big-hearted, but foolhardy, gesture of defiance, to mark his departure from the town. After a deliberate pause Mulcahy turned to Oliver. His companion handed over the plastic bucket from Tom Giblin's front garden. Mulcahy took the bucket, stepped forward and emptied the contents along the marble counter. A swineherd pouring out swill.

"Spend, and the Lord will send," he declared.

Coins of every denomination rolled across the bar counter and fell on the floor. At the sight of this glittering jackpot amongst the loose flakes of Indian meal, Tuttle's face cracked into its first recorded smile. There was a rush towards the bar with the boycott officially lifted.

Oswald and Leddy did a quick about-turn and escaped discreetly out the door.

Sally Holmes came around from behind the counter with a pint of stout reserved for Oliver. Her face turned pale when he shook his head.

"Are you not well?" she asked, flabbergasted.

"Give that pint to Mulcahy," the words burst from his mouth. "I've made an eejit out of myself too often. From now on I'm going to walk straight and drink water. Good clean water from the river," he said, amazed to find it wasn't so impossible to speak to her after all.

Sally raised herself up on tip-toes, gave him a big hug and kissed him on the mouth. "You're a dote," she said.

She looked around to offer the pint to Mulcahy, but he was surrounded by well-wishers.

Grace pushed through the tightly packed drinkers in an effort to reach Mulcahy. As she struggled across the room, there was a sound of heavy machinery in the town square. The noise was loud enough to lure everyone out on to the pavement to investigate. Grace was carried along in the crush.

The earth-moving machines from the mountain, a convoy of heavily loaded trucks and vans and a four-wheel drive jeep with dogs in the back, was passing through the town. Those on the pavement who still wore their warrior costumes waved the drinks Mulcahy had bought for them and heckled the procession to hurry the retreat. Youngsters ran after the last truck tossing home-made spears.

After the mining company machinery left the square, the crowd noticed that the crane from the harbour was also on the move. Mulcahy's Black Pig had been removed from Tom Giblin's front garden.

Oswald and Leddy and Tom Giblin stood beside the plinth signalling directions to the operator. The pig floated high above the square, and the extended boom swung around to centre the monument carefully above the plinth. All that remained was to set the permanent direction the monument would face. In a hurried conference, between Giblin and the two official committee members, it was decided Oswald's cement store should have the pig head on. Leddy's bed and breakfast would have the side view. Which left Tuttle with the rear end.

Oliver and Sally joined Sam at the front of the crowd. His old black umbrella had been discarded, and someone had given him a new, brightly coloured version.

"It's a pity Theo had to die for this to happen," Oliver said.

"Just count your blessings we're all alive and well to see it," Sally answered.

"I wouldn't go that far," Sam remarked, and began to laugh as soon as he had said it.

Grace appeared beside them. Her eyes followed the Black Pig as it hovered dramatically over the square. It was a special moment, full of consequence and history, and she was proud of the role she had played in bringing to completion this public monument dedicated to her grandfather. She had every reason to feel happy, and to be grateful for the new direction her life had taken, but Mulcahy's absence overshadowed everything.

A boisterous, high-spirited dance started. The costumed warriors pressed around the monument with their firebrands raised. The jostling dancers crushed Grace up tight against the man standing next to her. When she turned around, the fiery light revealed Mulcahy.

"I'm sorry," he said.

"What?" she cupped her mouth up close to his ear. "What did you say?"

"Do I have to shout it from the rooftops," he roared to be heard over the noise of the revellers swarming all around.

"Shout it."

"I said, I'm sorry. I'm truly sorry."

"What?"

"I love you."

"That's better."

"I really love you, Grace."

"Louder."

"I love you and I want you to stay."

"Is there room for one more in the workhouse?" she cried.

He threw his arms around her. An impulsive and homecoming embrace. Two lovers amongst the crowd. Their lips meet at the moment the Black Pig reached the plinth. Or so the legend would have it.